The Wild One

Janet Gover

Book 2 in the Coorah Creek Series

Where heroes are like chocolate – irresistible!

Published 2015 by Choc Lit Limited
Penrose House, Crawley Drive, Camberley, Surrey GU15 2AB, UK
www.choc-lit.com

A CIP catalogue record for this book is available
from the British Library

ISBN 978-1-78189-266-4

Printed and bound by Clays Ltd

The Wild One

For John

Acknowledgements

In researching this book, I read the stories of people caught up in the wars in Iraq and Afghanistan – both civilians and servicemen on both sides. I want to thank them for sharing their experiences and helping me to understand that the wounds we can't see are often the hardest to heal.

The issue of feral horses in Australia's national parks is very real. Horses, camels, rabbits, foxes and other introduced animals do enormous damage to the landscape and native wildlife. Culling is one solution often used. It's not an easy solution or a good one. Brumbies can be and have been domesticated. I have ridden one. She was lovely. I wish more of her kind could find the sort of home she did.

I would like to give special thanks to my friends Jean and Rachel – who always help me more than they know with both their knowledge and their love.

Working with Choc Lit is a great joy. The editorial team is wonderful and the authors are the most supportive group of people I have ever met. Thank you all.

Thanks also to the Choc Lit Tasting panel members – Emma M, Jennie A, Claire W, Betty, Liz R, Jane O, Liz W, Leanne F and Lucy M.

Thanks go to all the friends and family who continue to love me, despite my habit of disappearing inside my head to talk to people only I can see or hear.

And most of all – thanks to my husband John, the only other person who sometimes seems to hear those characters whispering inside my head.

Chapter One

Dan Mitchell was sweating by the time he reached his vantage point, high on the side of the steep sandstone cliff. He lowered himself into the gap between two big rocks, where he had the clear view he needed. He laid his rucksack and rifle on the baked red earth and pulled out a bottle of water. He took a long swallow of the warm liquid, then settled himself comfortably to wait. He maintained the kind of immobility that only comes with rigorous training, very aware that even the slightest movement could jeopardise his mission. As he had done so many times before, in places half a world away, he tried to empty his thoughts of everything but the task he was facing.

The sun was sinking rapidly now, but the day was still hot. A small breeze wafted through the gorge, rippling the water on the billabong below him. In the distance, a kookaburra laughed. At the water's edge, a small mob of grey kangaroos raised their faces to the east, ears flicking back and forth. Listening. Waiting. The sun dropped lower, sending a shaft of golden light through the gorge, setting the deep red cliffs on fire. The silence was broken by a low rumbling sound. With a raucous cry, a crow launched itself into the air. The kangaroos bounded away, their tails high to balance the thrust of their powerful hind legs. The noise grew, echoing through the cutting, shattering the peace.

The wild horses burst over the top of the rise. They swept down the gorge like a leaping, living wave. Black and brown coats rippled as muscles strained. Flashes of white glowed like molten silver in the dying light. As one,

1

the brumbies raced towards the billabong, hard hooves hammering the dry ground until the very earth itself seemed to vibrate with the joy of their passing.

Dan watched them, his sharp blue eyes narrowed against the sun's glare.

The lead mare tossed her head, scenting the sweet water. She slowed, bringing the rest of the herd to a halt. With much snorting and fighting for position, the first few mares waded into the billabong and began to drink. As they lifted their heads between mouthfuls, sunlight sparkled on drops of water falling like diamonds back into the quivering surface of the water.

There were about forty horses of all ages milling about. Some of the mares had foals clinging close to their sides. The youngsters looked well grown and healthy, but none ventured too far from their mothers. Yearlings hovered on the outskirts of the herd.

Dan was no expert, but to his eyes, the horses looked beautiful. Brumbies were supposed to be mean creatures, in-bred and ugly. Badly conformed and useless. But not these. These creatures were beautiful. Dan remembered a story told to him by an Iraqi child during his last tour of duty. The child explained that Allah had created the horse from the South Wind, saying 'You shall be Lord of all animals and you shall fly without wings'. As he looked at the brumbies, Dan could believe the legend.

This was not the first time he'd come to watch the horses, and he knew that one was still missing. Dan had still not seen the leader of the herd … the one responsible for the broad white blaze that ran crookedly down the faces of the foals and the yearlings. He searched the gorge, waiting. The stallion was always the last to enter.

Something moved in the deep shadows where the sun no longer reached. Dan tensed, waiting. At last the stallion stepped forward into the sunlight. His hide glowed like a blood red ruby in the golden light. A blaze of white ran down his face, and over one nostril, almost as if an artist had slipped while applying paint. His thick mane wafted in the wind as he stood watching his harem at the water's edge. The big horse tossed his head, scenting the wind. He was tall and well-muscled, with fine strong bones and an elegant head. He might run with brumbies, but somewhere in his not-too-distant past there was thoroughbred blood. He was as fine an example of his breed as Dan had ever seen. Strong. Intelligent and alert. Fabulously alive.

After surveying his domain for a few more seconds, the stallion turned towards the billabong. As he trotted past, the mares gave way to make a path for him. He waded into the water, but even as he drank, he remained alert for danger, constantly lifting his head to scent the wind.

The sun was sinking lower now, the shadows in the gorge lengthening. When darkness came, it would drop quickly, like a cloak to cover the animals in the bottom of the gorge. It was now or never. Dan felt sweat break out on his forehead. His palms were slick with it and he wiped them quickly on the leg of his blue jeans before lifting his rifle to his shoulder. He relaxed into a stance as familiar as it was hateful to him. He looked down the long grey barrel, smelling the oil he'd used to clean the weapon just a few hours ago. He closed his eyes for an instant, knowing that image of the blood bay stallion would haunt him. The horses didn't belong here. They damaged the park and threatened its native inhabitants. They had to go. He understood that. And orders were orders. But this was wrong. There must be another way.

By the waterside, a young colt squealed – an excited, high-pitched sound that was almost human. Almost like the cry of a child. It was the cry of an innocent, from another time and place not so very different from this. When the same sun raised sweat on his brow, but his hands held another weapon. A time when very different brown eyes looked back at him through the sights of his rifle.

'Take the shot. Damn you. Take it!'

'But, sarge … the child …'

'That's an order, soldier. Take the shot!'

Dan's finger tightened on the trigger. He opened his eyes, squinting to get a clearer sight in the gathering dusk. The stallion turned its head to stare up at the side of the gorge. It was almost as if he knew Dan was there. The horse's huge dark eyes seemed to look right back at him. Right through him. See him as he really was …

'You're a coward, Mitchell. You make me wanna puke.'

The smell of spicy food cooking somewhere out of sight. Voices. The sound of an engine.

'He's gonna get away. Take the shot. Someone take the bloody shot!'

The loud crack of a rifle close by.

Screams. The smell of blood seeping into the hot desert sand …

'Shit!'

Dan's finger tightened on the trigger. He wouldn't miss. He was too good for that. He was cursed with an instinctive knowledge of distance and speed and wind. He knew how to send that small but lethal round unerringly to its target. He also knew how small a movement of the rifle barrel could send the shot wide.

The sound of the gunshot cracked through the still air, followed by a ping as a bullet ricocheted off rock. The stallion flung up his head, rolling his eyes in alarm as he flung himself sideways. In an instant the mob was racing away, the thunder of the hooves louder than before.

Nostrils flared as the smell of the cordite wafted down from the side of the gorge. The stallion was behind the mob, teeth flashing as he drove the mares to even greater speed.

In less than a minute, they were gone. The echoes rumbled around the red cliffs for a few seconds, and then they too faded as the dust raised by the swift hooves settled back to earth. The gorge was empty and still. The sun dropped the last few inches, and darkness fell.

Above the rocky outcrop, Dan's rifle slipped slowly to the ground. His hands were shaking as he ran his fingers through his tousled red hair. As he had done so many times before, he closed his eyes against the suspicion of tears.

Although he no longer wore a uniform, he knew a lot about orders. Orders that should be obeyed. Orders that shouldn't. Orders that would haunt a man for his entire life.

And now it was happening again.

Chapter Two

The town seemed to grow out of the shimmering sea of the heat haze. A few wooden buildings that would soon, hopefully, give way to something a bit bigger. With at least a petrol station and hotel. Quinn allowed herself a slow sigh. She flexed her fingers on the wheel and eased her stiff shoulders. She had been driving since early morning, and she was sick of it. Not that she disliked driving. Quite the reverse. She was happy behind the wheel of her customised Humvee. She loved the big former military vehicle, with its very non-military metallic gold paint and dark brown leather seats. The custom built lockers in the rear held all her belongings. It was more than a home away from home – it was her only home. The place she lived. But the big Hummer was kitted out for off-roading and she was sick of long straight flat roads.

A sign flashed past as she eased off the accelerator. Coorah Creek. At last! Whoever coined the phrase 'beyond the black stump' must have been thinking of Coorah Creek. Driving to this tiny outback town in the far west of Queensland had taken two long days. The next stop on this road was Birdsville, the last outpost of civilisation before the great central Australian desert.

She drove slowly through the 'suburbs' – a few blocks of family homes set on wooden stumps as most buildings were in this part of the outback. The houses were for the most part well kept, but lacked much in the way of lawns and gardens. That wasn't surprising. This close to the desert there wasn't enough water to spare for luxuries. The town, however, wasn't as depressing as some she'd seen. There were signs of prosperity. The school looked well equipped and well attended. It even had a small swimming pool. The main street boasted a few shops, none of which were particularly flash, but all of which looked to be getting along all right. There was even a single red brick building overlooking a small patch of green lawn with a statue at the centre. That would be the town hall.

She guessed the prosperity was due to the mine. While she was here she would have to see if she could get access to the big open cut uranium pit. Mines were always good subjects for her work. But she doubted they would let her in. Uranium mines generally were not fond of photographers.

The Coorah Creek Hotel looked as if it had jumped from the pages of a travel book or from a postcard. Painted a pale cream, the building boasted a classic two storey design. Both storeys were completely encased with wide, shady verandas which were, in turn, edged with intricate wrought-iron railings. A set of wide wooden stairs led from the baked ground onto the veranda, and to a pair of double doors that were propped wide open. Every one of the big windows on the ground floor was also open. Obviously, the Coorah Creek Hotel did not have air-con. That was a shame. It was hot. Still, it did look clean and well-kept, for which Quinn was thankful. She had certainly stayed in much worse.

A few cars were parked in front of the hotel, nose-in to the kerb. Most were four-wheel-drives or battered utes. All were covered with red dust. The Hummer fitted quite easily beside them. Quinn ran her hands through her short blonde hair, and then opened the car door. Before leaving the Hummer, she slung a rucksack over one shoulder and a big camera bag over the other. Not that Coorah Creek looked like a hot-bed of crime, but her laptop and her cameras were her whole life. Almost literally. She never left them behind.

The long bar was dark after the brilliant sunlight outside. It was also surprisingly cool. Three large fans spun briskly overhead. Behind the bar, a grey-haired woman was polishing glasses. There were four men on bar stools and each turned to watch Quinn come in. That was not surprising. There wouldn't be a lot of tall blonde strangers in this part of the world.

'Hello.' The grey-haired woman smiled broadly. 'Welcome to Coorah Creek. Why don't you pull up a stool? Can I get you something to drink? It's hot enough to fry eggs out there and you look like you've come some distance. Of course, everyone who comes here has travelled a fair distance. We are a long way from pretty much anywhere here at the Creek.'

'I'd like a beer, please.' It wasn't easy to get the order in. The woman barely stopped speaking long enough to take a breath.

'One beer coming right up. Extra cold. I hope you're happy with Fourex. It's all we have. We've normally got Fosters as well. The keg's here, but it's not on tap yet.'

The beer looked good as it slid across the polished wood of the bar, leaving a damp trail to mark its passing. Condensation slid slowly down the glass.

'You wouldn't be Rachel Quinn, would you?'

'People just call me Quinn.' The answer was as swift as it was automatic. 'I've got a room booked.'

'I thought so. Pleased to meet you. I'm Trish Warren. I own this place. Well, with my husband Syd. He's out back changing that Fosters keg.'

'Nice to meet you.' Quinn took a long pull of her beer, hoping that might discourage the woman from talking for just a few seconds. The beer was ice-cold and crisp as it washed away the dust of a long journey.

'I've reserved you the biggest room,' Trish Warren

8

continued. 'Your e-mail said you weren't sure how long you would be staying, but that's fine. We don't have any other guests at the moment. We don't get a lot of visitors.'

'Thank you.'

'So, what brings you all the way out here?' Trish asked, casting a meaningful glance at the rucksack and camera bag.

Quinn paused for a few seconds before she spoke. It was clear she wasn't getting away without paying her dues in conversation. She could understand that any stranger would be of interest in a town as remote as this one, but she spent so much time alone, conversation didn't always come easily to her. 'I'm a photographer. I thought there might be a few good shots to be had around here.'

'A photographer! My. Isn't that interesting! What sort of photographs?'

'Mostly scenic shots. The outback. Rocks. Wildlife. That sort of thing.'

'Like that guy ... oh, what *is* his name? Does calendars and things. I bought one once. The problem with calendars is that when the year is over, they are just so much rubbish. But I kept this one because the photos were so lovely. '

'Steve Parrish?' Quinn offered.

'That's him.' Trish sounded triumphant. 'Do you do stuff like that?'

'Yes, a bit like that.'

'Well, you've come to the right place. A lot of photographers go to the Diamantina Park just north of here. There are some beautiful spots there.'

Quinn imagined there were, but doubted that her idea of beautiful was quite the same as Trish's. There were plenty of photographers around who could and did photograph the outback. They went to the national parks and the well-known beauty spots. Quinn wasn't interested in that.

Anyone could take a beautiful photo of a beautiful place. Nor was she interested in fashion photography. She'd done it for a time. She'd even done a little modelling herself. But there was no skill in making beautiful women look good. The skill lay in finding something ordinary and making it extra-ordinary. Of finding beauty in places that were plain or even ugly. That was her talent. And she made a good living at it. She wasn't rich, but the income from the images she sold, and from her books made it possible for her to live the life she wanted, looking for the places no one else had ever photographed.

Looking for that one moment of space and light and time that spoke to her alone.

Looking for beauty where no one else could see it and preserving that beauty so it would never be lost.

Capturing a perfect moment in an imperfect world.

Making time stand still.

'... the ruins. A lot of people say that's an interesting place, although I've never been there.'

Quinn snapped her attention back to Trish, who had been chatting happily without seeming to expect an answer.

'I like to find places that are a bit out of the way,' she said to stem the vocal tide. 'Places only the locals know about. Places other photographers haven't been.'

'Instead of the Diamantina Park, you could try Tyangi,' offered a male voice.

A man appeared behind the bar. His hair was as grey as Trish's, and when he stepped to her side, Quinn felt as if she was seeing two halves of a coin re-joined.

'Hi. I'm Syd Warren.'

'Pleased to meet you,' Quinn said.

'I heard you telling my wife you're looking for out of the way places. You should definitely try the Tyangi

Crossing National Park, north of here. It's a lot smaller than Diamantina, and not as well-known. It doesn't get as many visitors, but I think it's more beautiful.'

'Tyangi.' The unfamiliar word immediately captured Quinn's imagination. 'Unusual name.'

'It's an aboriginal word,' Syd said. 'There's a legend associated with it. If you go to the park, Dan Mitchell can tell you all about it. He's the park ranger. He can probably also tell you where to find the brumbies, if that interests you.'

'Brumbies …' Quinn had never photographed wild horses before. The idea was rather appealing. She had set out on this trip with no specific purpose in mind. Just a desire to get away from civilisation for a while. She'd chosen Coorah Creek because it was almost the end of the west-bound road. Places didn't come much more remote than this. She was keen to get back to the wild places – where she didn't feel hemmed in and there were no people to make demands on her. Wild horses would suit her mood very well.

'Yeah. Ask Dan about them. They're feral, of course. Not supposed to be there. If they don't interest you, there are some pretty amazing rock formations in the park too.'

'Thanks for the suggestion. I might head out there tomorrow.' Quinn drained the last of her beer.

'Why don't you get your bags,' Trish said with a smile. 'I'll show you your room. My guess is you'll want a shower after the long journey.'

The room was on the top floor. It was larger than Quinn had anticipated, with a door opening onto the veranda. The double bed was also large. The bathroom wasn't, but it was clean and that was all that really mattered to Quinn. More importantly, there was a small desk, and Trish had boasted proudly that the hotel had just installed Wi-Fi.

Quinn tossed the rucksack of clothing onto the bed, and plugged her laptop in to charge.

She thought about a shower. She could certainly use one. Summer was still a couple of months away, but the temperatures were already high enough to raise a sweat. She thought about checking her e-mail. Then rejected both ideas. She felt the familiar restlessness return and glanced at her watch. In mid-October the sun didn't set until about seven o'clock. There was plenty of daylight left and sunset was always a good time for photography. She could drive to the park and check it out. She might try to find this park ranger – Dan Mitchell – and ask about brumbies.

She slipped her camera bag back over her shoulder.

Chapter Three

The park wasn't hard to find. Following Syd's directions, Quinn headed north from Coorah Creek. Almost an hour later, she saw the turn-off with the sign pointing to the park. That road quickly disintegrated into a gravel track. No wonder the park didn't get many visitors. A lot of people would have been deterred by the potholes and dust. Not Quinn. Tracks like this often led to extraordinary places. Her Hummer handled the road with ease, and Quinn felt a familiar sense of excitement. This was what she loved more than anything else in the world. Finding new places. Exploring the beauty of nature. Driving her big Hummer through the wilderness, she felt alive and free. There was no one to expect anything of her. No one to be disappointed when she failed.

The further she went into the park, the more she thought the publican was right. The park was interesting. She was crossing a flat, dry plain dotted with gum trees and Melaleuca scrub. There was nothing uncommon about that. Over to her left was a single sandstone monolith, rising from the plain in a quite spectacular fashion. Like Uluru, only smaller and more angular. But something extraordinary was waiting for her just a few miles ahead. A great sandstone plateau, rising maybe three hundred meters above the surrounding plain, dominated the view through her windscreen. It wasn't a single rock like the one that drew tourists to Alice Springs. This vast plateau would be a maze of gullies and gorges. And it stretched for kilometres. Quinn had never seen anything like it before. As the sun rose, those red cliffs would blaze with colour. As it set, the deepening shadows would create fantastic shapes where gullies split the rock. And if she was lucky enough for it to rain ...

Quinn's fingers were eager for the feel of her camera.

But that could wait. Those cliffs had been there for a millennium and they weren't going anywhere in the next few hours. First she had to find the park ranger.

The ranger station was a small cluster of buildings surrounded by a patch of bare earth that Quinn recognised as a firebreak. Bushfires were a very real danger in arid country and the firebreak was well-tended, as were the buildings. That would be a lot of maintenance for just one man. The park ranger was obviously a hard worker.

She pulled up outside what was plainly an office. The long low wooden structure had a wide veranda along the front and big sliding glass doors. When she stepped up to the doors, Quinn wasn't surprised to find them locked. She had already noticed that the covered carport beside the office was empty. A path led away from the office towards a small house, built of timber and raised on stumps in the traditional outback fashion. It too had a wide veranda with a wooden squatter's chair and table. Quinn could imagine sitting there watching the sun rise or set and listening to the birds. It would be so very peaceful.

She turned back to the office building, and the sign fixed to the door. It listed emergency numbers to call, but noted that mobile phone coverage in the park was patchy and unreliable. On the wall, a huge noticeboard featured the regulations governing use of the park. There was a fire danger notice – set to high. And beside that a map of the park.

The park was roughly square in shape, with the huge plateau covering the northern section. The map confirmed her suspicions, showing a maze of gullies. A person could easily get lost there. A set of caves was marked – annotated with a warning that the cave system was dangerous and anyone wishing to enter must first report to the ranger. Caves sometimes offered good photo opportunities, but Quinn was really interested in the brumbies. Horses needed water. And grazing. Quinn studied the map, looking for creeks or rivers. There weren't many, and at this time of the year, the smaller ones would be dry.

Quinn raised a hand and placed her finger on a point west of the ranger station. The map showed a billabong at the far end of a long deep gorge. That was the most likely place for permanent water, which also made it the most likely place for the wild horses. She glanced up at the sun. There was enough daylight left. Wild animals tended to gather at waterholes at dusk and dawn. If she could get to the waterhole before the sun sank, maybe she'd see the wild horses when they came down for an evening drink. She pulled her phone from her pocket. The sign was right. There was a very faint signal and she had a feeling that once she moved away from the ranger station, even that would vanish. Despite that, the phone still had its uses. She took a photo of the map and turned back to her vehicle.

According to the map, a four-wheel-drive-only track ran on the far side of a high ridge almost opposite the billabong. The Hummer would make short work of that. She found the track and, a few kilometres down it, noticed a flat area scoured with tyre tracks. Guessing this must be close to the billabong, she left the car there. Settling her camera bag comfortably on her back, Quinn clipped a water bottle to her belt and set out to climb the ridge. Her heavy hiking boots made short work of the rough terrain, but it was hot, and she was sweating by the time she reached the top of the ridge. She sat on a rock and took a swig of the warm water.

The view below her was much as she had expected. Between the high red stone cliffs, the large billabong looked cool and inviting. Trees threw shade over the water, and she caught a sudden flash of brilliant colour as a kingfisher darted between the trees. She was too far away to see details, but bare patches of worn and disturbed earth at the water's edge suggested she had found the brumbies' watering place. If the wild horses didn't come here to drink, some large animals certainly did. She would be interested to see them too. She found a good vantage place and, ignoring the discomfort of sitting on hard rock, she opened her camera bag. Selecting an appropriate lens, she clicked it into place and did what she had done so many times before – she waited.

The air was hot and still. She could feel the sweat trickling down between her breasts. And still she waited, motionless except for the slow rise and fall of her chest as she breathed.

They came slowly and nervously.

A single dark shape appeared on the very edge of Quinn's sightline. Slowly the mare moved forward, her head tossing as she scented the air. Another appeared. And then another. This one had a colt at foot, following close behind. Quinn raised her camera and zoomed in on the faces of the leading horses. With the aid of her powerful lens she could see the mares rolling their eyes, their nostrils flaring.

They were nervous. Frightened.

That didn't seem right to Quinn. The horses were on their home territory. Wild animals were always alert for dangers, but in this place, when they came to drink, they should feel relatively safe. She had photographed enough wild animals to know that something had spooked the herd. And recently.

She lowered the camera, just as the stallion appeared. He trotted past the mares and propped to a halt, head flung high staring down the gorge at the billabong. Every sense alert, he pranced from one side of the narrow pathway to the other, searching for danger. He was obviously thirsty and keen to get at the water, but fear was holding him back. At last, finding no visible threat, he began to move forward. The rest of the herd followed, but every single animal was tense and ready to flee at the slightest sign of danger. As they approached, Quinn could hear the nervous snorts and heavy breathing. They were very scared. Only the need for water was drawing them closer.

Quinn wondered what could have spooked the horses. There wasn't much that should frighten the wild herd in a place like this. There were no large predators to threaten them. No other large grazing herds to challenge them. The only threat they faced was from man.

Slowly Quinn turned her head to search the surrounding rocks. At first she saw nothing. Then out of the corner of her eye, she caught just a hint of movement. She lifted the camera again, twisted her powerful zoom lens and turned it towards a dark shape high in the rocks almost directly opposite her. For a few seconds she searched in vain, and then she saw him, almost hidden in a shadowy cleft in the rocks. Her fingers sought out the focus ring on her lens, turning slowly until the distant figure leaped into sharp outline.

The man was down on one knee. A broad-brimmed Akubra hat shaded his face. Even with the powerful lens, she couldn't see his eyes or even the colour of his hair. She couldn't guess his age, but something about the way he held himself told her he was young and fit. As she watched, he lifted something from the ground. Quinn could see all too clearly what he held in his hands. A rife. A large, powerful rifle with a hunting scope.

Quinn frowned. This was a national park. Hunting wasn't allowed in a national park. And what would he be hunting?

Even as Quinn watched, the man put the rifle to his shoulder and sighted down the barrel. Quinn lowered her camera as the terrible truth struck home.

The brumbies! The bastard was going to shoot the wild horses.

No!

Quinn didn't hesitate for even half a second. Taking a firm grip on her camera, she leaped to her feet.

'Ha!' she yelled at the top of her voice. Not at the man. At the horses. 'Ha! Get out of here. Go!' She darted forward down the slope slipping and sliding on the loose surface. Small pebbles and rocks clattered down the slope adding to the racket she was making. She waved her arms wildly, but there was no need. The wary horses had already seen her.

The bottom of the gorge erupted into a flurry of movement. The brumbies shied away from the noise and spun around, leaping into a wild gallop. The stallion screamed – a harsh, angry and almost human sound as he drove his herd away from the danger.

There was no need for Quinn to keep running, but she did anyway, yelling with every stride.

By the time she reached the bottom of the gorge, the horses were gone. A cloud of dust was the only evidence of their passing. The world was silent, except for the sound of Quinn gasping for breath as she stumbled to a halt. She bent forward, resting her hands on her thighs as she took a few moments to collect herself. It wasn't so much the physical exertion that had taken her breath as the realisation of what had almost happened.

At last, she wiped the sweat away from her face and looked up.

A man was walking quickly down the steep slope on the other side of the gorge. He moved towards her with precision and speed, as one used to rough going. Everything about the taut carriage of his body told her he was angry. Very, very angry. And that anger was no doubt directed at her. She still couldn't see his face, only the rifle that he held in his hands.

Chapter Four

Dan was angry. His cowardice had cost him a week that he didn't have. The shot he'd sent over the stallion's head had spooked the horses so badly, they hadn't returned to the billabong for two days. When thirst finally drove them back, they had come under cover of darkness. Dan didn't have a night scope on the rifle. He wouldn't take the shot unless he was sure he would hit his target. A clean hit. If he had to do this terrible thing, he would do it right. He would not have the animals suffer.

Today the horses had finally come back in daylight. Today he could have taken the shot. He'd had almost a minute of clear view of the stallion. He was a trained sniper. A minute was about fifty-eight seconds more than he needed.

He could have taken the shot. Should have taken it. But he hadn't. His palms had begun to sweat, and his hands to shake. He just couldn't do it.

Which only went to prove the sarge had been right. He was a coward.

He was ashamed of his cowardice. And he was angry with himself for not taking the shot. Once the stallion was gone, the others should be easier targets. He knew what he had to do. He just had not done it. And when the horses spooked and bolted, he'd felt an immediate surge of relief. They were beyond his reach for a few more days. He was spared this awful task once more. That relief had simply fuelled his anger and shame.

When he looked down into the gorge he saw a target for his anger. The person who'd caused his latest failure. Some idiot who took delight in frightening wild horses.

The idiot was waiting for him now, standing in the shade of a tree near the edge of the billabong. Dan marched steadily towards him, wondering what he was going to say. As the park ranger he was supposed to remove anyone who disturbed the animals. But by disturbing them, this idiot had actually given both the horses and Dan a reprieve. A part of him wanted to say thank you for that.

'What the hell were you doing?'

The shouted question shocked Dan into stillness. The idiot was a woman?

'This is a national park. You can't shoot here. I'm going to get the ranger.'

The woman stepped forward out of the shadow into the bright glare of the sun. Dan blinked in surprise. Whatever he had expected, it was not a tall and slender blonde, with a face that was strong yet intensely feminine with arched brows and a mouth that would no doubt be sweetly curved, when not clenched in anger. A touch of sunburn highlighted the woman's cheeks – or was the flush just another part of the fury that he saw sparking in her tawny eyes? He instantly recognised the jacket she was wearing. The press photographers embedded with his unit in Iraq had all worn the same sort of thing. He knew the many small pockets would be filled with batteries and lens covers and other paraphernalia he didn't understand. But she would. Everything about the way she stood and glared at him said this woman knew exactly what she was about.

Except for one small thing ...

He knew the exact second when she realised that he was wearing a uniform. He saw her eyes flick to the insignia on his shirt. The small embroidered possum stared right back at her.

'You're the park ranger?' Her disbelief was very apparent in her voice.

'Yes.'

'Then what the hell are you doing shooting horses?'

During the past few days Dan had asked himself the same question more times than he cared to count.

'That's park business ... Miss?'

'Quinn.'

Dan blinked. His mind raced as he took in the photographer's jacket and the expensive professional camera the woman in front of him was carrying. Surely this couldn't be ...

'Miss Quinn. I'm Dan Mitchell.' He thought about offering his hand for her to shake, but decided against it. Nothing about this woman suggested she was in the mood to be friendly, or even polite.

'It's just Quinn,' she said absently, as if by habit before getting back to the matter at hand. 'Why would a park ranger be shooting horses?' she asked again.

When she wasn't angry and yelling, she had a voice as interesting as everything else about her. Low and strong. Sexy too, if he allowed himself to think about it. Which he wouldn't.

Dan cast a glance back down the gorge. The horses were long gone. He could forget about them for a while. Which meant he could turn his attention to the more pressing matter of Quinn.

'This is park business, I'm afraid,' he said, not really believing for an instant that she would let him get away with that.

'It's my business now.'

'No, it's not. But even if it was, I could point out that the brumbies are not native creatures. They are feral and they do a great deal of damage to the park. They are big, hard-hooved grazing animals in a place that can't support them. They chop up the edges of the waterholes. They loosen the rocks and soil in the gullies and cause erosion. They overgraze the open plains. The National Parks and Wildlife Service is committed to preserving the native species and the wilderness here. That's not something we can do if the brumbies continue to breed in the park.'

Even to his own ears it sounded like he was reciting some official line out of a parks department policy statement. Which, of course, he was. He didn't believe in what he was doing. The brumbies did damage the park, but that was no excuse for the orders he'd been given. There had to be some other reason behind the deadline he faced; a reason known only to the man who had given the order. It wasn't the first time some faceless official had given him an order that left a bad taste in his mouth.

'So you're just going to shoot them?' He could hear the contempt in her voice.

'If you want to write to the Parks Minister, or take it up with your M.P, that would be your right. But in the meantime, I am just—'

He stopped speaking. He had been about to say following orders. But that was no excuse for violence and cruelty. He'd fought that fight once before, in the dust of Iraq. He'd disobeyed his orders and his brothers-in-arms had paid dearly for that disobedience. He saw a small frown crease Quinn's forehead. She could probably guess what he had not said but she could never understand what had stopped him from saying it.

'I assume you have a vehicle parked nearby,' he said.

Quinn nodded.

'It will be dark soon. There are campgrounds in the park. You need a camping permit if you want to stay. I can arrange that for you. If not ...'

She glared at him for a few seconds, and then turned on her heel. Dan watched her walk away. He could read the

22

anger in the stiffness of her back and the clipped strides she took. She climbed back up the rock strewn slope. That was a tough climb. But not once did she pause for breath. He guessed it was her anger propelling her forward. But still, he was impressed.

He had a feeling he hadn't seen the last of her.

His own vehicle was parked at the top of the plateau behind him, not all that far from the rock where he'd taken up his sniper's position. He walked back to it, deep in thought. The drive back to the ranger station was so familiar he didn't have to give it much conscious attention and before too long he was back at the place he called home.

He walked to the overflowing bookshelf and pulled out a large hardbacked volume. He put it on the coffee table, where it fell open to a well-thumbed page. The photograph showed a waterfall plunging down a red rock cliff in a wild place not all that different from the gorge he'd just left. The sky in the photograph was impossibly blue. The water was so white it seemed to glow. He took a slow deep breath as he looked at the photograph and remembered the first time he'd opened this book.

Six months out of the military. Eight months back from Iraq. He hadn't been adjusting. It wasn't just the nights that were hard to take, although they'd been the worst. The nights when a girl's dark eyes haunted him and he woke sweating, hearing her screams. The days were pretty rough too, when he had to try to lead a normal life, among people who didn't know what it was like to fear for your life every second of the day. Who didn't know what it was like to have blood on your hands. Loud noises bothered him. Silence was equally hard to take. He hadn't needed the doctors and counsellors to tell him what was wrong. He knew only too well.

He had walked the streets of Sydney like a man lost, staring down at the pavement so he didn't have to look at the faces of the people around him. His unorthodox discharge had separated him from his military brothers and the help he might have received there. The reasons behind that discharge separated him from everyone else. His family tried to understand, but they couldn't. How could they? They had never stared down the barrel of a rifle and been ordered to destroy an innocent life. He was slowly being smothered by a world that no longer seemed to have a place for someone like him.

Then one day, by chance, he'd found himself staring at a book in the window of a bookshop. It was propped open to show two glorious colour photographs. One photo was of a red rock gorge, with a narrow waterfall. The falling waters looked like a ghostly veil over the face of the cliff. At the base of the waterfall, the vegetation was dark green velvet. It was a beautiful image, and powerful. Something in that photograph spoke to Dan and before he really knew what he was doing, he was inside the shop, paying a ridiculous amount of money for a large glossy coffee table book even though his tiny flat had no coffee table. In fact, his tiny flat had very little to make it seem like a home, because it wasn't a home. It was just the place where he ate and slept. He'd taken the book back to those empty rooms and stared at the photos for hours. That night, the nightmares had been just a little less violent. Just a little less painful. The next day he had sought out the National Parks department and applied for a job.

He flicked the pages of the book on the coffee table. Something about these photographs had spoken to him. Had somehow reached into the darkest parts of his battered soul and lit just the smallest spark of light. They had led him to this place of sanctuary. Over the months, his nightmares had eased. The girl's face still haunted him, but there were moments when he could almost forget what had happened that day in Iraq. Almost forget what he had done.

He traced the name at the base of the photo with one finger. Quinn. There was no author photo in the book. It had never occurred to him that Quinn might be a woman. A beautiful woman with hair the colour of a Banksia flower and eyes that could warm a frosty morning. A crazy woman who would face down an armed man in the middle of nowhere, without a second thought, to save a wild horse.

She had saved him once too, without knowing it, when her book led him here.

Today she had saved him again, by sending the brumbies beyond the reach of his rifle. At least for the next couple of days. After that …

It was too much to hope she might do it again.

Chapter Five

How did a man like that get a job as a park ranger? What sort of a park ranger shoots horses?

Quinn was still running a full head of steam as she parked the Hummer outside the Coorah Creek Hotel. The drive back had been uneventful, if probably faster than was entirely legal. When Quinn was angry she didn't pay much attention to things like the speed limit. In her head she re-ran the confrontation with Dan Mitchell – again and again. Getting a little bit angrier each time.

Shooting horses? That wasn't what being a park ranger was all about. He should be preserving the wildlife, not killing it. Just because the brumbies weren't native, that was no reason to slaughter them! And if Dan Mitchell thought she was just going to sit back and let him do it, he was very much mistaken.

The bar was almost empty when she walked in. There was no sign of Trish Warren, for which Quinn was thankful. Not that she had anything against the publican's wife; she just wasn't in the mood for her chatter. She took a few minutes to fetch her laptop from her room then found a seat at one end of the bar. A man she hadn't seen earlier approached.

'You must be Quinn,' he said. 'The Warrens told me to expect you. They are out this evening. I'm Jack North, filling in as barman. What can I get you?'

'A beer, thanks.' Quinn pulled out her camera. In a few moments she had the camera and laptop connected and was downloading the day's photos. Not that she had taken many. It was just something she trained herself to do. Every night she compiled that day's shots. Most days there was nothing there to excite her interest. She was a professional photographer. Most of her shots were good. But good wasn't enough. The sort of shots she was looking for were rare, but when they came …

'Here you go. I'll just put it on the room tab.'

The beer was very cold.

'The Warrens said you were out at Tyangi,' Jack said.

Did everyone in this town talk incessantly? Quinn made a non-committal noise of agreement.

Jack took the hint and moved away to serve one of the other patrons.

Sipping her beer, Quinn began flicking through the day's shots. She had taken a few general views of the gorge before the brumbies appeared. There was nothing there to excite. She moved on to the shots of the wild horses. There weren't many. There hadn't been enough time. There were no special shots – but there were enough good shots to bring back the emotions she had experienced when she first saw the wild horses.

Like most young girls, Quinn had gone through a pony phase. She'd read books about ponies and dreamed dreams about ponies. But growing up in an inner Brisbane suburb did not lend itself to pony ownership. When she was about thirteen, she was given the gift that changed her life. Her father gave her a small camera. Ponies were instantly forgotten in her wonder at this new toy.

But today that girlish love of ponies had been stirred again – not by some child's fantasy of a well-groomed, ribbon-winning pet, but by horses that were truly wild creatures. Something about them had moved her. Despite their unkempt manes and dusty coats, they were beautiful in their own way. Slowly she flicked through the photos. There was a shot of a mare, bending her head to gently touch her foal. Another of a young colt, hovering on the edge of the herd like a teenager seeking approval. She clicked to the next shot. She had captured the stallion close up. His broad strong head with its dramatic white blaze was quite spectacular. He looked arrogant and proud. She liked that. What she hadn't liked was the fear that showed in their body language and faces as they made their way carefully towards the water. They'd been hesitant and wary. Wild creatures shouldn't be afraid. They should own the wilderness they were a part of. Quinn now knew the source of their fear.

She clicked the next shot onto her laptop screen as her anger flared again.

The man's face was hidden in the shadow cast by his broad-brimmed hat. He was crouched, half hidden behind a dark red chunk of sandstone. The rock was almost the colour of dried blood. While the man was just a dark silhouette, the rifle in his hands was not. The barrel of the gun was as clear as the threat it represented and it was pointed down into the gorge, where the horses were gathered just looking for something to drink. Quinn felt her anger flare anew as she looked at the photo.

She wasn't going to let that man shoot those magnificent horses.

'Can I get you another?' The barman was back. 'Are you looking to eat?'

'Is Ellen cooking?' a voice called from the other end of the bar.

'Yep,' Jack answered. 'More of her beef bourguignon.'

'I'll have some of that,' another man chimed in quickly.

'There's plenty to go around,' Jack replied. He leaned forward to get a clearer view of Quinn's laptop screen.

'Is that Dan Mitchell?'

'Yes.' Quinn didn't even try to keep the disgust out of her voice.

'What's he doing?'

'He's shooting the brumbies – or, at least, he was going to but I disturbed him.'

'He was afraid that was going to happen,' Jack said.

'You know him?'

'Sure I do. Around here, everyone knows everyone.' Jack grinned. 'He's relatively new. Only been here for three years. He's a good man. I helped him pull an injured girl out of the Tyangi caves last year. He loves that park. Works really hard to keep it safe. We haven't had any big bushfires out there since he took over. He keeps a pretty close eye on the tourists. Not just to keep them safe, but also to make sure they don't do any damage.'

'Oh.' After what she'd seen today, Quinn had trouble believing such a glowing reference.

'Yeah. He's known for a while that he has to do something about the horses. They're really a problem. No predators, you see. They just breed unchecked. When the population gets too big, they do a tremendous amount of damage to the park. But the horses suffer too. They starve to death in the dry years. The parks department is looking for an easy way out. Shooting is the quickest and cheapest way of dealing with it. Tyangi is a small park – not one of the famous ones. There aren't many horses there. Dan was hoping they might just let it be. Looks like he was wrong.'

Quinn didn't respond. Dan Mitchell might have hoped he wouldn't be ordered to shoot the horses, but from what she'd seen, he had been. But that didn't mean he had to do it. Nor did it mean she had to sit by and watch.

'So, do you want some of the beef?' Jack asked. 'If you do, tell me now. When Ellen cooks the food vanishes pretty fast.'

It was served pretty fast too. Just a few minutes later a small blonde woman appeared carry a steaming plate. As she walked in, Jack's face lit up and his smile grew even broader. Ellen smiled back. Quinn noticed the woman's shape. She was obviously pregnant. Very pregnant. Maybe that explained the glow on her face. A glow that was reflected in Jack's eyes.

Quinn felt a familiar cold shaft of pain. The memories were never very far away. She closed her eyes for a second, forcing those memories back into the tiny locked corner of her brain where they didn't hurt very much. She tried to avoid looking at anyone as she ate.

The food was good – much better than she had expected in a small outback pub. She drank another beer and began to focus on the job at hand. Making full use of the Wi-Fi the publican had been so proud of, she started with the simplest of Google searches that led her on and on. She learned a lot about brumbies and national parks and why the two did not get along. And she started thinking.

Close to ten o'clock, Jack indicated that it was almost time to close the bar. Quinn suddenly realised that her day had been very long. She desperately wanted a hot shower. But she knew she wouldn't sleep. She walked out to her Hummer. The back of the vehicle was lined with custom-built polished wood lockers, and the boxes that filled every bit of space were of the same make. It was an efficient and clever use of every available square centimetre of space. Quinn hadn't built the interior. She'd bought it like this from another photographer, but it suited her perfectly. Those boxes and lockers contained everything she needed, from a camp stove to knitting needles. She opened one of them to remove some clothes and her wash bag. From another she took a cloth bag, from which dangled a length of soft yellow wool. Her fingers passed briefly over a parcel wrapped in plain brown paper in the same locker, before she locked the car again and headed up to her room.

The hot shower was as good as she had hoped. She slipped into a pair of cotton shorts and a tank top, and opened the door onto the wide veranda. The night air slowly seeped into the room, bringing with it the night sounds of the outback. She could hear the ticking of the tin roof cooling after the day's heat, and in the background the cicada song, waxing and waning as more insects joined the nightly chorus. What she did not hear was the sound of traffic. Or other people. She liked the peace and quiet.

Sleep was going to elude her. There were too many thoughts racing through her mind. She opened the bag she had retrieved from the car and removed needles and a ball of pale yellow yarn. She ran her eyes over the small garment slowly taking shape, and settled herself into a chair.

The sound of the clicking needles floated out into the night.

Chapter Six

Dan was about to walk out the door, when the ringing of the phone stopped him. He turned back to answer it.

'Tyangi Crossing ranger station.'

'Is that Dan Mitchell?'

'It is.'

'This is Thomas Lawson.'

Dan's heart sank. He recognised the name. It had been at the bottom of the e-mail that had launched this new nightmare. If only he had left a few minutes earlier.

'Hello, superintendent.'

'I'm calling because you have not replied to my latest e-mail. About the brumbies. I want to know what's going on.'

Dan's mind raced, looking for a suitable reply.

'I've been working on it, sir.' He sounded like a raw cadet trying to make excuses to a superior officer.

'And?'

'I have found where the brumbies go to water. I was there last night, but I was interrupted by a park visitor.' That wasn't a lie.

'Be careful. We want to avoid any bad publicity. You have my authority to close the park, if necessary, for a day or two. Just get the job done.'

'Yes, sir.'

'You have a deadline, Mitchell. This has to be dealt with before the Minister's visit at the end of month. He needs to announce that the park is free of feral animals. It's an important part of his re-election campaign.'

'Yes, sir.'

'Then get it done.' The call ended abruptly.

Dan hung up the phone then stood looking at it for a few moments. Lawson had given Dan an order. He should obey. He would – but not today.

He headed outside. On the way, he retrieved an axe from his tool shed. He walked around to a section of scrub that was beginning to encroach on his small house. He found the biggest, toughest looking tree in the area. With smooth fluid movements he lifted the axe high over his right shoulder. He held it at the apex of the swing for a heartbeat, and then swung it with all the force he could muster. The iron blade cut deep into the Melaleuca trunk with a satisfying thud. Small chips of wood flew and shards of bark fell to the ground at his feet. Dan pulled the axe free and swung again. And again, cutting deeper and deeper into the trunk. Finally, the tree began to give up the battle. At the slow creaking of the tearing timber, he stood back to watch the tree crash to the ground.

With a grunt of satisfaction, Dan pulled his shirt over his head and used it to wipe the sweat from his face and arms. He didn't bother putting it back on. Then he picked up the axe again. He attacked the next tree with the same intensity as the first.

The noise of it crashing to the ground wasn't enough to drown out his thoughts.

Dan stood for a few moments, taking long slow breaths, his chest heaving slightly with the exertion. He took a long draught from the water bottle he always kept to hand, then picked up his axe and moved on to the next tree. Cutting timber in this heat was hard work, but it was good honest work. And the sweat pouring from his body was clean sweat, triggered by physical labour – not by memories.

The little girl had come back to him last night. And the night before; so real he could almost feel the desert heat again. Every night since he'd received the e-mail ordering him to shoot the brumbies, she had denied him any rest. Ever since he looked through the sights of a rifle again and tightened his finger on the trigger, the little girl had haunted him. Her huge dark eyes accused him of breaking his oath. In the depths of the still night he would hear her screams and wake drenched with sweat. Overcome with guilt and remorse.

In another remote place, when he wore a different uniform, he had been ordered to use his rifle. He'd been good at it too. Good enough to attract the attention of his superior officers. There were times he'd used his skills as a sniper to protect his comrades. That he was always willing to do. Other times he'd been ordered to target enemy combatants and terror suspects. He'd felt less comfortable with that. Shooting someone in cold blood just did not seem right. But he was a soldier. And that was what soldiers did. And then he had been ordered to shoot a father while he held his child in his hands ...

That had been a step too far for Dan. He'd made a decision – and was still living with the consequences.

Shooting a wild horse was not the same as shooting a human being. But violence was violence and he had sworn never to take that path again. He had promised a dead girl that he was done. That he would never pick up a rifle again or harm a living creature. Now he was being forced to break that promise. He could refuse and walk away, but there would be consequences to that decision too. Last time, a girl died a terrible, painful death.

He was damned, whatever course he took.

With an angry swipe of the back of his hand, he dashed the sweat from his face, shouldered his axe again and moved to the next tree.

'What sort of a park ranger *are* you?'

The sharp voice caught him in mid swing. The axe

completed its arc and cut into the bark with a decisive thud. Dan pulled it free as he turned to see a beautiful angry woman standing a few feet behind him.

'You shoot brumbies. You cut down trees. Are you sure you're a park ranger?'

'And you think nothing of sneaking up on a man armed with an axe – or a gun. That sort of behaviour could get you in serious trouble.'

'Was that a threat?' Quinn demanded.

'No. Just an observation.'

A tense silence settled between them. Dan waited for Quinn to make the next move. He had all the patience in the world.

'Why are you cutting down trees?' she finally said. Her voice was a fraction calmer.

'I'm making a firebreak around the ranger station,' he said slowly, not at all concerned that he might sound smug or superior. 'It's the sort of thing park rangers do.'

He was rewarded with just the hint of a blush on Quinn's face. Today she wasn't wearing her photographers' vest, and this time there was no chance he could mistake her for a man. She filled out a pair of faded jeans and a tank top in an extremely feminine fashion. He must have been pretty out of it yesterday if he hadn't noticed those long lashes fringing her tawny eyes. Or the way the sun glinted on the short blonde hair that framed her face in a most angelic fashion. He was pretty sure angelic was a word seldom used to describe Quinn. But he kind of liked it.

'I've been reading about brumbies,' she said, obviously deciding to let the small matter of the trees pass. 'The National Parks department is trying to get them out of all the parks. Because they cause damage.'

'That's right,' Dan said. He studied her face and saw that she was genuinely interested. He'd been struggling with this for a while now. Maybe talking it through with someone would help him understand what he had to do and why. 'It's not an easy call to make. But most conservationists agree with the department. The brumbies do untold damage to the parks and the native plants and animals.'

'I can see that now,' Quinn conceded. 'But why shoot them? You could just move them.'

They were heading into dangerous territory. Lawson's warning was fresh in his mind. Dan knew he shouldn't be talking about this. Especially not to a photographer. She wasn't press, but he would bet she had contacts in the press. It was more than his job was worth to find himself at the centre of some newspaper crusade to save the horses. Among those orders he'd received was one about not talking to the press. To anyone. If he was going to start disobeying orders again, he might as well start with that one.

'It's not quite that simple,' he said.

'Tell me.' She sounded quietly determined. He liked that too.

Dan suddenly found himself wanting to talk to her about the horses. It was such a small part of the burden he carried, but it was the only part he would ever be able to share with anyone. And she would understand. No one who took the sort of photographs she did could fail to understand. And just maybe she might have some useful ideas.

He glanced up at the sun. It wasn't yet noon, but already the day was blisteringly hot. He suddenly became aware that he was shirtless and sweating. Not that Quinn seemed to be bothered by it. Or even to have noticed it. He reached for his shirt.

'Let's go inside out of the heat.'

He could have led her to the ranger station. He should have led her there. This was, after all, about park business. But he didn't. Instead he took her behind the office to his small house. As he did, he realised that in all the time he'd lived here, he had never had another person inside his home. He'd never let anyone get that close. But Quinn was different. She was already part of his life, although she didn't know it. She had been a part of his life for a long time.

At the bottom of the steps leading to the door, he gestured for her to precede him. The front door wasn't locked. His living room was clean and tidy – one of the military habits he'd never lost. Only one thing was out of place. A book lying open on the coffee table, where he'd been reading it last night.

'Oh!' Quinn stopped when she recognised the book.

'I was hoping you might sign it for me,' Dan said.

'I guess that depends,' Quinn replied.

'On what?'

'On what happens to the brumbies.'

The book had been a surprise. Quinn sat on the small but comfortable couch leafing through the pages. Every one of the photographs was familiar to her. She remembered taking each one. She remembered the thrill when she had looked back at the images and seen that extra something that turned a good photograph into something special. That trick of light. The clarity of colour. And the occasional bit of luck, like when a bird flew into frame at just the right second.

'How do you have your coffee?' Dan called from the kitchen.

'Black,' she replied, turning another page in the book.

Quinn wasn't particularly vain, but there were times

when she looked at her photos and felt a thrill of pride that she had added some small portion of beauty to the world.

And speaking of beauty ...

'Here you go. Coffee. Black.' Dan placed the steaming mug on the table in front of her.

He'd obviously taken a few moments to wash while he made their drinks. The sweat stained shirt had been replaced with a clean crisp one. Quinn felt a twinge of regret that he'd bothered with either. Shirtless, sweating and swinging an axe he'd made quite a striking picture. Quinn was a person who appreciated beauty, and Dan Mitchell had a beautiful body. She had noticed a couple of small scars on his back and chest, but that had done nothing to mar his attractiveness. In fact, the small imperfections had simply thrown his other attributes into sharp focus. He was taut and muscular, but not overly so. He moved with strength and grace. His eyes were a fabulous shade of blue. Quinn had never been fond of red hair on men – but on Dan Mitchell it looked right. His hair was a sandy-red, not unlike the sandstone cliffs of the park. It was straight and a little long and fell over his face in a most appealing fashion. If ever she wanted to give up nature photography and start photographing people instead, Dan would be a great subject to start with. It would be a challenge to see if she could properly capture the substance of the man, as well as the stature.

'I wonder why it is that we enjoy hot drinks in a climate like this,' Dan said with the hint of a smile as he sat down in the armchair opposite her.

That was a challenge too. She would like to see what he looked like when he really smiled. Or when he laughed out loud with joy. Although something in the lines of his face suggested he didn't laugh all that often.

With some reluctance Quinn dragged her thoughts back to her reason for being here.

'The brumbies,' she said. 'You can save them.'

'Nothing would please me more,' he said with transparent honesty. 'But they can't stay in the park.'

'I understand that now,' Quinn said. 'But some of the other parks have simply moved them. You could do that.'

'Assuming I could catch them, where would I take them?'

'There must be somewhere. This is the outback. There's plenty of room.'

'It's not like the east coast,' Dan said. 'Back there there's rich grazing. A few horses don't count for much. Out here, this close to the desert, every blade of grass is needed for the stock. There isn't food or water to waste on brumbies.'

'But if you give them to the graziers, they can train them. Free working horses.'

'That's true – but for the most part, around here, work horses are not in short supply. Motor bikes and helicopters do a lot of the work. Those who need horses usually have more than enough.'

'We could send them east. Find homes for them there.'

'We?' Dan raised an eyebrow. 'I thought this was my problem.'

Quinn gave him a withering look.

'We could,' Dan continued. 'If we can catch them. And tame them. I don't know much about horses, but that sounds like a lot of hard work. We need someone who can handle horses. And we need time. I don't have a lot of that.'

'Why not?'

'The Parks service has given me a deadline. The end of the month.'

'Couldn't you just … you know … not tell them until we've had a chance to organise something?'

'You mean lie?' He raised one questioning eyebrow.

Quinn almost said no, but he was right of course, she did mean lie. 'When you say it like that …'

'If I do that, I'll lose my job.'

'There are other jobs,' she said.

'True.'

To Quinn, it sounded as if he didn't believe her. As if this was the only job for him. And that couldn't be right. Surely someone like Dan would be able to work anywhere.

'If I don't shoot them, someone else will,' Dan continued. 'And I won't allow that to happen. At least I can make it quick and clean.'

'So, you're that good with a rifle, are you?' Quinn felt her lip curl a little in disgust at the thought of how many animals must have died for him to become a good shot.

'The army thought so.'

Quinn felt her cheeks redden again. Of course he was ex-military. She should have recognised it in the way he moved and that incredibly fit and controlled body. It would also explain the scars she had seen on his back. He must have been wounded. She could usually pick a military or ex-military man a mile away. It was something to do with the confidence that almost bordered on arrogance that most of them displayed. But she hadn't seen that in Dan. He was different. Not soft … Just different. She looked up at him, and for the first time their eyes really met. Somewhere behind those brilliant blue eyes she could sense there was so much more he wanted to say, but couldn't.

She took a deep breath. 'Give me a few days.'

'To do what?'

'I'm not sure. If I knew, I wouldn't need a few days.'

He smiled again. Small lines formed at the corners of his eyes and he suddenly looked younger, as if a tiny fraction of a great weight had been lifted from him. But only for a moment.

'The brumbies are spooked,' he said. 'After your efforts yesterday they won't be back for a couple of days. I couldn't do anything, even if I wanted to.'

'Three days,' Quinn countered. 'Please, promise me you won't do anything for three days.'

He hesitated. Quinn held her breath and waited. At last Dan gave a sharp nod.

'All right. Three days from now I have to be back at that gully as the sun goes down. You've got until then.'

Chapter Seven

22 … 24 … 26 … 28 … Nothing. She had nothing.

Quinn let her hands fall. One of the plastic knitting needles dropped to the polished wood floor, landing with a subdued clatter. Quinn looked down at the soft pale yellow yarn in her lap and sighed. Knitting was supposed to help her relax. Help her think. But it wasn't working this time. She had spent two days sitting in this hotel lounge, on the Internet. Researching. She had sent e-mails to organisations and people she had never heard of before, asking for their help or their advice. Some had even replied. But at the end of two days, in real terms, she had exactly nothing.

Tomorrow Dan Mitchell was going to start shooting the brumbies – unless she could come up with an idea. And preferably one with some small chance of succeeding.

She picked up her needles and started counting stitches again. If she could just get her brain to think about something else for a while, maybe she'd have some sort of a light bulb moment.

22 … 24 … 26 …

'Here's your dinner, Quinn.'

Biting back her frustration, Quinn tossed the knitting onto one end of the table, as Trish Warren set a plate in front of her. On the plate sat a burger, dripping with tomato sauce, and a huge pile of fries. Quinn took one of the fries and started eating it. When she was frustrated, she ate.

'This is so pretty,' Trish Warren said, hovering at the end of the table, reaching out to not quite touch the pile of yellow wool. 'I was never any good at knitting. Tried it, but never got the hang of it. People say it's restful, but for me it was just the opposite. As soon as I started talking to someone, I'd lose track of what I was doing.'

And Trish Warren would always be talking to someone, Quinn thought as she devoured another chip. When it came to talking, the woman was unstoppable. And as Quinn was the only person in the lounge at the moment, she was the target.

'Of course, it might have been different if Syd and I had had kids. There are such lovely little things to knit for kids. Like this little thing you are knitting. Who is it for, dear?'

There it was again. That knife in her heart. Time had not in any way made it any less sharp. Quinn wished Trish Warren would fall down some deep dark hole. Then, chiding herself for her lack of charity, she forced a smile onto her face.

'Not for anyone. I just like to knit. I do find it relaxing. In fact, it's nearly done. So if you know anyone who might like it ...'

'You mean you'll just give it away?'

'Yes,' Quinn said.

'Well, that's generous of you, dear. I do know someone.'

'Trish,' a voice called from the bar, where there were a few people drinking and chatting. 'You've got some more food orders.'

'Coming!' she called back. 'Sorry, dear, I've got to go. Enjoy the burger.'

The older woman walked away.

Quinn opened her laptop. She could eat and surf at the same time. She took a deep bite of the burger. It was good. Balancing it in one hand, she typed 'brumby' into her search engine with the other.

'Hi. Remember me? Jack North.'

Quinn looked up to see the barman she had met two nights before smiling uncertainly down at her.

'Of course. I also remember your wife's cooking. Not that there's anything wrong with this burger – but is she coming back soon?'

'Ellen works most of the time at the other pub. The Mineside. She just cooks here occasionally.' Jack hesitated and looked a little embarrassed. It looked a bit strange on a man of his size. 'Sorry to disturb your meal, but Trish said I had to come out here and ask you about ... well ... knitting?'

Quinn finally put two and two together. 'Of course, you're expecting a baby.'

Jack nodded. 'And Trish said ...'

Quinn smiled. He was such a large man to be bullied by a small woman with silver-grey hair. But then again, Trish Warren was pretty formidable. Quinn decided to put Jack out of his misery.

'I would be very happy if you would take this,' she waved at her knitting, 'when it's done. I've got a bit of work still to do, but I think I'm going to be here a bit longer than I expected. Long enough to finish this, at least.'

'And you really want to just give it away? After you've put so much hard work into it?'

Quinn nodded. She couldn't explain to a stranger why she knitted baby clothes. Or why she gave them away. All except the delicate pink knitted lace jacket that lay safely wrapped in tissue in her Hummer.

'Well, thank you. It's beautiful and I'm sure Ellen will love it.'

'You are welcome.' Quinn glanced back at her laptop. She didn't want to be rude, but she had work to do ... and a deadline. Not to mention a burger to eat.

'So, you are trying to find a way to save the brumbies,' Jack said.

'Yes,' Quinn admitted slowly. 'How did you know?'

Jack nodded at the website displayed on her laptop. 'Word gets around.'

Trish Warren, Quinn guessed. Not that she had said much to her, but the older woman could probably hear her thoughts – or at least look over her shoulder at the websites she was visiting. Trish was more than capable of putting two and two together as well – but she'd probably get five.

'So, what do you need?' Jack posed the question in such a straightforward manner, as if he expected there to be easy answers. And Quinn knew there weren't.

'Not much,' she said ruefully. 'Some way to catch a herd of brumbies. Then I have to get them out of the park once they are caught. I need somewhere to put them where they are safe but don't damage the natural environment. And, oh yes, someone who knows something about horses to help me.'

'Well, that doesn't sound impossible,' Jack said with a simplicity that surprised her. 'In fact, here's someone who might be able to help with the last one. Adam!'

Quinn saw a tall man with curly dark hair approach. He was wearing an open-neck white shirt over his faded blue jeans. The woman with him was plainly dressed in jeans and a white T-shirt, but she had a beautiful face. Quinn knew it would photograph well. But everything about the woman suggested she probably didn't care.

'This is our doctor, Adam Gilmore and his wife, Jess. Jess flies the air ambulance. Adam, Jess, this is Quinn.'

'The photographer?' Adam grinned. 'I heard we had someone famous in town. Pleased to meet you.'

Quinn shook the hand he offered. Jess smiled her welcome.

'We need some ideas, Doc,' Jack said. 'To save the brumbies out at Tyangi.'

'Tell me more.' Adam pulled up a chair. Jess and Jack did too. Quinn gave up on her burger. She wasn't hungry any more. For the first time since she'd started this, she was beginning to feel a spark of hope.

'Quinn needs someone who knows something about horses,' Jack said. 'I was wondering if Carrie Bryant might help.'

'I'm not sure.' Adam's brow creased slightly. He exchanged a look with his wife. Jess frowned and Quinn sensed an unspoken message pass between the two.

'Who is Carrie Bryant?' Quinn asked.

Jack chuckled.

'What's so funny?' she asked.

'Around here it's pretty unusual for someone to ask a question like that. Especially about a famous jockey who happens to live here in town.'

'She's a patient of mine,' Adam cut in. 'Or she was. She was a jockey. A very good one. But she got hurt last year at the Birdsville Races.'

'Would she be willing to help?'

'I don't know.' A frown creased Adam's brow. 'She's fine now, physically. But she isn't involved with racing any more. She moved into town to work at the feed store. It's possible she could help you.'

'Adam, are you sure she's up for this?' Jess asked.

'Maybe something like this is just what she needs to get herself back on track,' Adam replied.

'There's only one way to find out,' Jack said. 'Ask her.'

That made sense to Quinn. 'We have to do it tonight.

Dan Mitchell is going to start shooting those horses tomorrow.'

'Maybe not,' a voice said behind her. 'Not if you can give me some other option.'

He hadn't been able to stay away. He told himself he should wait for her to come back. Because one way or another she would come back. She didn't look like the sort of woman to give up easily.

But two days had seemed such a long time. The firebreak was finished. There were no campers in the park. He had gone back to the billabong last evening to wait for the brumbies ... without his rifle. He watched the sun sink and heard rather than saw the brumbies come to the billabong to drink well after it was dark.

He sat there, perfectly still, listening to the horses splashing in the water and snorting. After a while the moon rose, gifting the scene with just enough light for him to see dark shapes milling around, drinking and eating the green grass that grew close to the water's edge. Dan found himself wishing that Quinn was with him. It was far too long since he'd had the pleasure of a woman's company. He wasn't thinking about sex – although that had been a long time too. He was thinking about how good it was to hear a woman's voice. To watch the laughter in her eyes. To know the scent of her hair ... of her body. He'd spent too much time alone. Or in the company of other men. He had loved his comrades-in-arms like brothers. But in this quiet moment, watching those beautiful wild creatures, as the cicadas' song echoed around and the breeze blew gently, Dan longed to have someone to share it with. A woman to share it with. A woman who would see what he saw in the quiet beauty of the night.

He spent the night at the billabong. He always carried

a sleeping bag in his Land Rover because he liked sleeping in the open. The dreams came less often when he slept outside. When he woke, he knew what he had to do.

That's why he was standing in the lounge of the pub, Quinn staring at him with a question on her face.

'I did a headcount,' Dan said, pulling a chair up to the table. 'We've got fifteen mares. Most of them seem to have foals, although they move about so much it's hard to be sure. The foals look terribly fragile to me, but they seem able to keep up. There's about another dozen others that hang out on the fringes of the herd. I don't know much about horses, but they look like youngsters. Then, of course, there's that stallion.'

'So, about forty,' Adam said. 'That doesn't seem too many to handle.'

'And there's a place further along the gorge, where it narrows,' Dan said, his eyes fixed on Quinn, who still seemed shocked to see him. 'It's got very steep sides. I think we could pen them in there. We'll need to fence it off somehow.'

'I can help with that,' Jack said. 'I can probably liberate some timber from the mine. I'll talk to Chris Powell. Maybe he'll help out with some labour too if we need it.'

'The mine?' Quinn finally seemed to catch up with the conversation.

'I do some work there,' said Jack. 'Fix things. Powell is the mine manager. He's all right. He'll probably be willing to help us. I'm pretty sure we can build a couple of sturdy fences. I guess you'll probably need gates too. I think I know where I can get a couple of those.'

'If Jack says he can build you a fence, dear, you better believe he can.' Trish Warren appeared with some glasses and a jug of beer. 'He actually keeps half the town running. God knows what Syd and I would do without him.'

Waving away the money Jack was offering her, Trish vanished again.

'Does she hear every word spoken in this town?' Quinn whispered.

The group around her all nodded, casting glances of mock terror over their shoulders.

Quinn's face relaxed and she smiled. Dan felt as if someone had turned on a bright new light in the room.

'So, back to Carrie,' Jess said. 'I guess you need to ask her if she'll help.'

'I guess,' Quinn said. 'Who knows her the best? Adam? Will you ask her for us?'

Adam shook his head. 'I think you should.'

'Me?' Quinn looked around.

'It's your idea,' Dan pointed out. 'Your crusade.'

'But she doesn't know me. Why should she even listen to me?'

'Because Dan will go with you,' Trish said, appearing once again without warning to clear away the remains of Quinn's dinner. 'And everyone knows Dan's a stand-up sort of a guy.'

Dan saw Adam and Jack exchange a glance. He knew what they were thinking. Trish was something of a matchmaker. She'd put her two cents worth in for Jack and Ellen. Also for Adam and Jess. All were now happily settled. It wouldn't work on Dan, of course. He wasn't marriage material. But if Trish's schemes gave him a little time with Quinn, that wouldn't be so bad.

'So, when do we do this?' Quinn asked, oblivious to the currents around her.

'No time like the present,' Adam decided. 'I can tell you how to get to her place.'

'All right. Give me a minute.' Quinn closed down her laptop and gathered her knitting into its bag. 'I'll be right back.' She headed in the direction of her room, but halfway across the lounge she stopped and turned back.

'Thanks for the help,' she said to them, but her eyes were on Dan.

Adam, Jess and Jack waved away her words.

Dan said nothing. She would never know it, but in his heart he knew the truth – he was the one who should be thanking her.

Chapter Eight

The light swinging across the lounge room curtains told Carrie she had visitors even before she heard the car easing down her long driveway. Her rented house was on the very outskirts of town. The only time she saw a light or heard a car was when someone was coming to visit her. That didn't happen very often. She reached for the TV remote and with a touch of her finger consigned the New York police and their latest investigation to darkness. She wasn't a particular fan of American police drama, but the sound from the television filled the silence in her house. And if she tried very hard, she might start thinking about their problems, rather than her own.

She eased herself out of her chair and walked to the window. She hated the way she peered through the curtains like some frightened old woman, but she seldom got visitors. And she was no stranger to fear.

The Land Rover pulling up outside had a logo on the door. She couldn't see it clearly in the darkness, but she recognised the man who got out. She'd seen the park ranger around. She remembered people talking about how he rescued an injured girl from the caves in the park. People said he was a good guy. A tall blonde woman got out of the passenger seat. Carrie had never seen her before, but there was a lot about her Carrie recognised. Her self-assured manner. The ease with which she carried herself. This was obviously a strong woman. A woman with things to do and places to go. The sort of woman Carrie used to be.

She stepped back from the window. For a fleeting moment she thought about ducking into her bedroom to change. But the knock on the door came too soon. Well, she would just have to answer the door wearing cut-off jeans shorts and a T-shirt. She flicked her brown hair behind her ears and reached for the doorknob.

'Hi, Carrie, I'm Dan Mitchell. I'm the ranger out at Tyangi Crossing National Park.'

'I know,' Carrie said brusquely.

'This is Quinn,' Dan continued. 'She's just passing through town. She's a photographer.'

'Hi, Carrie.' Quinn smiled and held out her hand.

Carrie took it reluctantly. She wasn't sure how to react to this beautiful, confident stranger. She didn't speak, waiting for her visitors to explain themselves.

'Carrie, we need your help,' Quinn said earnestly. 'It's about the brumbies in the park. Dan's been ordered to shoot them.'

'What?' Carrie was truly horrified. She turned to Dan. 'Why?'

Dan didn't answer, and the way his mouth twitched into a harsh line made her think he was as shocked as she was by the thought of such slaughter.

'It's a long story,' Quinn said. 'But the most important thing is we want to save them. And we need your help.'

'Can we come in and talk to you about it?' Dan asked.

Carrie stepped back to allow them inside. Quinn smiled in an encouraging way. The lounge room had only two armchairs. Quinn took one. After a moment's hesitation Dan took one of the two chairs from the small dining table and pulled it up next to Quinn. Carrie looked around the room, seeing it as Quinn and Dan must be seeing it. Sparsely furnished, the room was clean and neat, but that neatness wasn't due to her housekeeping skills. Mostly it was due to the total lack of clutter. There were no framed photographs. Very few books on the bookshelves, and no mementoes or souvenirs. No trophies, either. Nothing to indicate that this was the home of someone who had been a brilliant young jockey, whose first seasons on the track had broken records and accumulated a host of wins. Looking around, Carrie realised the room was totally impersonal. There was nothing of her here. This was a house where she lived, but it was not a home.

She propped herself on the edge of the other armchair. 'So, what's this all about?'

They told her. As they talked, Carrie could feel it all coming back to her. The beauty and strength of the horses she loved. The soft touch of equine lips on the palm of her hand, delicately tasting the treat held there. The silky sheen beneath her fingers as she stroked an arched neck. The feel of a thoroughbred racing beneath her. The glorious power of strong muscle and ever stronger heart. The wind in her face and the smell of leather and sweat. The roar of the crowd and the thunder of hooves entering the home straight. The heart-stopping moment when the horse beneath her faltered and fell ...

'So we need someone who knows about horses,' Quinn was saying. 'Someone who knows people who know horses. We need help catching the brumbies. And we need somewhere to put them. The doctor ... Adam ... thought you might be able to help us.'

Adam ... his voice reassuring her. His hands holding a needle explaining how he had to extract the air from her chest. The memory of him thrusting that huge needle into her body still woke her at night. And when it did, there were tears on her face.

Carrie suddenly realised that the others were looking at her, as if expecting an answer.

'I'm sorry. I don't think I can really help,' she said. 'I'm not a jockey any more. I don't move in that world ... not now.'

'But you did.' Quinn leaned forward eagerly. 'You know people. And you know about horses. I've never ridden a horse. I don't think I've even patted one … except maybe at a school fete when I was small. There's a lot you can do to help us save those brumbies.'

'No!' Carrie bit back the panic that was starting to rise. 'I've got a job now. I work at the feed store. I haven't got the time. I'm sorry. Really I am. I hope you find a way to save the brumbies. I really do. But I can't help you.'

She got to her feet and quickly moved towards the door, hoping her guests would take the hint.

'But …' Quinn appeared set to argue, but Dan interrupted her.

'I'm sorry you feel that way,' he said as he stood. 'If you change your mind, or if you think of anyone who might be able to help us, we really would appreciate it.'

Carrie nodded. She stood rock still, pushing her hands deep in her pockets as Dan opened the front door.

'Thanks for your time, Carrie,' he said in a gentle voice. His blue eyes held hers for a moment, and she thought she saw a shadow behind his smile. Then he ushered a reluctant Quinn out and closed the door behind them.

Carrie let out a huge sigh and turned back towards her empty living room. She dropped back into the chair, but didn't reach for the TV remote. No fake crime drama was going to distract her now. She felt desperately sorry for the brumbies. And for the man who had been ordered to shoot them. It was wrong. But there was nothing she could do to stop it.

She raised her hands in front of her face and looked at them. They were shaking. She clenched her fists to try to stop them, but it didn't work and the tears began to well up in her eyes. She wanted to find the person she used to be. Was this her chance? She looked at her shaking hands again and knew that it was not. She could never be that person again. She didn't have the courage.

'I really don't understand,' Quinn muttered to herself. 'She must love horses. Why won't she help us?'

The hotel bar was deserted. Quinn was seated on a stool, a glass of orange juice in front of her, continuing her fruitless searching for help on the web. Before returning to the park last night, Dan had promised her another day or two to find someone to help them save the brumbies. But, he'd warned, after that he would have no other option but to follow his orders. As he'd spoken the words, Quinn knew he was as eager as she was to find another answer.

Trish Warren was polishing glasses in anticipation of the late afternoon rush of business, which was due to start shortly.

'You know she was hurt,' Trish said. 'A fall at the Birdsville Races last year. Adam and his wife, Jess – you know she's the pilot of the air ambulance – well they flew her to Mt Isa Hospital. Something to do with her breathing. From what I hear Carrie never went back to racing after that.'

'Oh.' That did explain the total lack of anything even vaguely related to horse racing in Carrie's home. House – Quinn corrected herself. There had been nothing homely about it. Quinn understood all about houses that were not homes. She felt a surge of sympathy for Carrie.

'She works at the feed store now,' Trish continued. 'Only part-time. But she would know some of the people who go there. There must be someone else. Let me have a think. I'm just going back to the kitchen to start sorting things out for the dinner rush. Syd will be back in a minute. But if someone else comes in, just give me a call.'

Trish vanished through the doorway towards the back

of the hotel, still talking. Quinn tuned the voice out and typed brumby rescue once more into her search engine.

'How many brumbies are there?'

Quinn turned around to find Carrie standing in the doorway of the pub. Quinn knew Carrie was in her mid-twenties, but at that moment, she seemed very young and very uncertain.

'Dan thinks there are about forty of them.'

'I'd like to see them.'

'Of course.' Quinn looked at her watch. 'They come to drink at the billabong at sunset. At least they have been. It'll take about an hour and a half to get there. We should make it just in time.'

'Dan isn't going to … tonight? Is he?'

'No. He's holding off as long as there is still some hope we can rescue them.'

Carrie nodded. Quinn had the feeling the girl was holding on very, very tightly to her emotions … and whatever those emotions were, Quinn would have bet money that fear was right on the top of the list.

Quinn quickly darted up to her room to put her laptop away and collect the keys to her HHcar. She thought briefly about trying to let Dan know they were on the way, but decided against it. She wanted to get back to Carrie before the girl changed her mind.

Apart from a brief exclamation of awe when she saw the Hummer, Carrie spoke very little during the long drive to the national park. Quinn didn't push her. When they reached the ranger station, one glance at the carport told Quinn that Dan wasn't there.

'He's probably at the same spot we're heading to,' Quinn told Carrie. 'He's monitoring the brumbies fairly closely.' She didn't want to tell Carrie how badly the horses had been spooked – and by whom.

They set off in the direction of the billabong. Quinn spotted Dan's Land Rover and pulled up next to it. She and Carrie climbed to the top of the ridge. Quinn noticed that Carrie made light work of the steep scramble. Whatever physical injuries she had suffered in that fall, she seemed to be completely recovered.

Dan was already there, hidden among the rocks. He was not carrying his rifle. Of the brumbies, there was no sign. Carrie barely acknowledged Dan's presence. She carefully and quietly lowered herself into position among the rocks, a little distant from the others, where she had a good view of the billabong.

Dan looked at Quinn, raising one eyebrow in question. Quinn shrugged. No one said a word. An almost tangible stillness settled over the three people as they waited for the herd to appear.

The sky was turning all shades of purple and pink when they finally came. They walked slowly down the base of the gorge, heads turning to look around them. They were still wary. The stallion brought up the rear, his shapely head tossing as he scented the air, alert for the merest suggestion of danger to his herd. His white blaze was easy to spot in the gathering twilight. Quinn's fingers twitched, aching for the camera that she had left in the Hummer. She hadn't dared risk it. The horses were so nervous now that even the clicking of a shutter would send them flying.

Beside her, Dan silently reached out and placed his hand on her arm. She turned to look at him. Silently he directed her gaze towards Carrie.

Carrie was staring down into the gorge, her face shining with emotion. Quinn thought she caught a glimpse of tears. She hoped that was a good sign.

Quinn turned back to Dan, and saw that he was smiling. A slow, satisfied smile that looked very good on him. Quinn became very conscious that his hand was still on her arm. His touch was warm. She felt slightly bereft when he moved it away.

The three sat in silence for what seemed like half a lifetime, as the horses drank their fill, then turned and made their way back up the gorge at a leisurely pace, picking at the vegetation as they went. The sun was long gone, and soon the horses faded into the darkness, leaving not even the sound of their passing.

Quinn sighed and got to her feet, stretching her cramped muscles. Beside her, Dan was doing the same when Carrie leaped to her feet.

'I know him!' she said, her voice brimming with excitement.

'Know who?' Quinn asked.

'The stallion. I know him. I've ridden his sister. She was just wonderful.' Carrie shook her head, as if she couldn't believe what she had just seen. She took a long slow breath to calm her emotions. When she spoke again, there was a firmness and confidence in her voice that Quinn had not heard before.

'I know how we can save them.'

Chapter Nine

Justin Fraser tossed his broad-brimmed Akubra into the air. The big bay gelding snorted in fear and leaped away. The reins in Justin's hand snapped tight, spinning the gelding to face him. The horse quivered with tension as it stared at the hat, now lying in the dust at Justin's feet.

'That was not so good,' he said in a low soothing voice. 'It's just a hat you know. It's not all that scary.'

The gelding seemed to disagree. He snorted again and tossed his head as Justin bent to retrieve his hat.

Chuckling quietly, Justin stepped closer to the horse, and threw the hat up into the air again. This time the gelding kept all four feet on the ground and contented himself with rolling his eyes in protest.

'That's better.'

Justin picked up his hat again. Instead of putting it on his head, he placed it against his saddle, and then began moving it over the horse's rump. The horse sidled away but Justin stayed with him, continuing to move the hat over the animal's side and onto its neck. When the horse had remained stationary for almost a minute, Justin tossed the hat into the air again. This time the gelding ignored it.

'Well done,' Justin said, stroking the bay's nose. A horse that spooked every time a man's hat blew off was no good to anyone. 'That's more the sort of behaviour we expect from a Fraser horse. You keep that up, and you'll go far.'

At least, Justin hoped he'd go far. And bring a good price at sale when he did.

Justin retrieved his old Akubra from the dust. The hat had been through the same process with quite a few young horses and looked very much the worse for wear. But it was comfortable and it still kept the sun off his face. He had his good Sunday hat, of course. Not that he used it often. Running a property like this single-handed was hard work. He seldom took a day off.

Beside him the big bay gelding raised his head and whinnied loudly, gazing into the distance. Justin followed the horse's gaze, taking in the broad flat paddocks, the scattered trees. The grass still retained a touch of green from the rain, while above the sky was a brilliant blue. He took a deep breath to breathe in the scent of the land. Fraser land. Land that he loved, as had his father and grandfather before him.

'So, feel like stretching your legs?' Justin asked.

In response the gelding tossed his head.

'All right, then,' Justin said. He swept the reins over the horse's head and moved to its side. Anticipating what was to happen next, the big gelding started to prance. Justin tightened the inner rein, forcing the animal to circle him, rather than step away. He lifted one booted foot to the stirrup and lifted himself smoothly into the saddle. The gelding humped his back and gave a small jump.

'So, that's how it is,' Justin said, closing his long legs firmly against the animal's sides. He seldom wore gloves when working a young horse, preferring to keep a more sensitive contact on the reins. His hands responded as the horse dropped its head again and bucked once. Justin held his seat easily. He urged the horse forward with legs and hands and body. The gelding complied. He pranced a few more steps before breaking into a long striding swift trot. Justin curtailed his own impatience for another two minutes, holding the horse at a steady speed to make sure the lesson registered. Then he nudged the animal gently with his heels.

The horse leaped forward. He stretched his legs into

a ground-eating gallop. Justin held himself easily in the saddle, his body completely in tune with the movement of the horse beneath him. This was the best part of his day. This was what made the sweat and the sacrifice worthwhile. This feeling. This was what made his heart beat and his lungs draw breath. This was why he was born. Justin lost himself in the joy of the moment.

All too soon, he began to bring the horse back to a slower pace. The gelding was young. He couldn't stand up to this hard pace across the dry earth for too long. But one day he would. Justin stroked the horse's neck, now dark with sweat, and the animal relaxed, its breath still heaving through flared nostrils. The gelding was a good horse. Not quite the quality Justin was striving for, but a good animal nonetheless. He would certainly make a good stock horse. Maybe even make a showing at campdraft competitions, or picnic race meetings. Justin would get a reasonable price for him. There were a couple more youngsters also showing promise. Maybe this year he'd have enough money for that infusion of new blood his stock needed. He'd prefer an infusion of old blood, but that just wasn't possible any more.

Justin was feeling pretty good as he rode back through the home paddock towards the yards and stables. He let the gelding relax, stretching its head long and low as it walked quietly. It was almost midday. Justin decided he'd have a quick look through the latest sales catalogues as he grabbed something for lunch. He had a couple of horses almost ready for sale, and it would be good to know what else was on offer, and what sort of prices were being paid. And there'd be listings of potential stud stallions for sale too. Even if he wasn't ready to buy yet, it couldn't hurt to know what was out there. This afternoon he had two more horses to work – and he wanted to check the water level in his dams. Then he needed to check the fence line.

The gelding lifted its head and whinnied loudly.

'Eager to get back?' Justin asked. Then he realised what had attracted the horse's attention. There was a vehicle parked in his stable yard. And three people obviously waiting for him. He didn't get visitors often – and now three in one go.

'I wonder what this is all about?' he mused.

He didn't hurry. As always, his first thought was for the animal he was training. That was always how it was. His father, the legendary trainer, Sean Fraser, had taught him well. Justin could no more have broken that rule than he could have caused rain to fall from the achingly blue sky above.

The gelding did not put a foot wrong as Justin opened the last gate without dismounting. They approached the stables at a walk. As he drew closer Justin recognised the National Parks logo on the door of the vehicle. He also recognised the park ranger. They had met once, briefly, while both were buying supplies in Coorah Creek, his nearest town just fifty kilometres away. He couldn't remember the man's name, but did remember his distinctive red hair. The tall blonde woman was a stranger to him. And the third ...

The gelding tossed his head as Justin's hands clenched on the reins. For once, Justin didn't instantly respond. His eyes were fixed on the third person waiting for him.

It was Carrie Bryant.

He'd seen her ride more than once. The first time was at Mt Isa Races. She was mounted on a big grey. The horse had been a top earner as a two-year-old, and was looking to set some records in its second year on the track. Carrie seemed so tiny up on his back, but she had been totally at home: moving with the horse and keeping it controlled until that moment when the barriers lifted and the horses flung themselves at breakneck speed down the track. That ride had truly been something to see. Carrie held the big grey just behind the leading pack until exactly the right moment, then unleashed the animal's power and speed. More than that, she had somehow managed to tap into the horse's psyche and desire to win. On the straight, Carrie steered her horse wide and they passed the pack as if the others were standing still. She won that race by more than two lengths.

Justin was one of thousands of people cheering her as she rode to the winners' circle. She removed her helmet and held it high over her head to acknowledge the adoration of the crowd. Her face was stained with dust and sweat. Her short dark hair stuck out around her head in a spiky mess. But her face was shining with sheer joy and Justin thought she was the most beautiful woman he'd ever seen.

On reaching the winners' enclosure, Carrie had leaped from the saddle and pulled her gear from the horse's back. In the few seconds before going for the official weigh-in, she paused long enough to stroke the big grey's face. When the animal lowered its head to accept her hand, Carrie had leaned forward and planted an exuberant kiss right on the animal's nose.

At that moment, Justin had fallen just a little bit in love.

He'd fallen a little further each time he saw her ride until that terrible day at Birdsville Races when her horse stumbled, sending her rolling beneath the flashing hooves of the racehorses. He'd watched helplessly as she'd been rushed to the air ambulance and flown to the hospital for surgery.

He'd only seen her once since then. At the back of the feed store, when he was picking up supplies. She had looked tired and thin and pale. Just a shadow of the woman she'd been. They hadn't spoken. He would not have known what to say to her.

And now here she was, standing in his stable yard. Waiting for him. She still looked a little pale and thin. He didn't like to see her looking so fragile. There was sadness in her eyes and his heart ached for her.

Justin halted the gelding and swung down from the saddle. As he did, the gelding took fright at some imaginary hazard and shied to one side. Carrie's face paled even more and she quickly stepped back. Almost as if she was frightened. Justin took a firmer grip on the animal's reins.

'I don't know if you remember, I'm Dan Mitchell.' The red-haired man stepped forward and extended his hand. 'I'm the ranger at the Tyangi Park.'

'Of course.' Justin took the man's hand.

'And this is Quinn. She's a wildlife photographer.'

Justin shook the woman's hand, impressed by the firmness of her grip and the clear friendliness of her eyes.

'And this is—'

'Carrie Bryant,' Justin interrupted. 'I know. I saw your ride on Hawkwood at Mt Isa a couple of years ago. It was really something to see. I lost a few dollars that day because I didn't have the sense to bet on you.'

Carrie smiled, but didn't step forward or offer to shake his hand. 'I'm sorry about that,' she said in a too quiet voice.

'Don't worry. I got it back next time you rode and I bet on you.' Justin watched her face for a few seconds, but apart from a quick glance up at him, she kept her eyes fixed on the horse moving restlessly at his side.

'So, what brings you here?' He directed the question at Dan.

'It's a long story,' Dan said. 'But we are here to ask for your help.'

Before Justin could respond, Carrie took a step sideways to put a greater distance between herself and the horse. Only then did she take her eyes off the animal to look at Justin. She fastened her deep amber eyes on his face as she said, 'We've found Mariah's son.'

A photo in a plain wooden frame sat in pride of place on the bookshelf in the spacious living room. It showed a tall thin man holding a horse at some event. The horse had a ribbon around its neck. The man had a smile that seemed about to split his face in two. He was an older version of Justin; tall and lean with a craggy and weathered face that could have been hewn from rock. Despite that, he was a handsome man, as was his son. Carrie picked the frame up and after a long look at the image of the horse, she passed it to Quinn.

'That's Mariah ... or to use her full name, Mariah's Light. Isn't she extraordinary?'

'I don't know anything about horses,' Quinn said as she passed the photo to Dan. 'She's beautiful, I guess. But I don't get it.'

'Is this Justin's father with her?' Dan asked as he looked at the photo.

'Yes. Sean Fraser. He was a great horseman,' Carrie said. 'He built this place, and a reputation for breeding the best Australian Stock Horses in Queensland. Among the best in the country. People would come from all over to buy his bloodlines. They were pretty successful rodeo and campdraft horses. Won more than a few amateur races. But they were good working stock too. Out here, that counts for a lot. People were willing to pay a lot of money for a Fraser horse. Some were even exported to other countries.'

'And this mare?' Quinn asked as she returned the photo to its place on the shelves.

'The whole Fraser bloodline was based on one horse – a big blood bay stallion called Finnegan. He was getting old and Justin's father needed to replace him. He bought Mariah and bred them. The first season they got a filly. She's racing now. I rode her once.' Carrie hesitated, fighting back emotions that threatened to surface at the memory of that glorious ride. Not now, she told herself. Not now. Not ever. 'What Sean really wanted was a colt,' she added.

'To take his sire's place.' Understanding was evident on Quinn's face.

'That's right. The next year Mariah was again in foal to Finnegan when a bushfire swept through this area. Several of the horses were injured – including the stallion. He had to be put down. In the confusion Mariah vanished. It was always assumed she went bush and died.'

'How do you know all this?' Quinn asked.

'It's a local legend among the racing fraternity,' Carrie replied. She ran her fingers through her hair. 'Sean Fraser was a great horseman. Fraser-bred horses were the best. Growing up, all I ever wanted was to own a Fraser horse.'

'What Carrie is too polite to say,' said Justin coming through the door, 'is that things went downhill for us after that fire. My father was diagnosed with Alzheimer's. It progressed rapidly. We weren't able to replace the lost stock … at least not with horses of similar quality. My parents moved east. I kept the place running, but most of the money went to Dad's treatment.'

Justin joined them at the bookshelf and picked up the photo of his father and the mare. 'He's gone now.'

Carrie heard the deep sadness in his voice.

'Mum moved in with her sister on the coast,' Justin

continued as he replaced the photograph. 'She said it was too lonely here for her without Dad. I'm trying to get the place back on a solid footing again. Which brings me to ask ...' He turned to look at Carrie, his green eyes troubled. 'What did you mean that you've found Mariah's son?'

Carrie couldn't hold his gaze. What if she was wrong? The thought hadn't even occurred to her until this very moment. What if she gave him hope – only to have it crushed again? She didn't want to do that. 'Have you got a photo somewhere of the stallion?'

'There's this.' Justin moved to the door next to the bookcase. He pushed it open and stood back so the others could see inside. It was a small room, obviously his office. There was a computer on the desk, and a selection of horse related magazines littered about. But that was not what caught her attention. Carrie's eyes went straight to the painting hanging over the desk. Done by an artist of some skill, it showed a thoroughbred stallion. His coat was such a rich dark brown it was almost black. His shapely head was held proudly – and a large white blaze ran down his face, sliding off to one side as if the artist had slipped while painting it.

Beside her, Quinn drew a sharp breath. 'But that's the spitting image ...' Her voice tailed off.

It was left to Carrie to speak the words. She turned to Justin, and spoke with absolute certainty. 'Mariah had a colt. He survived and now he's running with the brumbies.'

Chapter Ten

'Are you sure?' Justin knew he'd asked the question a dozen times already, but he couldn't help himself. The wait at the top of the gorge was killing him.

'I'm sure,' Carrie said softly.

He hoped she was right. If she was she had just changed his whole world.

Careful not to make a noise, Justin eased his weight on the rough sandstone rock and stretched his legs for a few blessed moments before dropping back into his hidden position. The four of them were settled among some big sandstone boulders near a billabong in the National Park. The moment Carrie had told him what she'd seen in this place, he'd practically forced them to bring him here. He had to know if his father's legacy was waiting for him among the wild horses.

He glanced up at the sun. 'They'll be here soon. If they are coming.'

The waterhole was deserted, except for half a dozen kangaroos picking at the short green grass at the water's edge.

'It's the best water in this part of the park,' Dan said. 'They'll be here.'

If they haven't been frightened away, Justin thought. Dan had told him the whole story during the hour long drive from his property to Tyangi Park. The authorities wanted the horses out of the park, and it was Dan's job to do that, one way or the other. Justin had been shocked to learn that the parks authority considered shooting the horses an appropriate solution. He was a horseman. He knew that brumbies were usually not the best examples of their species, but even so ... they deserved better than that. He understood Dan's reluctance to carry out his instructions. He was looking for a way out and Justin was going to help him. Even if the stallion wasn't Mariah's colt, he would try to save the brumbies.

Justin felt a sudden cold shiver run up his spine. Dan had confessed to almost shooting the stallion. If he had ... and the stallion really was Mariah's colt ... Justin did not want to think about how close he may have come to losing this chance.

The roos by the waterhole paused in their grazing, their pointed faces turned towards the faint sound of hoof beats approaching from the west. The leading horses came into view. Two mares led the brumby herd at an easy walk. Both had foals at their sides. And both foals had a distinctive white blaze down their faces.

Justin stopped breathing as a yearling trotted past the mares, heading for the sweet smell of the water. He was a chestnut, with one white stocking and that same crooked blaze down his face.

'There he is,' Carrie whispered beside him. Justin instinctively reached for her hand as he watched a ghost walk into the gully.

On Justin's thirteenth birthday his father had walked with him down to the stables where Finnegan was waiting. Unlike some of his contemporaries, Sean Fraser believed his stud horses should also be ridden. Justin had spent hours watching his father and the big bay stallion with the crooked white blaze. Together they formed that rare thing – a perfect partnership of horse and rider. Justin's young heart yearned to be that good; to have the same close connection with such a magnificent horse. On this momentous day, Sean had saddled his stallion and led him from the stable yard. With no ceremony at all, he simply handed the reins to his son. Justin's heart was pounding with a mixture of fear and excitement. He was really too short to ride the big thoroughbred, but that didn't bother him. With the skill of a born horseman honed by years of his father's training, he had managed to swing onto the horse's back. There had followed the best forty minutes of his young life, basking in the glow of his father's approval.

That day he had found his life's purpose on the back of a horse they were to lose so terribly during the bushfire. Every day since then, Justin had worked to become as good as his father. To carry on after his father was gone. Today, for the first time, he saw the possibility of achieving those goals as he watched Finnegan's twin walk towards him.

There was absolutely no doubt in his mind. This was Finnegan's last son. Mariah must have survived the fire and foaled in the wild. Most of the herd was visible now, milling around at the water's edge. He ran his eye over the mares, but the one he sought was not there. That was tragic. She had been a lovely creature, beautiful to look at and equally so in her nature. She might not have survived the rigours of life in the outback – but her colt had. Survived and more. Justin could hardly believe what he was seeing.

The stallion was spectacular. He was the spitting image of his sire: in the way he moved and the arrogance of his carriage, not to mention that distinctive blaze on his face. There was something of his dam in him too. Mariah's gift was the underlying red gleam of his unbrushed coat and the elegance in the fine bones of his legs.

Justin closed his eyes as emotion took him.

I wish you could see him, Dad. He's everything you said he would be. And more.

When he opened his eyes, it was Carrie he saw. Her eyes were bright with unshed tears. She smiled at him, the first genuine happiness he'd seen on her face since her race fall.

Carrie had found Mariah's son and brought Justin here. She had opened a door that he had believed was closed to him forever. In just a couple of hours, she had changed his life. He didn't know how he would ever express his gratitude.

He suddenly realised he was still holding her hand. He clasped it with both of his and squeezed ever so gently. He looked into her eyes and slowly smiled.

'Thank you,' he whispered in a voice so low only Carrie would hear.

For a dozen heartbeats they stayed like that, then a squeal from one of the colts dragged their attention back to the waterhole. Reluctantly, Justin released Carrie's hand and gave himself over to watching the stallion. He had sought higher ground, standing guard over the herd as they relaxed by the waterhole. His intelligent face turned to look for danger, as his nostrils flared, reading the wind. Satisfied, the stallion finally relaxed and moved towards the billabong so he too could drink.

Justin could have watched them for hours.

When at last the horses started moving away, Justin turned to Dan.

'Okay,' he said. 'I'm in. There's no doubt in my mind. That is Mariah's son. And I want him back. I'll take the foals as well, if you like. In fact, I'll take them all, if you're happy with that.'

'I was hoping you'd say that. They're all yours. If we can catch them.'

'I don't suppose there are any stockyards in the park anywhere?' Justin said, thinking out loud.

'Nope.' Dan shook his head. 'But I have an idea.'

'Tell me.'

'It would be easier to show you. Follow me.'

* * *

As he led the others away from the billabong, Dan felt the first stirrings of hope. Getting Justin on the team was a big leap forward. He and Carrie had the necessary skills to pull this off and save the horses. And Justin had just solved the issue of what to do with them once they were caught. Maybe, just maybe, he was going to be spared.

'Dan, why don't you ride with me?'

Quinn's question caught him a little off guard. Earlier this afternoon, he'd left his park vehicle at the ranger station. It was almost out of petrol, and rather than waste time while he refuelled, he had travelled the rest of the way in Justin's ute. Both women had followed in Quinn's Humvee, which she had stubbornly refused to leave behind. Dan had assumed the same arrangement would apply as they made their way to their next stop.

He looked at Quinn and raised an eyebrow.

By way of an answer, she just nodded to where Justin and Carrie were walking together, deep in conversation.

'I guess we should let the experts start planning,' he said. Quinn gave a derisive snort that left him totally baffled.

The two vehicles were parked in the shade of a small clump of acacia trees, where there was no danger the horses would be spooked by them. The long, low square shape of Quinn's Humvee was as familiar to Dan as his own face. This one was painted in a shiny golden metallic gloss paint, not desert camouflage, but in the dim light and covered with red dust it didn't look all that different to the Humvees he had spent so much time in during his tours. Except for the roof. There was no weapons shield.

No heavy machine gun.

No MK19 grenade gun.

But guns were no protection against an IED.

A roadside bomb.

The sound was deafening, and the shockwave

pummelled his body like an iron fist as the Humvee shot into the air and rolled, coming to rest on its side.

The smell of smoke. Of flesh burning.

The screams were dim at first. As if coming from a distance. But as his ears cleared, they were closer and closer. All around him.

The screams were his screams too, as they dragged him from the Humvee ...

Lying on the sand as his unit opened fire.

Blood and pain ...

'Dan ... Dan!'

He blinked and the pain and confusion and noise in his head faded to be replaced by the slow peaceful sounds of twilight in the outback. Beside him, Quinn stood with her head on one side, her brows creased.

'Dan, are you—'

'Sorry,' he said hastily. 'I was daydreaming.'

The narrowing of her eyes told him she didn't believe that. She was too smart a woman not to suspect that something was wrong with him.

Before Quinn could ask anything more, Dan moved swiftly to the passenger side of the Hummer. He already knew Quinn well enough to know she wasn't about to relinquish the driver's seat. And besides, he thought as he reached for the door, it was better that the driver's hands were not shaking the way his were.

He fought the memories down. This was a different Humvee in a different time and place. There was no threat here. He opened the door and got in.

The inside wasn't like any Humvee he'd ever been in before.

It wasn't just the lack of armour. Or the comfortable seats. The back of the vehicle was fitted with built-in cabinets in polished wood. There was a bedding roll and what looked like a folding table and chairs. Everything was neat and in its place. This was set up so its owner could live out of the back with ease and a certain degree of comfort. This car was every camper's dream.

And there was something else that drew a sharp line between this Hummer and the ones he'd been so intimately familiar with in Iraq. There was nothing here of the grunts he'd served with. No sweat. No taste of rifle oil and cordite in the air. No blood ... There was only the softest hint of some sweet smell.

The other door opened and as Quinn slid in next to him he recognised the smell.

That soft, sweet scent was Quinn. Not some perfume that she wore ... Quinn herself.

Dan felt the past recede.

'So where to?' she asked.

The route was circuitous. They had to circle around a deep gully and cross a dry riverbed. But eventually Dan directed Quinn to stop. Justin pulled up next to them and all four of them walked into a narrow gorge.

'You're the experts. What do you think? Will it do?' Dan pushed his hat to the back of his head and looked at Carrie and Justin.

Without answering, the two of them began to walk. Just ahead a river had once cut through a high sandstone ridge. It was dry now. A sandy bed maybe fifteen meters wide, with a few scrubby plants growing there. The important part was the banks. The sandstone rose sharply to form what could only be described as cliffs. Cliffs far too steep for a horse to climb.

'How far are we from the place where they come to drink?' Justin asked.

'Maybe two miles,' Dan said. 'It's an easy two miles though. The horses wouldn't have to come the way we did in the cars. There is a gully that leads directly here. I thought … well, hoped, that maybe you could herd the horses down that gully to this point.'

'If we could build a couple of good fences – make a yard …' Justin had caught Dan's idea. 'You say it's a couple of miles directly from the billabong to here?'

'Yes.'

'Let's go take a look.' Justin set off eagerly.

As the four of them set off down the gully, Dan suddenly realised they were walking as two couples. No. Not couples, he thought. Not like that. Justin and Carrie were their experts. They knew about horses so it was only sensible that they should be walking together, discussing the problems they faced.

As for him and Quinn … they certainly weren't a couple. They weren't even friends. Barely acquaintances, really. And when this was all over, she would move on. She wasn't for the likes of him. A woman as beautiful as her could have any man she wanted. A man worthy of her …

He was suddenly aware that Quinn had stopped walking. He turned back to see her standing slightly off to one side, her camera to her eye. He followed the direction of the lens. Quinn was taking shots of Justin and Carrie walking down the centre of the dry riverbed in the shadow of the red rock walls that were growing ever higher and steeper on either side of them.

'What's that for?' he asked as Quinn finished her shots and fell back into step beside him.

'I just want to document this.'

'Why? Trying to get me into trouble?'

'No. Quite the reverse. I have a feeling something rather special is going to happen here. And there needs to be a record of it.'

Chapter Eleven

Carrie sat outside the pub, staring at the light streaming through the open doors. Even from inside her car she could hear the sound of voices. She was supposed to meet Justin here tonight. And Dan and Quinn too. They were going to work out a plan to rescue the brumbies. To rescue Justin's heritage.

She so wanted to be a part of that.

She was so very afraid to be a part of that.

She wrapped her right arm protectively around her ribs, mentally bracing for the pain, but there was none. She had totally recovered from her fall at the Birdsville Races, thanks to Dr Adam and his pilot, Jess. At her final appointment, Dr Adam had told her there was nothing to stop her riding again. Her collapsed lung was healed. She had her strength back. She was ready to ride.

But she wasn't.

Dr Adam and Jess had been married a couple of weeks after that appointment, just as Carrie moved into Coorah Creek to work at the feed store. The wedding had distracted most of the town. No one, not even Dr Adam, had asked why she had taken that job rather than return to the racetrack, and for that she was grateful. By the time the wedding fuss was over, people had become used to her presence. She had never had to explain to anyone ... just herself.

She'd seen the press photos of her fall. They were quite shocking. They showed a dark shape that was her own body flying through the air as her horse fell. Even now she shuddered when she thought of that newspaper clipping, long since torn up and thrown away.

Sitting there in her car, Carrie could hear voices floating out through the windows of the hotel. And laughter. The laughter was harder to take than the pain. Carrie closed her eyes as she remembered.

She had been so very eager to get back to riding. The day after Dr Adam declared her fit she drove out to the stables at daybreak, looking forward to getting on with her life again. Horses she knew and had ridden before were waiting for their morning exercise. She parked her car in a familiar spot and got out, breathing deep the much-loved smells of horses and hay and listening to the voices of the stable boys as they went about their morning tasks. It felt so good to be back where she belonged.

She was welcomed with much enthusiasm by the trainer. She was his top jockey and she had been missed. Carrie Bryant won races. Having her as part of his team ensured he was offered the top young horses to train. She was money in the bank.

He signalled one of the stable boys to bring out his newest charge. The horse was beautiful. A golden chestnut filly, young and elegant, brimming with energy and power. Carrie watched her approach, waiting for that familiar lifting of her heart that always came at moments like this.

But it didn't.

Instead her legs suddenly felt too weak to hold her. Her palms began to sweat and her hands to shake. Her breath caught in her throat as she struggled to draw breath, just as she had all those months ago lying in the sand at Birdsville.

The horse tossed its head and pranced a few steps, revelling in the cool crisp air and the promise of a chance to stretch her lovely long legs on the exercise track.

Carrie took a quick step backwards and almost stumbled.

The trainer had turned to her, his brow furrowed.

As the stable boy led the filly closer, Carrie's crippling panic had begun to overwhelm her. She stumbled backwards, conscious of the shock on the trainer's face. She heard something else too – the whispering of the stable boys. Then one of them had laughed. At her. Without saying a word, she had turned and fled, tears of shame pouring down her face.

She had never gone back.

Carrie reached out to turn the key in her car's ignition. She didn't belong here. The others had asked her to join because they needed someone with her horse handling skills — the skills that had made her a top jockey. But she wasn't a jockey any more. She couldn't work with horses any more. Just being around one was enough to set her hands shaking. She thought back to the day she met Justin. Having his gelding so close had almost paralysed her with fear. That gelding was well bred and trained and no doubt far gentler than any racehorse she'd ever ridden. But even so, she had almost fallen apart. She was not a horsewoman any more. She wasn't anything.

'Hi, Carrie, are you just getting here too?' The voice at her open window froze her hand half a second before she could turn the key to start her engine and back away.

Justin opened her car door, and stepped back to allow her out. He smiled down at her with those sparkling green eyes, looking as if he were genuinely pleased to see her. If he knew what was in her heart, he wouldn't look at her like that. He'd turn away in disgust. Or worse, he'd laugh at her like the stable boys had.

It was too late now for her to back out. To simply drive away and find some excuse. She pulled the key from the ignition and stepped out from behind the wheel.

'Hi, Justin,' she said.

'This is just great,' he said as they walked up the steps together. 'Adam said Jack North was going to be here this evening too. You know Jack, don't you?' He barely waited for her nod. 'He does the maintenance on the air ambulance. And at the mine. He can turn his hand to anything.'

Justin paused on the veranda. He turned to look down at Carrie.

'You know, Carrie. I am actually starting to believe this is real. For such a long time I've wanted to re-invigorate the bloodlines Dad worked so hard to establish. Now, there's a chance to do that. And with the very same horse that Dad had centred his plans around! That's almost too much to comprehend. But it *is* real. And that's all thanks to you.'

His excitement shone out of him like sun after a rainstorm. He was practically quivering with energy and eagerness to get started. Walking beside him, Carrie felt like the worst kind of cheat and coward.

'It's nothing to do with me,' she said, stepping forward into the doorway of the pub. 'You are just so lucky Mariah's colt survived.'

'Hello, Carrie. And Justin. How nice.' Trish Warren grinned in a knowing way as she walked past holding two huge plates of food. 'Nice to see the two of you here … together.'

Carrie felt her face begin to redden. She opened her mouth to say something, and just as quickly closed it again. She hadn't lived in Coorah Creek long, but she knew Trish Warren's reputation already. She was a kind soul, everyone said, but there was no keeping a secret from Trish. Not that Carrie had a secret to keep. Well, not one that involved Justin. They were just friends. Not even friends, really. They'd only just met. And it certainly wasn't going any further. Not when he discovered that the jockey he'd admired was now … nothing.

'The others are in the lounge,' Trish said as she turned back towards the kitchen, having delivered her load to two men sitting at the bar. 'Now that you're here, tell them I'll be over in a few minutes to see what they want to eat.'

'Carrie, can I get you a drink?' Justin asked.

She hesitated, and then decided a drink was just a drink. Especially if it wasn't really a drink. 'Just some coke, thanks,' she said.

'Right. Do you want to join the others and I'll be right over.' Justin turned to the gleaming wooden bar, greeting one or two of the other patrons as he did.

Carrie stood for a moment, watching the ease with which Justin chatted to the men he knew. They seemed pleased to see him, shaking his hand and sharing a few words. He was so much at ease with himself. She used to be like that. She turned towards the lounge.

'Hey, Carrie,' Quinn called.

They were clustered around a big table. Quinn and Dan were both there, as was Jack and a tall tanned man she had never met before.

'Do you two know each other?' Jack asked as Carrie sat down.

She shook her head.

'This is Chris Powell. He's the manager at the Goongalla Mine. He's going to help us out with building some stockyards. Chris, this is Carrie Bryant. She's our horse handler.'

Chris held out his hand. Carrie took it, biting back the urge to shout that she wasn't their horse handler. She was nothing more than a cheat for taking a place at this table. She wasn't even sure why she was there.

She looked up and saw Justin heading their way, glasses

in his hands and a broad smile on his face. He dropped on to the seat next to her and slid over her glass of coke.

'I was just telling Carrie that Chris is going to help out with the building work,' Dan told Justin.

'I can give you some timber and rails. I guess you'll want a couple of wide swinging gates. I can't help with those, I'm afraid. But if you can source them somewhere, I'll take them on my trucks with the lumber.'

'I can talk to my boss at the feed store,' Carrie said tentatively. 'We've got swinging gates. I might be able to convince him to lend us a couple.'

'Great.' She felt absurdly pleased when Justin smiled at her like that. It made her feel almost like she belonged.

'Once we have them penned in that gorge, I'll need to spend a few days settling them before I try to get them home. Obviously the stallion is my priority, but I can take them all unless anyone else wants any of them.'

'What will you do with them?' Dan asked. 'I don't know much about horses, but I guess some of them can't be much use to you.'

'You'd be surprised,' Justin said. 'I can probably train most of them and sell them on. I can promise you that none of them will be destroyed.'

'That's good enough for me.'

Carrie saw the look the two men exchanged. There was agreement. Respect. Perhaps the beginnings of friendship.

Quinn didn't say much during the discussions that followed. The others talked about rails and wire, about transporting feed and water. It seemed to her that re-homing the brumbies was a pretty complex business. She hadn't thought past catching them. But then they had to be fed and watered until they had become used to their captivity. Justin was giving the brumbies a home, but getting them to that new home would not be easy. Quinn heard talk about trucks and loading ramps. About mustering and driving the horses cross-country like cattle. Each suggestion seemed to raise another wave of problems. Quinn decided she should take a back seat and let those who knew what they were talking about take over.

The people of Coorah Creek all seemed to want to help. Several men dropped by to offer help with various parts of the enterprise. The teacher from the school joined them briefly talking about getting her kids involved in a project about brumbies. At one point an older man joined in the conversation. He was introduced to Quinn as the mayor. He was obviously a little on the wrong side of sober as he shook her hand and gushed his approval for the project.

Quinn used his arrival as a cloak to slip away in the general direction of the bathrooms. When she was sure no one was paying her any attention, she darted back up the stairs and collected her camera from her room. From the darkened stairway, she snapped a few shots of the meeting in progress. The story she was going to photograph wasn't just about the horses. It was about these people. This community.

She caught a shot of Jack North sketching some plan on the table top with his finger and the moisture from a cold glass of beer. The water would dry and the drawing would fade, but the idea wouldn't. Nor would the hope she saw on Justin's face every time he mentioned the stallion. She twisted her zoom ring and shot a quick close-up of Dan's face. She could see the lines etched around his eyes. And the crease in his forehead which suggested he frowned far too much. And his eyes. The brilliant blue that went so well with his shock of hair the same dark red as the desert sand. She clicked her shutter once more, suddenly aware that Dan was staring back at her through the lens.

She lowered the camera as Dan rose from the table to join her.

'I think we are go,' he said softly. 'We seem to have everything we need. And if we don't, I have a feeling Justin and the others will find it. Thank you.'

Quinn frowned, very aware of how close Dan was standing to her. The two of them, set apart from the community and the plan it was hatching. 'There's nothing to thank me for.'

'You are the one who got this started,' Dan said. 'If you hadn't ... I might have ...' His voice trailed off and Quinn could sense the pain in him.

'No. I don't think you would. You would have thought of something.'

His eyes searched her face for a few tense moments. He didn't smile. 'I'm not so sure. I was in the military. We were taught to obey orders – not to think. Even then, it's not always as clear-cut as it seems.'

And he was gone, slipping out the door before she could ask what he meant.

Chapter Twelve

Quinn was amazed at how quickly it all came together. It seemed that when the people of Coorah Creek decided to do something, everyone joined in.

The morning after the meeting she headed down to get some breakfast, only to find the pub kitchen was already a hub of activity. Trish was pulling food from her huge freezer. Ellen was packing it into several ice-filled cool boxes.

'The eskies should keep the food good for a couple of days,' Ellen said. 'Then we can restock for you.'

Quinn raised her eyebrows. The discussion the night before had included talk about setting up a camp at the national park. It was easier than spending hours each day travelling to and from town. Justin's place was a little closer, but it would still be more convenient to stay in the park. It would give them more time to work, and also accustom the brumbies to their presence. After the others had left, as she sat up knitting, Quinn had decided to move out to the park today to try to photograph the brumbies before they were moved. But no one knew that yet. She had imagined she would have a day or two of solitude before the others joined her. Apparently not.

'I've put in some frozen steaks,' Trish told her. 'You probably should eat them tonight. The dishes of frozen stew will be slower to defrost. So that should do you for the second night. I talked to Ken at the store and he's just dropped by with some stuff. It's in the bar. There's a box of canned food. Bread, too. Tea, coffee and sugar. And some cooking implements.'

'That's a lot of food,' Quinn said.

'Dan and Justin will be working hard. They'll need a good meal at night,' Trish declared. 'So will you. And there'll be others too. Carrie will be driving out later with a load from the feed store. Jack and Chris Powell will be bringing timber and tools from the mine. The bushfire brigade is lending you a water tanker for the horses. Your own water ...'

Quinn blinked, wondering when all this had been organised. She'd once photographed a military exercise. This was starting to sound very similar. Her little camp was not going to be as small or as private as she had anticipated.

'... will be coming back and forth the most. So he can fetch anything else you need.' Trish stopped talking and looked at her. 'That's okay, isn't it?'

'Of course.' Quinn wasn't sure exactly what she'd agreed to, but she was sure that if Trish Warren was doing the organising, it would be exactly what was needed.

'Excellent.' The older woman almost glowed with satisfaction. 'I'll fix you some breakfast.'

'Just coffee and toast will be fine.'

'Rubbish,' came the declaration from the depths of the fridge. 'Who knows how long you'll be camped out there. This may be your last good meal for a while.' Trish emerged loaded down with bacon, eggs and sausages which she set down by the big stove.

Quinn thought about mentioning that she was a very capable camp cook, and had managed not to starve on many other trips to places even more remote than the national park. Then she caught Ellen's eye. The pregnant woman was trying hard not to grin as she placed a few more items into a box filled with enough food to feed a small army on bivouac.

Quinn made to get to her feet. There was no way she was going to let a pregnant woman lift that heavy box.

But Trish was one step ahead of her.

'Don't you lift that box, Ellen,' Trish said without turning away from the stove. 'Leave it and Syd can carry it out to Quinn's car later.'

Eyes in the back of her head, Ellen mouthed at Quinn.

Just then the door burst open and two small children entered at a run.

'Mum, look! Jack got me a new comic. It's Donald Duck!' The little boy held his prize aloft, a huge smile splitting his face.

'Quinn, this is Harry and Bethany,' Ellen said as she ruffled the girl's blonde hair. 'Kids, this is Quinn.'

Two pairs of huge blue eyes looked up at her. She hadn't seen eyes that blue since … well, for a very long time.

'Hello.' Bethany looked up at her from under her fringe and smiled such a sweet, trusting smile. A part of Quinn wanted to wrap her arms around the little girl and hold her. The other half wanted to run from the room so fast her memories wouldn't catch her.

'Hello, Bethany,' she said quietly.

'I've got to get this pair to school,' Ellen said. 'So I'm off now. Let me know if you need anything else, Trish.'

'I will,' Trish replied from the direction of the stove, where her sizzling pan was starting to exude lovely cooking smells.

'And Quinn, good luck. I really hope this works. I would hate to see those brumbies killed.'

Quinn had barely finished the huge cooked breakfast when the door opened and another familiar figure appeared.

'Glad I caught you before you left,' the doctor said as he came into the kitchen.

'Coffee, Adam?' Trish asked, already reaching for the electric kettle.

'No, thanks. I can't stay,' Adam answered. 'I just wanted to give this to Quinn.' He dropped a bulging rucksack on the table and pulled up a chair.

'And this is …?' Quinn prodded it gently.

'First aid kit. With the sort of work you'll be doing, there are bound to be a few cuts and bruises. I can't come out. I have to stay close to base. And we don't have a nurse.' The doctor's voice softened as he said those words, and Quinn felt an aura of sadness about him. Trish laid a hand briefly on his shoulder as she moved past him to start clearing away the breakfast things. 'Anyway, I guess you'll have to tend your own injuries, unless it's something serious of course.'

'I hope there won't be any need for your services,' Quinn said.

'Me too.' Adam got back to his feet, smiling. 'There's a phone at the ranger station. Call me if anything serious happens.' He raised a hand in farewell as he walked out the door.

'He's the only doctor in town?' Quinn asked Trish.

Trish nodded, sadness reflected on her face too. 'We used to have a nurse. A medical nun. Sister Luke. She and Adam were very close. But she passed away a few months ago.'

'I'm sorry to hear that.' Although the response was automatic, Quinn could feel the very real affection Trish had obviously held for the woman. She was beginning to think that Coorah Creek was a family as much as it was a town.

'We did get a new nurse,' Trish said. 'Not a nun this time, an ordinary nurse. She was a nice young thing but she didn't like it out here. Too remote. It doesn't suit everyone. She left after a few weeks. The second one did too. I don't imagine Adam is proving an easy boss, and Sister Luke left some pretty big shoes to fill.'

Trish dashed a hand across her eyes and resumed her customary demeanour. 'If you want to get your things together after breakfast, I'll get Syd to help you load this stuff in your truck.'

Quinn knew better than to say she didn't need any help. 'I'll get all my things out of the room,' she said instead. 'And settle my bill.'

'Leave anything you want in the room,' Trish said. 'It's not like we'll need it. This is not a busy time of year. And as for the bill, don't you worry about that. There are more ways to pay than with money. You're already in credit with us.'

Quinn removed all her things from the hotel room anyway. It wasn't that she didn't trust the Warrens, but she didn't want to be beholden to them. To anyone. Her whole life fitted into the back of the Humvee and that was where she liked to keep it. Once it was all carefully stowed, there was even enough room for the boxes of food, first aid kit and cookware. Quinn had her own camping cookware, but she didn't want to disappoint Trish by refusing her offer. And besides, she only had enough to cook for one, and it was becoming obvious she would not be alone.

Once everything was on board, Quinn backed the Hummer out of the parking place and turned it in the direction of the Tyangi Crossing Park.

Standing just inside the door of the feed store, Carrie watched the gold Humvee drive past. Its brilliant metallic paint was already starting to dim under a layer of dust. The Hummer was a lot more showy than the farm vehicles and sensible four-wheel-drive utes that were most often seen in town. The car suited the owner, Carrie thought. Quinn was everything she herself was not. Strong and competent. Confident. Happy. All the things she used to be, but had lost.

'You're nearly set, Carrie,' her boss, Paul Summers, called from the back of the store.

Carrie walked through the building to the loading bay. Paul was tying down a load of hay bales on the flat bed of the store's truck. There was enough there to keep the brumbies fed for at least a week.

'That Trish Warren is hard to say no to,' Paul said as she approached. 'She wanted me to give you time off with pay – but I can't do that.' He tugged the last knot tight and turned to face Carrie. 'Sorry, Carrie, but I really can't. You know how tight things are here.'

'I know,' she said. While the mine brought jobs and money into the town, Coorah Creek was not rich. Nor were the properties that surrounded it. They got by, but there wasn't a lot left over. 'I didn't expect you to.'

'Maybe you didn't, but Trish did.'

'I'm sure she meant well.'

'She always does.' Paul smiled. 'I can't pay you, but do take the time off if you like. If I need you, I'll get a message to you.'

Carrie wanted to say no. She wanted to say that she would keep working, not join the mission to rescue the brumbies. It wasn't about the money. As a successful jockey, she had saved enough to get by. But working in the store was safe. It allowed her to stay at a distance from the horses she once loved. Allowed her to stay at a distance from her fears. And then there was Justin. If she stayed away, she wouldn't let him down. She had seen the admiration on his face when he talked about her riding. She didn't want to see that replaced with pity and disgust.

'If you're sure you are okay with that,' she said.

'I am. Now, I've got two swing gates here for you. Let's get those tied on.'

It didn't take long, and then she was ready to go.

'I do need the truck back today,' Paul said. 'After you've delivered the feed, can you come back?'

'Sure.' Returning the truck would give her an excuse to leave. She could drive her own car back ... if she decided to go back.

'Great. Well, you're set. Good luck.'

Paul stepped back and Carrie opened the truck door. She set one foot on the step and lifted herself up. Standing there, she turned back to her boss.

'Thanks, Paul.'

'Go on. Get going. I need that truck back,' he replied gruffly as he walked away.

Carrie slid into the driver's seat and started the engine.

An hour later, as she was driving the long straight road towards the park, she saw another truck in her rear-view mirror. Unlike the one she drove, this one was modern and looked very well kept. It caught her easily, but rather than pass, it fell into place behind her. It was then she noticed there were actually two trucks. The colour scheme of one instantly identified it as a Goongalla Mine truck. The second was smaller and painted the distinctive bright yellow of the Rural Fire Brigade. It looked to have a water tank on its flat bed.

'We got ourselves a convoy,' she said in a shockingly bad American accent to the wide open spaces beyond her windscreen. Her own joke made her smile, and with her heart lifting, she hummed a few bars of the song as she led the small convoy through the gates of the park.

As she approached the ranger station she saw no sign of Dan's car and kept going, heading down the dirt track that led to the gorge. Three vehicles were already there ahead of her.

'Hi,' Quinn called as Carrie stepped down from the cab of her truck.

'Hi.' She looked around for Justin and Dan and spotted them a bit further down the gorge. They had obviously heard the vehicles and were heading their way.

The trucks had pulled up close by. Jack descended from the cab of the fire brigade tanker and Chris Powell from the mining company truck, which was loaded with timber and tools.

'Where do you want this?' Chris asked.

'I'm not sure,' Quinn said. Her camera hung around her neck. She walked a few steps away and snapped a couple of shots of the trucks.

'That hardly seems worth photographing,' Carrie said.

'Maybe. But you never know. I want to make sure I don't miss anything.'

'Hey!' Justin called as he approached. 'Carrie. Good to see you.'

'Hi,' she replied.

'Now that we've got our horse team here,' Dan said, 'we can get down to the details.'

Carrie flinched. She wasn't part of any 'horse team'.

Dan crouched and picked up a small stick. He swept a hand over a patch of ground to smooth the dust, and began to draw a rough map.

'We are here,' he said. 'The billabong is a couple of miles away. The ridge lines run like so.'

'That'll help us keep the herd heading in the right direction,' Justin said.

'So, you're happy with building the yard here?' Jack asked, looking at Justin.

'I think so. If we fence across the gully here.' He added another line to the dirt map. 'And here – then we can use the side of the gully as natural barriers.'

'We need to make sure there's no permanent damage to the park,' Dan added.

The others murmured their assent.

'Then let's get these trucks unloaded.' Dan rose to his feet.

While the men started unloading the timber from the mine truck, Carrie began unloading the hay bales. Despite her small size, she had been hefting hay for most of her life, and could balance the heavy bales on her shoulder with ease.

Quinn spent a few minutes snapping photographs, then returned to a sheltered place in the shadow of the ridge, where she was setting up a substantial camp. She had already erected two tents and built a fire pit.

Carrie was just finishing her load when Justin appeared at her side.

'I was wondering if I could ask you a favour.'

'Sure.' Carrie wiped the sweat from her brow.

'Well, I was wondering …' Justin hesitated.

Carrie realised that he was embarrassed. That rocked her a little. If anyone had cause to be embarrassed it was her. She was the one who was here under false pretences.

'I'll be spending a lot of time here,' Justin continued, avoiding her eyes. 'But there is still a lot I have to do back at my place. Horses to be fed. Exercised. There hasn't been enough money for a jackaroo or stockman for a while and I'm on my own. I'd have more time here if maybe you'd be willing to help me out there. When you can.'

He finally met her gaze. She saw more than his discomfort there. She saw need. And hope and something she really wasn't quite sure what it was – but maybe there was a hint of a reflection in her own face as she realised that she wanted Justin to like her. To think well of her.

'I need to be home for a few hours each day,' Justin explained. 'I thought we could head back in the late afternoon and feed and exercise in the evening then stay the night and repeat the process next morning early before we come back here. That way we could spend every second night in the camp.' He smiled. 'And to sweeten the deal, you'd get a hot shower every second day.'

She returned his smile. 'Of course,' she said, and was rewarded with a look of pleasure that spread slowly over his face.

'That's great. Thanks. I'm really looking forward to it. And it will be great having you ride my horses. Perhaps I can include that in my sales brochure – Carrie Bryant trained.'

Carrie knew he was joking of course, but the look of admiration on his face was real. It was a long time since anyone had looked at her like that. She felt such a fraud.

A yell from Dan sent Justin heading back to help the others. Watching his back recede, Carrie found her hands starting to shake.

What had she done? Agreeing to Justin's request just so she could see approval on his face? He'd soon find out the truth, and when he did, that approval would be quickly replaced by contempt.

Chapter Thirteen

The little bay filly had her sire's crooked white blaze running down her nose. She stretched her neck and blew a long slow stream of air out of her nostrils. The young kangaroo flicked its ears back and forth, and then stretched out its front paw. The joey touched the foal's nose. A brief, gentle touch. The filly gave a tiny squeal and shook her head. The joey bounced a few feet away and looked back over its shoulder. For an instant the filly looked set to turn and run, but she didn't. She squealed again, pawing at the ground as she would when playing with another of her own kind.

From her position on the rocky ridge, Quinn kept her finger on the shutter release button of her camera, hearing the shutter click again and again. She knew she was witnessing something quite rare and very precious. The experts might argue that feral horses destroy a park. They might argue that the native wildlife could not co-exist with imported animals. But sometimes, experts were wrong. Quinn didn't doubt the need to find a better home for the horses, but at the same time, she couldn't help but wonder what the experts would say if they could witness these two joyful young animals at play.

The filly took a couple of tentative steps forward, and reached out to sniff the tip of the joey's tail. The little kangaroo spun to face the brumby, and the two eyed each other in a classic stand-off.

Quinn kept shooting, knowing that one of these images might be something quite extraordinary.

'I guess no one told them they can't live together.'

She almost jumped at the soft, deep voice so close

behind her. But the gentleness and wonder in his tone told her that Dan was enjoying this moment as much as she.

'I didn't hear you coming,' she whispered as he lowered himself beside her on her rocky seat.

He shrugged and she realised his stealthy approach probably owed much to his military training.

On a patch of short green grass beside the billabong, the filly was joined by another foal about the same age. This was too much for the joey, which bounded away to dive in a neat somersault into his mother's pouch.

Quinn laughed. 'They look so cute when they do that. I never get tired of seeing it.'

'I guess you spend a lot of time in the bush?'

'I do,' Quinn said. She lowered her camera and rested it in her lap. She had taken the best shots she was likely to get today, but she kept it close. Just in case.

'So, where do you actually live?' Dan asked.

'In my Humvee.'

'I gathered that. It's very well equipped for camping. Did you do all that?'

'No. I bought it off another photographer. He built it.'

'It suits you. But what about when you are not on location? Where's home?'

Quinn took a deep breath. She'd had this conversation many times in the past. She usually didn't care too much if the listener thought her strange. This time was different. She wanted Dan to understand the choices she had made – as best anyone could.

'I don't have any other home. I live in my Humvee. I have some things in storage, but pretty much everything I own, or need, is there.'

'But you must have a house or a flat. A base of some sort. Somewhere for the mail to be delivered.' Dan sounded confused. 'Everyone does.'

Quinn shook her head. 'My business mail goes to my agent or my accountant. If I have to give an address, I use them, or occasionally my parents. But why should I pay rent or a mortgage on four walls that I don't want?'

'When you put it like that …'

'When I'm working, which is most of the time, I live in the Hummer – camping or staying at a hotel. Between jobs, I sometimes stay with my parents. But that's never for very long.'

'I guess that makes sense.' He didn't sound convinced.

'Walls don't define a home,' Quinn said.

'I don't know many women – many people really – who would agree with you. Most women seem to want the sort of stability that comes with four walls.'

Except it doesn't, Quinn wanted to say. Four walls guarantee nothing. 'I'm not most women,' she said instead.

'I can see that.'

'And I would never want to give this up.' Quinn nodded down towards the bottom of the gorge where a couple of horses had waded into the billabong, pawing playfully at its sparkling surface. In the several days since they had been disturbed by humans, the wild horses had allowed their guard to drop. They were once more relaxed and at home in the gorge. As Quinn and Dan watched, one of the mares folded at the knees and lowered herself into the watering hole. She tossed her head and snorted, enjoying the cool caress of the water, before lurching back to her feet. She walked out of the billabong and shook herself, much as a wet dog does.

Dan chuckled. It was a deep throaty sound that Quinn guessed he made far too infrequently. 'I wouldn't mind doing the same thing myself.'

She knew exactly how he felt. 'We worked hard today.

But I guess we'll be working even harder tomorrow when we start building the fences.'

'We're going to have to work hard. We haven't got a lot of time.'

Quinn lifted her eyes from the animals below them and looked at Dan. He had left the campsite when the trucks were emptied of their loads, following Jack and the others back to the ranger station for a short time to check on things there. Something in his demeanour made her ask, 'Has something happened?'

'No. Not really. Just another e-mail from the department. Wanting to know where things stood with regard to removing the brumbies from the park.'

'Wanting to know how many you had killed,' she said with a bitter taste in her mouth.

'Probably. I replied that I was making progress, but left it deliberately vague.'

'You said there was a deadline for getting the horses out.'

'Yes. The Minister is heading out here on his election campaign. He wants to be able to announce that the parks are cleared. Which is ironic when you consider he's not coming anywhere near Tyangi.'

'I never really liked politicians,' Quinn declared.

'Me neither.' They shared an understanding smile. 'We've got a few days' leeway now. They won't contact me again until after the weekend.'

'It's the weekend?' Quinn raised her eyebrows, genuinely surprised.

This time, Dan laughed. It was a soft warm sound, like the feel of suede or the taste of fine whiskey in front of a roaring fire.

'It's easy to lose track of time out here,' he said.

As if prompted by his words, the sun began to dip below

the crest of the ridge, shooting pink and yellow flares into the darkening blue of the sky. The horses lifted their heads. In a sudden flurry of movement, the mares made way for the stallion as he trotted away from their watering hole. He tossed his head and gave a little buck, before easing into a long slow canter.

'I don't know anything about horses,' Dan said. 'But he's beautiful to watch.'

Quinn agreed. She raised the camera to her eye again and snapped a couple of quick shots, knowing as she did that the light was all wrong. But it gave her a few moments to think. About Dan. About the promise of cool refreshing water. And their lack of swimming costumes.

She finally lowered the camera and turned to face Dan. He looked pensive. A little sad. She supposed that was not unexpected given the circumstances. But she wanted to see him smile.

'Well,' she said. 'I am ready for that swim now. What do you think?'

Without waiting for his answer she picked up her gear and began to make her way between the boulders and down the ridge towards the inviting dark blue water of the billabong.

Dan stood for a few seconds watching her go. How he admired the energy in her step. The joy she seemed to take from every moment of the day. This from a person who had no home.

Slowly he began to follow her down the slope.

He had never before met someone who deliberately chose to be without a permanent home. In the service, many of his comrades had no permanent residence. The single servicemen moved from base to base, living out of their duffle bags. But for them the army was their home.

Quinn didn't have that. She had nothing. Nothing but freedom. That didn't sound a bad thing at all.

Quinn had reached the edge of the water. As Dan watched, she carefully laid her camera to one side and with easy, unconscious movements, began to remove her clothes. She used her many-pocketed jacket to protect her camera, and then slid out of her hiking boots. Her thick hiking socks were dropped inside the boots, and she began to unbuckle the belt of her jeans.

Dan lowered his eyes. Quinn was totally unselfconscious. Far less than he was. He lifted his eyes again. Quinn was wading into the water, clad only in her underwear and tank top. Even at a distance she was lovely, her body as slender and strong and perfect as the wild animals they had watched earlier. When she was waist deep, she raised her hands and shallow dived into the water. She swam halfway across the billabong with strong, sure strokes. Then she turned to float on her back, her arms outstretched like a starfish as she gazed up at the darkening sky.

Dan smiled at that.

He had to do something. He couldn't just stand here and watch her. He had to either join her or leave.

His first thought was to turn away. To head back to the camp – or better still, the ranger station. Where he could be alone. Safe with his memories and the faces that haunted him. Then he shook his head. Just this once he was not going to let his demons control him.

Before he could think better of his decision, he stepped away from the safety of the rocks and headed for the water's edge. He was even quicker than Quinn to shed his clothing. The boxers he wore were not all that dissimilar to swimming trucks. The self-consciousness he felt as he slid into the water had nothing to do with his attire.

He dipped under the water, feeling the stress and sweat of the day wash away. As Quinn had, he began swimming with long slow powerful strokes that carried him swiftly across the billabong. At the far end, the water lapped at the base of a red sandstone cliff. He drew close to the cliff and began to tread water in this, the deepest part of the waterhole. He turned to find Quinn doing the same close behind him. They both turned and swam back the way they had come, until Dan knew his feet could once more easily touch the bottom. He stood up and shook the water from his hair. Tiny water droplets sprayed from him, sparkling in the fading glow of the sunset as they fell back into the water. They fell onto Quinn's damp, velvet skin as she emerged from the water beside him.

'That feels wonderful,' she said, flicking her hair back from her face. The wet tendrils clung to her neck, sending a trail of water trickling over the tanned skin of her shoulders and arms. Dan watched the water run over her skin, wishing he could follow that same trail with his hands. Or his lips. With a start he realised what was happening to him, and quickly raised his eyes again, to find Quinn meeting his gaze.

Her tawny brown eyes glinted with a hint of gold as they stood looking at each other, both so very aware of soft water on bare skin. Of a heat that emanated as much from them as from the setting sun. There was invitation in her eyes. In the subtle sway of her body towards him. All he had to do was raise one hand to feel that silky skin. Take one small step toward that slender body. To lower his head and taste those soft lips.

From behind, a sudden sharp noise, rock falling on rock. Instinct and training took over. Dan spun around, pushing Quinn behind him to shield her as his fingers twitched to hold the rifle he no longer carried. His eyes flew to the source of the noise. Looking for movement. For the glint of sun on metal or the shape of a man.

'It's just a kangaroo.'

Quinn's voice steadied him, and he followed her pointing arm to see the creature bounding away through the rocks. Not a threat. Or an enemy. Just a harmless animal. The rock wall once more became just an outback landscape, no longer an ambush. Dan shook himself, trying to avoid looking back at Quinn. He knew what he would see.

The army doctors had called it PTSD. Post Traumatic Stress Disorder. Not unexpected, they said, given what he'd survived in Iraq and Afghanistan. Treatable, they said. With time and care and drugs. Nothing to be ashamed of. But that was easy for them to say. He knew what lay behind his nightmares and he was ashamed.

Behind him, he heard Quinn splash playfully in the water, inviting him to turn around and finish what they had just started. But a few moments ago, he'd seen desire in Quinn's eyes. He didn't want to look at her again and see that pity had replaced it.

'We'd better get back to camp,' he said shortly and began to wade out of the billabong.

Chapter Fourteen

Justin kept one eye on the long driveway as he walked down to the stables. Carrie should be here soon. She'd taken the borrowed truck back to her boss and was due to return with whatever she needed for a few days' camping in the gorge, or here with him. He was grateful she had agreed to help. She understood how important this was to him. He still found it hard to believe. Mariah's son – out there all this time. It was the answer to a prayer.

'I'll bring him back, Dad,' he said under his breath as he swung open the first metal gate. 'People will soon be talking about Fraser horses like they used to. You just wait and see. I'll make you proud of me.'

A loud nicker from the direction of the stables was his answer and it made him smile. Now he was going to be able to carry on his father's work the way it should be done.

A new sound from the direction of the driveway caught his attention. Carrie was here. She parked closer to the stables than the house, and raised an arm in greeting as she got out of the car. She was wearing faded blue jeans and a plain shirt. Dressed for work, not to impress. But despite that, Justin felt his heart give a tiny kick. Whoa, he thought. What's that all about?

Carrie started walking his way. Justin paused by the gate to give her time to reach him.

'Hi,' he said. 'Thanks for helping me out like this.'

'It's no problem,' she responded with a small smile.

'Shall we get right down to it – or would you like some coffee?' Justin hadn't planned on going back into the house before starting work, but his subconscious seemed to have its own ideas about playing host to Carrie.

'I'm fine, thanks.'

'Well then ...' At once thankful and disappointed, Justin led the way to the stables. 'I've only got two horses in work that we need to ride this evening. And the stallion needs to be lunged. The mares will need feeding and there are four stalls to muck out.'

'I could do the feeds and muck out while you were riding,' Carrie said.

'Why don't we ride together? Then we can share the mucking out.'

'No,' Carrie answered very quickly. 'You ride. I'll do the rest. Then we can get back to the camp.'

Justin didn't understand why she would say no to a late afternoon ride. It was his favourite part of the day and barely counted as work next to the messy job of cleaning the stables.

'Are you sure?'

'Yes.'

'All right then.' Justin felt curiously deflated. He had been looking forward to riding with Carrie and showing her the land that meant so much to him. 'But next time it will be my turn to do the dirty work.'

It took just a few minutes to show Carrie the stables, feed room and the horses, before taking his saddle out of the tack room. A few moments later, he was riding away on his big bay gelding. The horse was eager to stretch his legs, and that matched Justin's mood very well. He was excited about the prospect of capturing the brumby stallion. Not a brumby – a thoroughbred. His thoroughbred, really. Mariah's son and his father's legacy. He was eager to get started on the plan he'd hatched with Dan and Quinn and Carrie.

He nudged the horse with his heels and it broke into a swift canter, as eager as its rider.

Carrie watched Justin ride away, admiring the way he sat the powerful young gelding. As if he belonged there. As if the two of them had merged into a single creature. She knew how good that felt. With every fibre of her being she longed to be there, beside him. Riding as she used to. Before ... But at the same time, she was weak with relief that he had accepted her offer to muck out the stables while he rode. It delayed for at least one more day the moment that he found out how she was lying.

She turned away from the sight of Justin and his horse cantering with easy grace and freedom across the brown earth.

Her first job was to feed the brood mares. There were five of them in a small paddock, with plenty of shade and safe fences for the two month old foals they had at foot. They needed hay and grain.

Carrie walked into the hayshed, and rolled a bale from the top of the stack onto her shoulder. With the ease of much practice, she balanced the heavy weight with one hand, and with the other she picked up a bucket of grain that Justin had already prepared for the mares. She walked down to the paddock and paused by the gate. This was the moment when she should simply pull open the gate, walk inside and lay out the hay for the mares. But she didn't. The horses, knowing it was feeding time, were milling around the gate. To get into the paddock, Carrie would have to push her way past them.

She dropped her bale of hay on the ground outside the gate. She flexed her shoulder once the weight was gone, pretending the weight was the reason she had stopped at the gate, and not just carried on with the job she was supposed to do. On the other side of the fence, the mares were becoming even more restless, eager for their food. The youngsters were jumping about, infected by their mothers' movements as they jostled for their dinner.

There was absolutely nothing to be frightened of. These were not the high-spirited racehorses she had once ridden. These horses were bluebloods, they were brood mares. Well accustomed to human company. As for the foals. For goodness' sake – they were smaller than she was and the only threat in them was the possibility they would trip over their own gangly legs and fall face first in the dust.

Carrie looked at her hands. They were shaking. All she had to do was open the gate and walk inside the yard. All she had to do was place the hay where the mares could eat. After that, she would empty the bucket of grain into the raised feed trough. It was a job she once would have done without thinking. The work of a minute or two. Not to be given a second thought. But here she was, one hand on the gate, frozen with fear. Afraid of a few gentle brood mares.

She wanted to weep with frustration. But she didn't. She had already shed far too many tears.

It should have been so easy to go back after the accident.

Her body had healed, but her mind – that was another matter.

Carrie took a deep breath and let the memories wash over her. The excitement of the racetrack. The satin smooth coats of the horses and her red and yellow and blue jockey's silks – so vibrant and soft. How she loved the excitement of it all. And the endless promise that seemed to vibrate around her as the horses entered the starting gates. Her favourite moment was that few seconds as she crouched low over her horse's neck, waiting for the gates to spring open. That was a moment where anything seemed possible. She always held her breath, feeling the coiled energy in the animal beneath her, waiting for that moment when the gates sprang open and the horses leaped out into a full gallop. Even now, her heart beat faster at the memory.

If only that was the only memory that made her heart contract. She could still see the look on Doctor Adam's face as he raised a long needle and prepared to plunge it into her body. She could still recall every terrifying moment of that emergency flight from the Birdsville Races to Mount Isa hospital. She had spent more than an hour strapped into a stretcher on the air ambulance. Sitting beside her, Adam Gilmore had held her hand and talked to her every moment of the journey. Reassuring her she was going to be all right. And then, at the hospital – the white coated surgeons ...

She heard a strange noise and realised it was the sound of herself, whimpering as the memories struck her with what was almost a physical pain.

She took a slow deep breath and pulled the pocket knife from the leather pouch on her belt. She cut the twine around the bale and began to pull it into slabs. As she did, she hurled each slab over the fence with a swift underarm swing that sent the hay many metres from where she was standing. Startled, the mares shied away from the flying slabs of hay, then, realising what it was, they moved swiftly over to begin eating.

The gate was now clear, as was the metal feed trough just beyond it. Carrie lifted the bucket of feed and, taking a firm grip on her fear, she opened the gate and walked through. She quickly emptied the contents of the bucket into the trough. As she did, the mares turned toward her, eager for the sweet taste of the grain. Carrie quickly moved back through the gate, slamming it shut behind her.

It was ridiculous that her heart was pounding and her breath was catching in her throat. She shook her head. If Justin saw her now, what would he think?

Something thumped her in the middle of her back. She jumped away from the fence and spun around. One of the foals, not interested in its mother's feed, had come to investigate this strange person leaning on the fence. It thrust its head between the rails, nostrils quivering as it stretched its nose out to sniff her.

A foal, Carrie thought. No more than eight or nine weeks old. She couldn't be frightened of a foal.

'Hello, there,' she said in a soft and gentle voice. 'You are a handsome young man, aren't you?'

The foal's ears twitched as it listened to her voice. It pushed even harder against the fence, stretching its neck to come just an inch closer to Carrie.

She reached out her hand and stroked the foal's nose. It was so soft. Its lips flicked against her fingers, checking for any source of food. Carrie let out the breath she hadn't even realised she was holding. With a little more confidence, she stroked the broad space on the youngster's forehead and pulled a leaf from its forelock.

It felt so good to be doing this. To feel a moment of pleasure instead of the fear.

A sudden movement from the feeding mares caused both Carrie and the foal to jump. The colt pulled his head back through the fence and, in response to a nicker from the direction of the feed trough, went trotting back to his mother.

Carrie picked up the empty feed bucket and set off back to the stables feeling almost pleased with herself. She had taken a step in the right direction. Only a small step, but didn't everyone say the first one was the hardest? Maybe she was ready to take another, slightly bigger one. The stable block was a huge shed, with tack and feed rooms at one end, and stalls for the horses down both sides. Not all the stalls were occupied. But the middle one on the right side of the shed housed Justin's stallion.

Dropping the bucket outside the feed room, she walked into the big tack room. It only took a moment for her to find what she was looking for. The stallion, Beckett, needed to be exercised on the lunge. There was no riding involved with that. All she had to do was stand in the middle of the round yard, and keep the stallion trotting in circles at the end of the long lunge rein. It was something the stallion did almost every day. He'd probably do it without any guidance from her at all. She could do that. She had to be able to do that. If she couldn't do that, she might as well just walk away now.

The stallion was waiting, his head over the stable door. Carrie stopped a few paces away.

'Well, Beckett, here we are,' she said.

The horse gazed at her. He was a nice animal, Carrie could see. But he wasn't in the same class as the stallion running with the brumbies. Mariah's son.

'I think you're about to be replaced, boy,' she said in a calm voice. She stepped forward, ignoring the churning in her gut, and stroked the stallion's face. He tilted his head, requesting a scratch behind his ear. Carrie obliged.

This was obviously a well-mannered animal. She should have known he would be, with Justin as his owner and trainer. He'd be no problem at all. Before she could talk herself out of it, Carrie slipped the lungeing cavesson onto the horse's head and attached the long rein. She unlatched the stall door and quickly stepped back. Beckett walked sedately through the door. He'd obviously done this a hundred times before.

This is going to work, Carrie thought. Her heart in her

mouth, she moved into position beside the horse's head and tugged on the rein. The big horse obeyed instantly, calmly stepping forward. Carrie went with him, but not too close. She could hear her own heart thumping as she approached the stable doors. Carrie blinked as they stepped out into the bright sunlight. They turned towards the wooden railed exercise yard, but the stallion suddenly stopped and flung up his head. He rolled his eyes and his nostrils flared as he sensed another horse. He lifted in a half rear and roared – a harsh masculine challenge that caused Carrie to flinch away from him, half raising her arm to cover her face from a danger that was mostly in her own mind.

The stallion's challenge roused the horses in the nearby paddocks. As they raced around the fences, Beckett's excitement rose a notch. Thoroughly agitated now, he started prancing on the spot, reefing at the rein in Carrie's hands.

She knew how to stop him. All she needed to do was tug his head back down. Assert her dominance over him and force him to focus on her commands, not on the other horses. It was so easy. She'd done it a thousand times before with horses far more uncontrolled than Beckett.

'I can't do this,' she sobbed as she fought the urge to just drop the rein and run. With the greatest effort of will, she maintained control of herself long enough to drag the stallion's head around until he was facing back into the stables. She tugged the rein and he reluctantly followed her, still tossing his head and trying to turn around. Carrie hurried a few steps ahead of him, then reefed on the rein again. The stallion lunged forward. She ducked out of his way and did the same thing again. This time, they reached the open door of his stall and the horse darted inside. Carrie let go of the rein, slamming the stall door quickly.

In a flash Beckett had turned around and was straining back over the gate, screaming his frustration. He lashed out with both hind legs, sending a loud crash echoing through the yard.

Carrie pressed herself back against the opposite wall of the stables and closed her eyes. Her heart was pounding and there were tears on her face. She couldn't do this. She really couldn't. She felt weak with disgust at her own cowardice.

What would Justin think of her?

At that thought, she opened her eyes and the first thing she saw was the stallion, still wearing the cavesson, the long rein dangling from it. That wasn't good. If the rein tangled around his feet, the horse could be injured. She couldn't allow that to happen. It took all the courage she had to cross the gap and place a hand on the stallion's neck. Whatever had upset him, he was rapidly calming down now he was in the familiar comfort of his stall. Carrie pulled the polished leather harness off his head and stepped back, reeling in the long lunge rein as she did.

There, it was done. She hung the cavesson next to the horse's stall and wiped her sweating palms against her jeans. The she turned away from the stall and the horse in it. Without pausing or looking back, she walked to the far end of the stables and picked up a rake and shovel. The stall where Justin's gelding lived needed cleaning out. Shovelling manure was all she was good for now.

At the other end of the shed, Justin remained motionless in the shadows, shocked by what he had just witnessed. He had returned from exercising his gelding far earlier than he normally would. Perhaps it was eagerness to spend more time with Carrie that made him do it. He'd tied the gelding to an outside railing, and was just entering the shed when he saw Carrie send the stallion back into his stall.

Carrie had been terrified. Even in the dimly lit shed, her face had been white as a sheet. He could almost feel the fear emanating from her in waves.

Justin knew the reason. Her terrible fall at the Birdsville Races.

It had never occurred to him that a fall might do such a thing to Carrie. He'd fallen – or been thrown – a hundred times or more since he had scrambled up onto the back of his first pony at the age of about three. Falling was part of working with horses. He accepted it in the same way that he accepted sore muscles at the end of a hard day's work.

But none of his falls had left him with more than a few scrapes and bruises, and some dents in his pride. Carrie had been seriously injured. If not for Adam and the air ambulance, she might have died. But that was months ago. Surely by now she had recovered. His heart went out to her. How terrible to have lost the thing that you loved the most. No one understood better than he how hard it could be trying to put a life – or your heritage – back together.

He wanted to take her in his arms and hold her until the fear went away. Until she stopped shaking. He wanted to tell her that it was all right. That she would find her way back, and he would help her. But he didn't. He quietly and slowly stepped away from the doorway and walked back to the gelding. He swung himself back into the saddle. He'd never let Carrie know he'd seen her like that. She would hate that he knew.

He would hide that knowledge. But he would find a way to help her regain what she had lost. To become again what she had once been. Powerful and strong. So beautiful. Whole.

Maybe in saving the brumbies, he could save both Carrie and himself.

Chapter Fifteen

'Here's to our success!' Justin held the beer can high, his face glowing in the firelight.

Quinn raised her can in salute, as did Dan and Carrie.

The four of them had gathered at the camp for this first night of their project. Justin and Carrie had arrived just after dusk, as Quinn and Dan were returning from their swim in the billabong.

It hadn't taken the four of them long to have the camp in order. Hoping not to spook the brumbies too much, they had set up right at the mouth of the gorge, placing the camp a short distance behind the area that would become their stockyard and brumby trap. Quinn was an old hand at setting up a bush camp, and she carried a host of useful things in the back of her Hummer. Dan's military background was showing too, as he quickly found firewood and lit the fire. Carrie was in charge of food and Justin had pulled camp chairs from the back of his ute.

Following Trish's instruction's, Carrie was now busy cooking steaks on a bed of glowing coals, while a billy hung above the flames bubbling away as their potatoes boiled. Quinn had her laptop open on her knees, loading that day's photos from her camera.

'We can take that back to my place when we go to work the horses tomorrow,' Justin offered. 'I can plug it in and recharge it for you.'

'Thanks for the offer,' Quinn said. 'But I have solar batteries in the Hummer. I can use those to recharge.'

Justin looked impressed.

'Food's ready,' Carrie called. She dished out steak and potatoes onto four metal plates and handed them around.

'Damn!' Justin said. 'We forgot the tomato sauce.'

'No, we didn't.' Quinn reached into their box of supplies and extracted the required red bottle. 'And when I say we didn't, I mean Trish didn't.'

The laugh they shared was full of affection for the woman who some people considered the heart of Coorah Creek.

Quinn took another drink from the beer can, still ice-cold thanks to her solar-powered cooler. 'Dan,' she said, 'I've been meaning to ask. What's Tyangi mean?'

'It's an aboriginal word,' Dan replied. 'Tyangi is a Dreamtime character. Part of the creation myth.'

'Tell us.'

'Well, apparently Tyangi was a man who fell in love with a beautiful woman from another tribe. But she was in love with someone else, and spurned his advances. So Tyangi waited until one day he saw her walking alone across the open plain. He kidnapped her and took her away from her tribe and the man she loved.'

'Not a nice man, then,' Justin interjected as he reached for another can of beer.

'No. Not really,' Dan agreed. 'Anyway, the woman was afraid and alone and she cried. Her tears formed a river.'

'Coorah Creek?' Quinn asked. She was fascinated by the story, and also captivated by Dan's voice and the firelight on his face. His respect for the aboriginal people and their culture was evident as he spoke. She liked that.

'Yes. Her lover, meanwhile, had gathered the men from his tribe and they came to get her back. Tyangi was killed in the fight and his spirit rose into the sky, to pay for his crime by shining a light onto the land for all eternity.'

Simultaneously all four of them raised their eyes to the sky above. Despite the light from their fire, the stars were clearly visible, scattered across the sky and shining like diamonds.

'I wonder which one he is,' Carrie said softly.

Silence settled over the camp as they finished their meal and began to clean up. Soon the work was done. The four of them settled again around the campfire, this time holding enamel mugs of coffee as the temperature began to drop.

'Quinn, are you planning a book of brumby photos?' Justin asked.

'I don't know,' she said honestly. 'I came out here with no particular project in mind. I just wanted to get out of the city for a while. Then I saw the brumbies – and Dan with that gun. I guess I'm a sucker for a cause.'

'It does seem so unfair,' Carrie agreed. 'It's not their fault. They're just trying to survive like all the other animals.'

'We have to take some responsibility,' Justin pointed out. 'We brought them here. We let them escape. And it's not just that they damage the habitat. It's not good for them either. They become inbred. In a drought, they suffer terribly because they are not adapted to this sort of country.'

'I don't want to shoot them,' Dan said slowly. 'But there is a very real threat that the parks service will step in. In other places they have used aerial culling.'

Quinn shuddered. The thought of shooting wild horses from the air was just too terrible.

'If it comes to that, maybe we could talk Jess into helping,' Justin suggested with a teasing grin. 'Use her plane to drive the shooters away. Our very own dogfight. Or brumby fight.'

His words lightened the mood a little, but a sombreness had come over them, each wrapped in their own thoughts.

'I guess we should hit the sack fairly early,' Justin finally said. 'We'll be up at sunrise and there's a lot to do.'

The inside of Quinn's tent was neat and comfortable. It needed to be. She spent a lot of time living there. Some of her assignments involved staying in first class hotels, but this was where she felt most at home. Where she felt like herself. Where she felt free. She didn't bother turning on a light. She simply slipped into her sleeping bag. She was as comfortable on her air mattress as in any bed. She settled herself and closed her eyes, listening to the night sound as she prepared for sleep.

But sleep didn't come.

After a while she gave up and unzipped her sleeping bag. She reached for her portable gas light and the bag with her knitting. As quietly as she could, she slipped out of her tent and moved away from the others. She found a corner where she hoped her light wouldn't disturb anyone and turned it up full. That was more than enough light to knit by. She pulled out her wool and needles. This jacket was nearly finished. By the time the brumbies were safe, she'd be able to give it to Jack and Ellen and start the next. There wasn't a lot more wool in the Hummer, but that was all right. She'd be heading back east soon, and there were plenty of places there to buy yarn.

She took a twist of wool around her little finger and started knitting.

Carrie heard Quinn leaving her tent. So she wasn't the only one who couldn't sleep. She closed her eyes again and willed her mind to blankness. It didn't work. The events of the day were spinning through her head. The smell and feel of the horses. Her fear of the stallion. Her relief when she realised Justin hadn't seen her failure.

She tossed in her camp bed, her movement restricted by her sleeping bag. She felt as if she were caged and reached for the zipper. Once she was free of that confinement, she stood up without thinking and unzipped her tent, the cool fresh night air calling her. The first thing she saw was the glow of Quinn's light among the rocks a short distance away.

'I hope I'm not disturbing you,' she said as she stepped into the light.

'Of course not,' Quinn said. 'Pull up a rock.'

Carrie settled onto a smooth sandstone boulder. As she did, a slight breeze carried a sound from the campsite. Someone was snoring quietly.

'Sounds like someone is getting a good night's sleep,' Carrie said.

'They'll need it,' Quinn replied, her fingers never ceasing in their rhythmic movement. 'There's a lot of hard work ahead of them. Ahead of us all.'

'I didn't know you were a knitter.'

Quinn hesitated and took a deep breath. Carrie sensed she had struck a nerve.

'It gives me something to do at night,' Quinn said in an offhand tone. 'And it's something that travels easily.'

'That's a very pretty jacket. It looks difficult.'

'Not really.'

Something in Quinn's tone told Carrie the subject was now closed. She bit back any more questions, but her curiosity was aroused. Quinn was such a strong and competent woman. Travelling alone. Taking those wonderful photos for her books. Carrie had looked her up online and been very impressed that someone who was successful to the point of being almost famous was becoming involved in their little town.

Yet there was something more here. She could sense it. Something that was connected to the pretty little baby jacket Quinn was knitting. Something responsible for the underlying sadness in her voice and her reluctance to talk.

Carrie realised she wasn't the only one with secrets. Quinn also had a past with painful moments she had to deal with. For some reason that gave Carrie comfort. If a woman as strong as Quinn was struggling with her past, Carrie's own struggle wasn't so shameful. She lifted her feet onto the rock and wrapped her hands around her knees.

'Do you really think we can do this?' she asked, thinking as much about her own battle as she was about the brumbies.

Quinn's voice was determined. 'Yes. I know we can.'

Chapter Sixteen

'We need to be certain this doesn't leave any sort of permanent impact on the park,' Dan said as he wiped the sweat from his eyes.

Justin grunted with effort as he thrust his fencing bar into the hole at his feet. Driven by muscle and two metres of heavy steel, the tapered end bit deep into the red earth. Justin used his weight to swing the bar back, causing the dry ground to crack and break. Nodding with satisfaction, he raised the digging tool from the hole. He let the tip touch the ground, and rested the bar against his shoulder.

'Does a hole count?' he asked, his dry lips moving in a weary smile.

Quinn's hands ached for her camera. Instead, she was holding a shovel.

'Isn't there an easier way to do this?' she asked.

It was hard to tell which of the four of them was sweating the most. Dan and Justin were digging post holes for the fence across the gorge. Carrie and Quinn were following behind them, upending the wooden fence posts into the holes, shovelling the dirt back in and tamping it in place. Carrie insisted that all the dirt should go back in the hole – despite the fact that a large wooden post seemed to fill most of the space. She wouldn't let them move on to the next until that goal had been achieved. Carrie seemed to know what she was doing. Quinn had surreptitiously leaned against one of the posts, testing it. It had not moved a millimetre.

For her part, Quinn was simply unskilled labour. Holding tools, carrying and fetching as she was instructed.

Despite all the time she'd spent photographing rural and remote places, she'd never built a stock fence before.

'Well, there are portable stockyards,' Carrie answered Quinn's question. She put down her shovel and reached for the canvas water bag hanging in the shade of a nearby bush.

'So why aren't we using those?' Quinn asked. 'That sounds a lot easier.'

'We are dealing with brumbies,' Justin said, moving to take the bag from Carrie. He raised it above his head and directed the stream of cool clear water into his mouth.

'So?' Quinn didn't understand.

'Domesticated horses understand and respect fences,' Carrie told her. 'As long as it looks solid, they won't test it.'

'But a wild horse—'

'Might just try to run straight through it. Portable yards might not be strong enough,' Justin finished for her. 'And there is one other small factor.'

'Which is?'

'We don't have any.'

'Ah. I could see that would be an issue.'

Quinn took the water bag and tried to emulate Justin's feat of directing the cool stream straight into her mouth. She almost succeeded. A thin trickle of water dribbled down her chin and she wiped it away with the back of her hand. Dan was beside her now, reaching for the water bag. Like the rest of them, he was wearing a sweat-stained hat to protect him from the sun, and as little clothing as modesty allowed. On him, it looked pretty good.

They'd been working since early morning. The plan was to build a substantial fence across the narrowest part of the gorge. Something with wooden posts and rails, high and strong enough to block the herd of galloping brumbies.

Where the sides of the gorge sloped steeply, but not quite steeply enough, Justin had decided that an easier fence of wire and metal posts would be enough to hold the horses. A second fence had to be built near the mouth of the gorge – to form the fourth side of their makeshift stockyard. This fence needed a wide gate that could be quickly closed after the brumbies had run through. It was hard, back-breaking work. And hot. But sharing made it seem easier. A sort of camaraderie was fast developing between the four of them as they divided the work according to their strengths.

Dan lifted his hat from his head and wiped his arms across his sweat-streaked face. He squinted up at the sun.

'We've got some time left,' he said, and placed his hat back where it belonged. He and Justin turned back to the hole they were digging, the last needed for the rear fence. Quinn caught Carrie's eye. She nodded in understanding and Quinn headed back to the campsite.

Quinn was an experienced camper. Despite her reservations about pitching camp in a dry creek bed, she had accepted Dan's argument that millennia had passed since this gorge last ran with any real amount of water. She paused beside her tent and reached inside the flap. Her camera bag was where she had left it, in easy reach. She opened it and removed her camera. She checked the battery levels. When she had a moment, she would have to set up her solar panels to recharge both the camera batteries and her laptop. At least she didn't have to worry about her phone. Out here there was no signal, so she had turned it off.

Moving up the side of the rocky slope, she took a couple of quick shots of the work unfolding below her. Still searching for the right angle for the best shot, she focussed on Dan. His muscles were clearly outlined as he swung a pick into the solid earth. He kept up the strong rhythmic movements for a few minutes and then paused, lifting his head to look up at the intensely blue sky. The strong lines of his face were silhouetted against the sky. His tanned skin glistening slightly with the sweat of labour.

Quinn's camera clicked. And again. She felt two kinds of emotion. She had just taken a couple of great shots. Portrait photographers longed for shots like that. But there was some other emotion there as well, emotion arising from Dan, not the photographs.

The harsh crack of metal on metal rang through the gully. Quinn jumped, but that was nothing to Dan's reaction. With movements almost too fast to follow, he spun and dropped into a crouch. In a second, the pick turned from a tool to a weapon. With her zoom lens, Quinn could see his face. There was a wildness there. And threat. Suddenly Dan looked like a dangerous man.

Quinn frowned as the loud metallic crack sounded again. Dan was looking carefully about, and suddenly his whole posture softened. Quinn followed his glance to the other side of the gully where Justin and Carrie were working on the metal fence posts. As she watched, Justin lifted a cylindrical post driver over his head, slamming it down again with enormous force and a loud crack.

When she looked back, Dan was back on the job, driving the pick into the baked earth with great strength. Quinn knew that the others hadn't seen what she had.

But what exactly had she just seen? And for the second time? Dan had reacted in a similar way back at the billabong when they were swimming. She hadn't given it much thought then. She'd been too disappointed that Dan had stepped away from her, when every fibre of her being had longed for him to kiss her.

Quinn had never been a war photographer, but she had travelled to a few disaster zones. She had seen the faces of people in shock in the immediate aftermath of a cyclone or fire. Dan's face had looked a bit like that, but overlaid with a readiness to fight. How long was it, she wondered, since Dan had left the army? She wondered where he had served. The scars on his body suggested he'd been wounded in action. That probably meant Iraq or Afghanistan. What could have happened to him there to leave such a terrible scar on his psyche?

Dan slammed the pick into the earth with all the force he could muster. He tugged the end free and swung it again. Sweat was pouring down his face, but he barely noticed. Again and again he swung the pick, before dropping it to begin shovelling the shattered earth from the rapidly growing hole.

Hard physical labour made it a little easier. When the sweat was in his eyes, he couldn't see the little girl's face. When his heart was pounding with effort, he couldn't hear her screams. At least, that's what he told himself. It didn't always work.

Behind him, the sharp crack of metal on metal snapped back at him from the walls of the gorge. With difficulty he ignored it and kept on digging. He hoped the others hadn't seen his reaction a few minutes ago. They were civilians. They could never understand. Hell, nobody did. The army doctors thought they did. But they weren't there. They didn't see or hear that little girl. How could they possibly understand?

'Hey, Dan. I think that'll do.'

Dan stopped in mid-swing. He looked at Justin and then down at the hole at his feet. It was a very deep hole.

'It's the last one. I wanted to be sure,' Dan said, stepping back. He laid down his shovel and he and Justin quickly heaved the fence post into place. It stood at a drunken angle against the side of the whole.

'Have you two got this one?' Justin asked, squinting up at the sun. 'Carrie and I need to get underway if we're going to get back to my place with enough daylight to do what has to be done.'

'Sure, we've got it,' Quinn said joining them. 'I'm an expert at this. So, Dan, if you're not sure, I can tell you exactly what to do.'

She was smiling as she said it. She was so obviously enjoying herself. Dan was amazed. Not many women he had ever met would have taken it upon themselves to organise a rescue mission for a herd of wild bush horses. Even fewer would have been prepared to get their hands dirty doing it. And Quinn was probably the only one who would look so good when she was that dirty and sweaty.

'Okay. We're off.' Justin started to walk away, Carrie a step or two behind him.

'See you two tomorrow,' Quinn called after them.

'Shall we get this done?' Dan asked as he picked up the shovel.

Quinn took hold of the post and pushed it until it was in a proper vertical position. Dan shovelled the soil he had so recently removed back around the base of the post. When Quinn was certain the post wasn't going to tilt, she picked up the fencing bar and reversed it in her hands. Then she began using the flattened end to tamp down the loose soil. They soon fell into a smooth rhythm. Dan shovelling and Quinn tamping. Dan was very conscious of Quinn's heavy breathing as she worked every bit as hard as him. Then it was done. They both stepped back to admire their handiwork.

The line of posts stretched across the gorge – perfectly straight. At least as far as the unaided eye could tell.

'Now all we need are some rails, and we'll be halfway there,' Dan said.

'Then there's just the small matter of catching the horses,' Quinn said, wiping the sweat from her face.

'Hey, that's up to Justin and Carrie,' Dan countered.

'I have a feeling it's not going to work quite like that.'

Taking the tools with them, they headed back towards their campsite, collecting the canvas water bag on the way. They quickly divested themselves of their tools, and both took long draughts of the cool water.

'Well, I don't know about you,' Quinn said easily. 'But I wouldn't mind washing off some of this sweat and dirt.'

'Do you want to go back to the ranger station? There's a shower there.'

'Not really. I was thinking we could use the billabong. Like yesterday. Then, if you're lucky, I might fix you some of the food that Trish sent.'

Images of the previous evening flashed through his mind. Quinn stripping off for her swim. The water on her silky skin. The unwanted feelings that she aroused in him.

He should say no.

'That's a good idea,' he said. 'Let's go.'

Chapter Seventeen

It was dark by the time they returned from the billabong, refreshed by the water and still dripping just a little.

'Let me get some dry clothes, and I'll see what Trish has in store for us for dinner.'

Quinn walked back to her tent and ducked inside. She quickly stripped off her wet tank top and bra. Her jeans were a bit damp from wearing them over her wet legs. She found some dry jeans and a cotton shirt. Before she ducked back out of the tent, she took a couple of minutes to comb her wet hair. Quinn had never been self-conscious. No one who worked in the fashion industry, even for a short time, could afford to be self-conscious. With models and designers and photographers of both sexes hurrying through the madhouse behind stage, modesty just wasn't an option. And most of those present cared more about the clothes than the bodies in them anyway.

But stripping to her underwear to swim this evening with Dan had been different.

Quinn's lifestyle didn't exactly lend itself to long term relationships. She had tried that once, and was still haunted by her failure. Now she seldom stayed in one place more than a few weeks. Any relationships she had forged were based on the unshakable fact that she would soon be moving on. Quinn knew she was attractive. She probably could have made a career as a model if she hadn't preferred to be behind the camera. In her travels she had met more than a few men who were happy to share a short term relationship. She enjoyed the best of the relationship, without a great emotional entanglement. Without any need to change who she was or the life she led. Without any call on feelings that she kept well buried. That suited her just fine.

Dan should have suited her just fine too.

He was a good looking man. Strong and intelligent. Interesting. As sexy as hell when he stripped off his shirt to swing an axe. The scars on his body only added to his aura of strength. The attraction was there. She felt it every time she looked at him. And she was pretty sure he felt the same. They were both loners. Neither of them looking for any sort of permanent relationship. So why was it that she kept her eyes downcast as he stripped down to his boxers? Why did she slide into the water and start to swim away from him, before he could look at her?

They had swum for only a short time. By some sort of unspoken mutual agreement, they gave each other a little more space than they had the day before. Quinn was the first to suggest they head back to the campsite. It wasn't that she felt uncomfortable swimming in her underwear. She certainly wasn't afraid of anything. Perhaps she was uncertain of herself. Or of Dan. And now here she was, hiding in her tent, actually wishing she had a mirror.

She was behaving like a bashful teenager.

Getting a firm grip on herself, Quinn ducked back out of the tent and disappeared into the bush to answer a call of nature. There was nothing like dropping your jeans behind a tree to take away all pretentions. By the time she returned, Dan had the campfire burning. Despite the heat of the day, it could get very cold at night. He looked fresh and dry and was staring down into the flickering flames. He was so lost in thought, he didn't notice Quinn. What was he thinking about, she wondered? Was he remembering his days in the military? It was clear from his reaction to unexpected noise that he had brought something back with him from that foreign war. Something more than just the scars on his back. Whatever it was, it still haunted him and left him strangely vulnerable for a man with so much strength.

Quinn felt herself longing to photograph him again. She seldom photographed people. She didn't find them as interesting as the wild spaces that usually inspired her. For some reason Dan was different. Such a portrait that would make. The handsome face so deeply thoughtful, illuminated by the flickering flames. So intent was Dan on his thoughts, she could have retrieved her camera from the tent and taken some shots without his knowledge. But she didn't. That would have seemed an intrusion on something private. Something personal. And not just for Dan. She felt it too.

Instead, she took a couple of steps towards the fire, making no attempt to mask her approach. Dan looked up but his face revealed nothing of his thoughts.

'I seem to remember you made mention of food,' he said. 'I hope you weren't joking. I'm starving.'

'Nothing like a good day's work to build an appetite,' Quinn said. 'Trish sent it, so it should be good.'

'You're not a cook then?'

'I can cook,' Quinn said. 'I enjoy it and I'm not bad at it either. Mostly I cook over a camp fire, and that doesn't lend itself to anything too fancy. What about you?'

'I have never poisoned anyone.'

'Didn't they make you peel potatoes in the army? As punishment?' Quinn stepped closer to the fire.

Dan hesitated. Quinn had a feeling she might have struck a nerve.

'They don't make you peel potatoes as punishment,' he finally said. 'That's only in the movies.'

The food Trish had sent was good. A thick meaty stew

with rice. Dan ripped the tops off two beer cans and handed one across to Quinn. They were sitting in camp chairs, eating by firelight. Dan was enjoying the food and the beer. He was also enjoying watching Quinn eat. He had never understood women who nibbled at their food, as if a good appetite was somehow a sin. Quinn ate the same way she did everything else – with great gusto and enthusiasm.

He liked that about her.

There were other things he liked too.

He liked the way she laughed. He liked the way she was willing to get her hands dirty for something she believed in. He liked the way she looked in her wet underclothes. He liked that very much. Quinn knew how to be silent. They had spoken hardly a word since they started eating. As a man who spent much of his time alone, he appreciated her ability to be silent. But he also liked the sound of her voice.

'How did you become a photographer?' he asked.

'I was a model before I was a photographer.'

'That doesn't surprise me. You're far more beautiful than most of the girls I see in magazines.'

'Not *that* sort of a model.' Quinn sounded indignant, and he smiled.

'Not *those* sorts of magazines,' he said. 'And honestly, I only read them for the articles.'

He liked her laugh too. It wasn't coy or pretentious. She enjoyed laughing. So did he, but he knew he didn't do it often enough. He decided he should do it more, because he liked the way her laugh harmonised so well with his.

'This sounds like a line, but I really was stopped in the street when I was still at school by a talent scout for a modelling agency. He was on the lookout for tall girls, and there I was.'

'Did you enjoy modelling?'

'Not really. I was far more interested in the photography than the clothes. I started working more and more as a photographer's assistant. And then as a photographer.'

'It sounds like every young girl's dream. Why did you give up such a glamorous lifestyle for a tent in the middle of nowhere, stew cooked on an open fire and served with warm beer?'

'I lost interest in making beautiful things look even more beautiful. I wanted to find beauty that wasn't manufactured by a make-up artist and a stylist. I wanted to find a perfect moment in time – and preserve it forever. So it can never be broken or taken away.' Her voice trailed off and she turned her gaze to the flickering flames.

'You don't miss it? Or miss having a home somewhere?'

'No. I love what I do. I don't like feeling ... trapped, I guess. I don't like having to live up to someone else's expectations.' She shook her head. 'Between jobs I stay with my parents sometimes. My mother and I ... well, I guess you could say we have our moments. I never lived up to her expectations.'

'And your father?'

'He's an art teacher. I guess that's where I got this creative streak from.'

'I'm sure he's very proud of you,' Dan said.

She didn't reply, just sat staring into the fire. Her mind seemed a long way away.

Dan watched her face. The easy smile had faded. There was a softness about her eyes that made him wonder what she saw when she stared into the flames. Everyone saw something different in the leaping red and gold. He saw the dark eyes of a dying girl. What was it that brought the sadness to Quinn's face?

'So, what about you?' She looked up at last. Her voice was bright, a forced gaiety that she couldn't hide. Dan was happy to let her change the subject, but given a choice, he would have sent it in a different direction.

'I joined the army straight out of school. A few of us did. We were all friends, hyped up by talk of terror attacks and weapons of mass destruction. We thought we were going to save the world.'

'And you didn't?'

'No. I served in Iraq and Afghanistan. It was ...' Words failed him as they had so many times before. When talking to his officers, military doctors and psychiatrists. Even his family. He had written reports, but he had never been able to talk about that time.

Quinn seemed to understand that words were difficult. 'I saw the scars on your back. You were wounded?'

He nodded. 'I.E.D.'

'Improvised Explosive Device,' she said. 'A roadside bomb?'

'Yes. I was one of the lucky ones. Some of my unit didn't make it.'

'It must have been terrible.'

Not as terrible as what came later, he wanted to say. A soldier expects to come under fire. That was what you signed up for. You know some of your comrades may be wounded or even killed. That you may be wounded or killed. A soldier is trained to deal with fighting a war. A soldier is not trained to deal with the thought of killing a child.

Dan closed his eyes. He knew if he looked into the flames he would see the girl's face looking back at him. He would see the blood on her cheek and her small hand moving weakly, trying to reach her father's hand where he too lay bleeding in the hot desert sand. Silence settled around him, broken only by the night sounds of the bush.

'And when you got back?'

'I saw your book. Those photos spoke to me. I needed a job and being a park ranger seemed to suit. There was a job going here. So here I am. Speaking of which, I should go back to the ranger station.' Dan got to his feet.

'I thought you were staying in camp tonight,' Quinn said, her voice registering her surprise.

'I have remembered something I have to do. You'll be fine here by yourself, won't you?'

'Yes, of course I will.'

'Fine then. I'll see you bright and early in the morning. Sleep well.'

He was running away. He knew it. But he was powerless to stop. The memories were back. Louder. Clearer. Harder than ever before. He knew if he stayed, the nightmares would take him. And he didn't want Quinn to see him like that. Better that she thought him rude than she knew him to be a coward.

Quinn sat staring at the fire and listening to the sound of Dan's Land Rover recede into the night. She wasn't sure quite what had happened. Obviously she had touched a nerve, one that triggered memories Dan found difficult to face. She understood that. Everyone had their own secrets. And for every secret there was a trigger that turned it into a different kind of I.E.D. She knew this because she had been very close to her own secrets tonight. She didn't like talking about her past. She almost never did.

Quinn got to her feet and walked over to her Hummer. She opened the back and delved into one of the compartments. She pulled out the small packet wrapped neatly in tissue. She rested her hand on it just for a moment, feeling the softness under the tissue.

'Kim,' she whispered.

Then she carefully placed the package back. Her eyes

were slightly misty as she returned to her tent for her knitting bag and gas light.

Moving her seat away from the fire and the risk of soot and smoke soiling her work, she pulled out her needles and held up the unfinished garment. The infant's jacket was pale yellow. A simple but lovely pattern that she had knitted before. She could knit this without too much thought and right now, thinking was something she wanted to avoid.

Knowing it would be a while before she felt like sleeping, she settled herself into the chair, and the soft click of the needles joined the other sounds of the night.

Chapter Eighteen

Carrie woke up in an unfamiliar bed. She lay staring at the bare white ceiling for a few moments before she remembered where she was. Justin's house. In his spare room. They'd come back from the park last night, arriving just on dusk. Together they had fed the horses. It had been easy enough for Carrie to maintain her pretence. She'd checked water troughs and distributed the feeds Justin mixed, without the need to actually handle any of the horses.

Afterwards, Justin had made them a simple but tasty dinner which they had eaten sitting at the big wooden table in his kitchen. Their dinner table conversation had been all about the brumbies. Justin was brimming over with plans that would begin when he recovered Mariah's son. He had already made enquiries about getting the horse registered in the stud book. Once that was done – and Justin's face had shone as he said this – he would train the stallion, and start competing on him. He had no doubt the horse would soon earn a name for himself both as a working horse and in breed shows. But, Justin said, for the first two years, he wouldn't stand the horse at stud to outside mares. If anyone wanted one of his progeny, they would have to buy a Fraser horse. In a few years, he was certain, Fraser horses would again become known as the fastest and smartest and best.

Carrie had barely sipped the wine Justin had poured for them both. She had played with the stem of her wine glass, twirling it between her fingers as she listened to him talk with such enthusiasm and hope. Each word was torture for her.

She had once had such dreams. Dreams of a life working with the animals she loved. Perhaps of sharing that love and life with someone – someone a lot like Justin. But she had lost those dreams under the flashing feet of the racehorses the day that she fell. Some dreams, once lost, can never be recovered.

Then Justin had reached out to touch her hand, his face intense and thoughtful.

'Carrie, I don't know how to thank you for this,' he said. 'If you hadn't recognised the stallion. Well, this wouldn't be happening. What you have done means more to me than I can ever begin to say.'

Even now, Carrie felt the heat of her shame.

She had mumbled something about being lucky and pleased she could help. A few minutes later, pleading tiredness after the long hard day of work, she had escaped into her bedroom, to lie awake a very long time, staring up at the ceiling and despising her own weakness.

Now morning had come, and with it the time for her to confess. She couldn't go on working with Justin – Quinn and Dan too, of course, but mostly Justin – under false pretences. Justin had so much riding on this plan of theirs. If she didn't tell him the truth now, she was putting everything at risk. In the long dark hours of the night, her mind had thrown up images of her own failure. If Justin relied on her at a crucial moment and she let him down – his whole future would come crashing down around him. And it would be all her fault. Far better to tell him now, so he could find someone else more fit to help him.

'Good morning. I've made coffee,' Justin greeted her as she walked into the kitchen. He was seated at the table, some papers spread in front of him, eating an apple, but he got to his feet as she entered and started to pour her a mug of coffee. There was a gentleness about Justin. Old-fashioned good manners. Carrie felt her heart contract. She liked the way his face lit up every time he saw her. She loved the way he treated her as if she was … as if she was who she had once been. And now she was going to destroy all that with a few words.

'Justin, there's something I have to tell you,' she said, slipping into a chair across the table from where he had been sitting.

He didn't say anything. He simply put the coffee in front of her, sat back down and looked at her with his lovely green eyes, waiting with the same patience he would show a frightened foal.

'I ...' Carrie took a deep breath. This was hard. Harder even than she had imagined. But she had to be honest with Justin. She knew she would regret it if she wasn't. 'I shouldn't be here.'

'Of course you should.'

'No. No. I shouldn't.' She turned her eyes down to the scrubbed wood of the table. A single grain of sugar, missed from someone's coffee, lay near her finger. She focussed on that, pushing it along the grain of the wood, as the words she hated slowly welled up from her soul. 'I have been lying to you, Justin. I can't help you with the brumbies. Because ... I can't ride anymore.'

Once the words were out, it was as if a dam had broken. Still staring at her hands, the words flowed from her to lie exposed in the air between her and Justin. 'I have lost my nerve. After the accident last year at the Birdsville Races, I was hurt and it took a long time to recover. Doctor Adam says I am fine, but I can't ... I just can't ride. I did try once. I went back to the racing stables. They were so glad to have me back, but as soon as one of the horses came near me, I burst into tears. I felt such a fool and I never went back. I know I am a coward, but there is nothing I can do about it. You'll need to find someone else to help you muster the brumbies. I lied to you and I am so very sorry.'

Only then did she look up, expecting to see disgust and anger on his face. She deserved it. But he was smiling at her gently. He reached out to touch her hand, stilling the fingers that were pushing the sugar grain back and forth. In a voice as soft as the first rain of a spring morning, he said, 'I know.'

Justin watched her face change. An expression of disbelief which was quickly replaced by something else. Confusion. He wanted to keep holding her hand, but he let go. Right now, he had to be what Carrie needed him to be. She needed more than just a friend to hold her hand. She needed someone who understood about horses. About loving them and about being afraid.

'You know?' Her voice revealed her shock.

He nodded. He had lain awake during the night, thinking about Carrie asleep in the next room, and wondering what to do. At some point, her fears would be revealed. The day of the brumby muster, if not before. In that moment should he tell her that he already knew? Would that destroy the friendship growing between them? In the early hours of the morning, he'd decided that he wouldn't lie to her. He valued her as a person, as a friend and just maybe as something more than a friend. He wouldn't betray her secret. He wouldn't even tell Quinn or Dan. But whenever she chose to confide in him, he would be honest with her and say that he knew. He didn't want there to be any lies or even half-truths between them. He just hadn't expected it to be this soon.

'I saw you the day before yesterday. When you tried to lunge Beckett.'

'Oh.' It was so soft he could only just hear the break in her voice.

'It's okay, Carrie.'

'No. It's not. I've lost my nerve. I can't ride any more. I've lost everything that was important to me. I have lost myself.'

The last words were an anguished cry, and Justin wanted nothing more than to take her in his arms and hold her until all the pain washed away.

'You haven't lost anything, Carrie,' he said. 'It's all still there inside you. All of it. It will come back. When you need it, you'll find it.'

She looked up at him, so lost it broke his heart. 'Do you really think so?'

'I know so,' he said, filling his voice with confidence.

She took a deep breath and brushed away the traces of the tears in her eyes. 'You're right,' she said, nodding with some signs of confidence.

Her voice betrayed her. The confidence was forced. That didn't matter one iota to Justin. Even pretending confidence took courage. Maybe that was a small step, but it was in the right direction. An idea began to form in the back of his mind. The more he thought about it, the better it looked. It would help them with the brumbies, but more importantly, it would help Carrie.

'So,' he said in a firm voice, 'we had best get started. We've a busy day ahead.'

'I'll muck out while you ride,' Carrie said.

'All right.' He wasn't going to push her too hard. But at the same time … 'We need to load one of the spare aluminium bathtubs into the ute today. To use as a water trough at the park.'

'Today? But we haven't even finished building the yard yet.'

'We will have to finish today because we're taking a couple of my horses to the park today too.'

'So soon?'

'Not soon enough really. If this crazy plan is going to succeed, and it has to, Dan Mitchell needs to learn how to ride a horse. And you are going to teach him.'

Chapter Nineteen

'I guess I'm as ready as I am ever going to be,' said Dan.

I wish I was, Carrie thought to herself as she pushed her clenched hands deeper into the pockets of her jeans and carefully composed a smile on her face. 'Well, let's get started.'

'Just tell me again why I'm doing this?'

'Because we need another rider,' Carrie said carefully.

Dan looked at her thoughtfully and she saw his eyes narrow. Did he suspect something? Not that it mattered. They would all know soon enough. Now that Justin knew, it didn't seem that important to keep the secret from the others. Justin was the horseman. If he understood, the others would probably simply accept it.

The stockyard was as good as finished. Both front and rear fences were in place, the timber posts and rails making a solid barrier that would stop even the racing brumby herd. There were a few places on the side walls that still needed some work, but that wouldn't take long. Right now, Justin was stringing wire on a secondary fence line; a smaller, less imposing yard was needed to house the saddle horses that he'd brought to the site that morning.

There were two geldings; Justin's big bay and a slightly smaller, lighter chestnut with a big white blaze lying slightly askew across his nose. Both horses carried some of the same bloodline as the stallion they were here to catch. The chestnut was a slightly older horse, and Justin had assured her that he was perfect for a novice rider. He hadn't said a nervous rider – but Carrie knew that was what he'd meant. He might have suggested she teach Dan to ride, but she could tell he still hoped she'd be riding with him when they went to muster the brumbies.

She wished the same thing, but she was a long way from being ready to ride. It was as much as she could do to teach Dan what he needed to know. But teach him she would. It was the least she could do.

'Okay, Dan,' she said, forcing confidence into her voice. 'You're going to be riding the chestnut. So, why don't you go and get him.' She tossed a bridle towards Dan, who caught it easily in one hand. He held it up and a frown creased his forehead as lengths of leather fell in a tangled mess from his fist, the heavy metal bit dangling at the end.

'I've got no idea how to put this on a horse.'

'Luckily for you, the horse does,' Carrie countered. 'It's no good me doing it, I already know how. You're the one who has to learn.'

Carrie heard a chuckle as Quinn eased into a spot next to her on the rails. Her camera was in her hands and Carrie guessed that Quinn was going to enjoy this far more than either she or Dan would.

'All right,' Carrie said feigning reluctance. 'Give it here.'

She took the bridle and quickly sorted out the tangled leather.

'This piece you slide up and over his ears,' she said, holding the bridle up. 'The metal bit goes in his mouth.'

'And how the hell do I get a horse to open its mouth?' Dan asked. 'Say open sesame?'

This evoked another chuckle from Quinn.

'He'll just do it,' Carrie assured Dan. 'Try not to whack the bit against his teeth. He won't like you for that. He's bigger and stronger than you are. You want him to like you.'

'Yes, ma'am.' Dan reset his hat squarely on his head and opened the wide metal gate.

No sooner had he stepped through the gate and latched it behind him, than both horses turned to look at him. Both took a step forward and halted, waiting for him.

'See what I mean,' Carrie said. 'They know how this is supposed to work.'

'I'm glad one of us does,' Dan muttered as he approached the animals.

'Just talk to them,' Carrie suggested. 'You could loop the reins around his neck to hold him while you get the bridle on, but I doubt he'll need it. Fraser horses are well-trained.'

She was right. Despite Dan's small fumbles, it wasn't long before the chestnut was wearing the bridle, and tied to a rail.

'You need to take Justin's horse out of the yard,' Carrie told him as she handed him another bridle. 'You don't want him in the way during your lesson. And the practice will be good for you.'

With both horses caught and tied up, Dan was ready for the next step.

'You need to learn how to saddle him too,' Carrie said.

'But you could do it for me.'

'I could, but if your saddle comes loose when you are out there somewhere, you need to know how to fix it,' Carrie pointed out. She meant it too. It wasn't just a way for her to avoid getting too close to the horses.

Dan looked up at her. His blue eyes held hers for a long minute. It seemed as if he could see straight through her bravado to the damaged soul underneath. He nodded almost imperceptibly, and something changed. Carrie knew he had once been in the military. Now, for the first time, she began to understand what that meant. Once he had decided to do this thing, he went about it calmly and with an enviable efficiency.

Following her instructions, he calmly and effortlessly swung the saddle onto the horse's back. With very little hesitation, he had the girth pulled tight and the animal ready to ride. When he swung into the saddle, Carrie caught her breath. It was hard to believe this was the first time he'd ever ridden a horse. He settled quickly into the right place on the saddle, his body held taut, but not stiff. He was totally under control of every part of his body. The hands on the reins were steady. His legs firm around the horse's ribs. There wasn't the smallest trace of uncertainty or fear on his face.

'Hands and legs,' she told him. 'You have to keep them steady and controlled. That's how you talk to the horse. You can use your voice too, but hands and legs are the most important. No sudden movements. Don't jar his mouth. Keep your back firm but not stiff and let your body feel the movement of the horse.'

Dan and the chestnut were moving around the yard now. Following Carrie's instructions, Dan turned the horse this way and that and then urged it into a slow trot. A few laps of the large yard and Carrie called for a canter.

Beside her, Quinn had the camera glued to her eye.

'I know nothing about all this,' Quinn said without lowering the camera. 'But it seems to me he is doing well.'

Well? That wasn't the half of it. Carrie had never seen anyone take to riding so easily. It was, in part, his fitness and the great control he had over his muscular body. It was in part a natural sense of balance and rhythm. Confidence and intelligence had a lot to do with it too. But there was something else as well – the willingness to understand and work with another living creature on its own terms.

Carrie fought down a wave of jealousy and self-pity. He made it look so easy, this thing that she had once loved.

This thing that had brought her so much joy and was now lost to her. Possibly forever.

'He'll do,' she said to Quinn.

At that moment their attention was diverted by the sound of an engine. Carrie glanced back towards the campsite to see Ellen and Jack emerge from the car he'd just parked under a shady tree. Ellen was moving a little slowly because of her pregnancy. Not so her kids, who took one look at the horses and raced towards the yard, excited yells preceding them.

Carrie felt her heart clench for a moment and looked back to where Dan and the chestnut gelding were circling at a slow canter. The horse's ears flickered and he tossed his head to get a better look at whatever was approaching with such noise. As if responding to an instinct, Dan closed his legs around the horse's side and forced it forward a few more strides until its attention was back where it should be. On him. Only then did Dan bring the animal to a halt and turn it so it could see the cluster of people by the stockyard gate.

Carrie put up a hand to try to calm the children. 'Whoa there,' she said as they slid to a stop. 'The first thing you have to learn about horses is that you don't run and yell around them. Got it?'

Two blonde heads nodded earnestly, identical blue eyes wide and serious.

'Good.'

'Sorry about that,' Ellen said as she caught up to her children. 'How are you, Carrie?'

'Fine thanks.'

'Trish wanted us to bring some more food out,' Jack said as he approached laden with a box.

'And I think she wanted a report too,' Ellen added with a grin. 'She hates it when she doesn't know if her plans are working out.' Ellen raised her eyebrows and cast a sideways glance at Justin as he approached, fencing pliers in hand.

'Can we ride the horse? Please?' Harry asked not to be deterred.

Carrie's heart clenched at the childish plea. Even these two had more courage than she did. She was trying to find a way to say no when a voice spoke close beside her.

'Of course you can. If your mum says it's all right.' Justin dropped his fencing tools in the dirt beside the gate.

'Mum. Pleeease!'

The little boy's heartfelt request was very hard to resist. Ellen hesitated, and then looked at Justin. 'If you are sure it's—'

'Carrie and I will take good care of them,' Justin said.

Ellen hesitated then nodded. 'Well, Harry, I guess if Justin says it's all right.'

Carrie glanced at Justin. The eagerness and hope in his eyes put that on the faces of the children to shame. Carrie took a deep breath. If the kids weren't afraid, she shouldn't be either. And if Justin was beside her …

'That sounds okay,' she said.

A loud cheer greeted her words.

'What did I say about being quiet?' she said with mock severity.

The children fell silent, but their faces were split by the widest grins.

Justin caught her eye, and Carrie felt a tiny thrill at the approval she saw in his eyes. She signalled Dan to bring the horse over, and took the reins from him without the slightest hesitation.

'Well, if you guys are stealing my horse,' Dan said as he ruffled a blond head, 'I guess I probably have to go and do some work.'

'I'll help,' said Jack. 'Just tell me where to leave the food and I'll grab my tools.'

As Dan stepped back, Justin led first Harry, then his sister forward.

'This is Finbarr,' he said. 'Say hello.'

'Hello, Finbarr,' the children chorused. The gelding reached out to snort gently in their hair, evoking more childish squeals.

'All right, now that you are acquainted ...' Justin lifted Harry then his sister onto the back of the big chestnut horse. Her heart in her mouth, Carrie stepped closer to the horse's head and took a firm grip on the reins, very aware that her hands were shaking.

'Let's go,' Justin said.

Carrie took a deep breath and began to lead the chestnut forward. Finbarr followed her without hesitation or complaint. They circled the yard with Justin walking beside the children, one hand on the saddle. The horse was totally relaxed, its head held low as it flicked its ears back and forth, listening to the steady stream of instructions and advice Justin was giving the children.

By the gate, Ellen was watching, her face glowing with pride. Quinn was, as always, taking photographs.

One full circuit of the yard went without a hitch, and Carrie's breathing was returning to normal.

'Can we do it again?' Harry begged, almost in a whisper.

'I think so,' Justin replied. 'What do you think, Carrie?'

'I think so too.'

Carrie was instantly rewarded with a whispered childish cheer, but more important to her was the nod of approval she got from Justin. The smile on his face was for her alone. As she set off on the second round of the yard, she looked down at her hands.

They were no longer shaking.

Chapter Twenty

The thick meaty stew bubbled in the pot, sending rich smells wafting on the night air. Quinn wondered what the local wildlife, out there in the dark, thought of that. The smell of smoke from the camp fire was probably more disturbing, she decided.

The stock horses didn't seem bothered. They were hobbled in the almost completed stockyard, dozing after a busy day. Ellen's kids were nothing if not energetic. They had ridden that poor horse in circles for what seemed like hours. Quinn was certain they would still be riding, had not Justin eventually decided the horse deserved a rest.

The kids had then turned their attention to the campsite, which involved a detailed examination of the tents and cooking arrangements and some far too detailed questions about how the campers went to the bathroom.

They were good kids. Intelligent and energetic and as well behaved as could be expected at their age. But the little girl with the big blue eyes had disturbed Quinn more than she liked. It had been such a long time—

Quinn shook her head. She did not want to go there. She looked around for Dan. He was filling a bathtub with water from the tanker they'd been given by the fire service. Justin and Carrie had decided to head back to Justin's place, after bedding down the two stock horses for the night. They needed to collect some more fencing wire, and tomorrow Carrie would bring her things to the campsite and she'd stay on to look after the horses, and continue her lessons with Dan.

Although Dan was eager to get the brumbies safely out of the park, they were planning to wait a few more days before trying to capture them. This would give Dan time to improve his riding skills, and allow Justin more time to plan what he was going to do with them after that. Moving them from the park to his land was no simple task. Justin had finally decided not to try driving them across country on horseback. It was too far, and there were too many places where they might lose the herd. A truck was the best answer, but loading wild horses onto a truck was not going to be easy.

Quinn was feeling restless. Before she and the kids left, Ellen had passed on a message from Trish. Quinn's agent had called the hotel, looking for her when he was unable to raise her on her mobile.

She'd call him back tomorrow. She had to go to the ranger station to get a signal, and she really didn't want to. She knew where the conversation would lead. He'd want to know how 'the brumby project' was going, and when it would be finished.

When she had first become involved in ... whatever this was ... she had told her agent there was a great story to be had. He'd been enthusiastic and certain he could sell her photo essay to a major newspaper or magazine. He'd even suggested *National Geographic* might be interested. He'd be anxious to hear when he would see some photos. When he could make his pitch and make them both some money.

Quinn should be as eager as he was. That was how she made her living. More than that, it was a career she had chosen for herself and loved. She would have made more money had she continued to model, but her photography fulfilled some basic creative drive within her. She was committed to her career – and had envisaged a significant story, not to mention some significant income from her photos of the brumby rescue.

But something had changed. It had become personal.

She no longer looked at the brumbies as just a story. She no longer looked at the other people involved as characters in that story. Justin and Carrie, Trish and Ellen and the others were, if not yet friends, rapidly becoming so.

And Dan? Quinn wasn't entirely sure. A part of her yearned to finish what had started at the waterhole. Her flesh still tingled when she remembered the way his eyes had followed the water trickling over her body. She had never felt so intensely feminine. So sexy, so desirable. A part of that was down to her own strong physical attraction to Dan. From the day they had met, when she'd watched him stride down the side of the gorge, angry and threatening and more male than anyone she had ever met before. He might not be as handsome as some of the male models she'd worked with – but he was more of a man than all of the pretty boys put together. And when they had swum half naked in the billabong, it was all she could do not to touch his body. To feel the hardness of his muscles. And the scars she'd seen had only added to the overpowering feeling of strength that oozed from his every pore.

So what was holding her back?

She thought she knew the answer to that. The scars on his body were not the only legacy of his military service. It was clear he carried emotional scars as well. That didn't make him any less attractive to her. Perhaps the opposite. Any man who could see and do what a war demanded and remain untouched was not for her. She desired a more thoughtful soul. A more caring heart. But it was plain Dan struggled at times with the past. He didn't need any other disruption in his life. And that's what she would be. A disruption. Whatever happened between them would end when she walked away. And she always walked away. Dan deserved better than that.

'That's probably cooked by now.'

'What …?' Quinn dragged her mind back to the present, and looked down at the pot bubbling madly in the fire in front of her. 'Sorry, I was miles away.'

She grabbed a couple of enamelled metal plates and began to spoon out two good helpings of the steaming food. The rich smell teased her nostrils as she handed one plate to Dan.

In return, he passed her a cool beer, with the top already open.

'Here's to the brumbies,' Dan said, raising his beer can to Quinn.

She nodded and raised her own beer in return.

Dan tasted the food and licked his lips in appreciation. 'Trish sure knows how to cook.'

'I think this one might be Ellen's doing,' Quinn said. 'She has a reputation as a great cook.'

They ate quickly, hungry after a day's hard labour. The stew was followed by some cake that was equally delicious, and finally both leaned back, replete.

'I was pretty impressed with your riding lesson,' Quinn said. 'You looked like you had done that before.'

'Never,' Dan said with a smile. 'I really enjoyed it though. It's not at all like I thought it would be.'

'In what way?'

'I suppose I thought it would be a domination thing. Force the horse to do what I wanted it to do. But that's not the way it was. It was more like working together. I liked that. You should have a go. I bet you'd do pretty well too.'

'I'm not so sure about that.'

'Don't sell yourself short. I think you'd do just fine.'

Quinn cast a sideways glance at Dan as he placed another log on the fire. The flickering flames enhanced the angles and planes of his face and gave a rich molten texture to his red hair. Her fingers twitched – but for once it was not because she wanted to reach for her camera. Because she wanted to touch him. And when he raised his eyes from the flames to look at her, she saw the same desire reflected back. All her reservations and doubts vanished in an instant. The need to be in his arms was the only thing that mattered.

Dan got to his feet, and held out a hand. Quinn placed her hand in his. In one single movement, she was standing and in his arms and their lips were seeking each other with a hunger as hot as the fire itself.

He tasted like a steamy summer's day. Like the tingle of electricity in a thunder storm. He was smooth strong chocolate and the sensuous feel of fine suede. His arms closed around her and pulled her close. She could feel his hard body pressed against hers and she lost herself in him.

The squeal from the top of the ridge tore them apart. Dan's heart, already pounding with emotion and desire, kicked up a gear as he spun to face the danger. He stepped in front of Quinn, his hand automatically reaching for the weapon that was not there. His head knew that there was no danger, but his instincts took over, his eyes searching the darkness for threat.

'It's the stallion.' Quinn's steady voice beside him was all he needed to bring him back to this time and place.

His eyes followed her pointing finger. Silhouetted against the bright stars of the night sky, he could see the stallion pacing along the top of the gorge, scenting the horses below. Finbarr and his companion were moving restlessly, hampered by the hobbles they wore. One of them whinnied, prompting an immediate response from the stallion, a hard fierce masculine challenge.

'He's checking out the newcomers invading his turf,' Quinn said.

'Do you think he'll come down?'

'I don't know. I kind of hope he doesn't,' Quinn said. 'I have no idea what to do if he does.'

'I suppose we could try to get him into the yard.' Dan sounded hesitant.

'Would he hurt Justin's horses?' Quinn asked.

Neither of them knew the answer to that.

The question was solved when the stallion squealed once more and with a final toss of his head, vanished into the darkness.

'I'll just check everything is okay.' Dan moved away from the fire towards the stockyard and the horses that were still showing some signs of restlessness.

He needed those moments alone in the darkness to compose himself. He was the one disquieted. Not by the stallion so much as by his own actions. He had sworn he would not give in to this overwhelming attraction he felt for Quinn. No good could come of it for her. If he was no good for himself, he was certainly no good to her either. What had he been thinking? Giving in to the urge to take her in his arms. She had looked so lovely in the glow of the fire. So close. So tempting. This beautiful woman who could have the world at her feet on a catwalk, but chose instead to look for beauty in the wild places she loved. Quinn wanted to save the world – or at least this small part of it. He admired that. He'd wanted to save the world once. That's why he'd signed up and gone to war. He had soon learned that saving the world was not what he'd thought. Of the two of them, he thought Quinn probably understood that far better than he.

Maybe she could save him too. She had already helped him once through that book of photographs that was one of his most valued possessions. But he would never ask her to do it again.

After checking the horses, he didn't walk back to the campfire, where Quinn was waiting. Instead, he turned towards the side of the gorge. It wasn't hard for him to climb to a vantage point halfway up the rock wall. From there, he could raise his eyes to look into the heavens and the dark sky, sprinkled with glittering stars. Or he could look down to the one bright light on the bottom of the gorge. The campfire, where he could see Quinn sitting on a fallen tree that had room for two. She was knitting as she waited for him to return.

The sarge was right. Back there in Fallujah. When he'd called Dan a coward. He was a coward. He was never afraid of the enemy he'd faced in the desert. He wasn't afraid of being injured. Or dying. He was afraid of seeing the disappointment in Quinn's eyes when she realised who he was and what he had done. Spending time with Ellen's kids today had brought it back with such sharp clarity. A child. He was responsible for the death of a child. That was unforgivable. He could never forgive himself – and nor would Quinn.

He stayed where he was for a long time. He watched the fire slowly die down to nothing. He watched Quinn give up hope. She stood up, checked the fire, and retired to her tent. Still he didn't move. The gas light Quinn kept in her tent came on. He could see her silhouette as she moved about the tent, preparing for sleep. Finally, the light died and darkness settled over the camp.

Dan still didn't move. He sat and listened to the small night sounds of the bush. He listened to the stock horses moving below him. He watched the moon float above the landscape. He waited for sleep to touch him – but it didn't.

Just before sunrise, Dan came back down into the gully.

Moving silently to avoid waking Quinn, he collected his car keys and walked to his jeep. He started the engine and drove swiftly away.

The brilliant headlights of the jeep cut through the pre-dawn darkness as Dan drove back to the ranger station. Knowing that it was pointless to try for even an hour or two of sleep, he went to his office to work. The e-mail from Thomas Lawson was waiting for him when he powered on his computer. He read the words slowly.

... departmental policy regarding eradication of non-indigenous animals ... immediate implementation in time for the minister's announcement at the end of the month... further delay will be seen as a refusal to follow direction and could result in dismissal ...

Hidden behind the formal language of the bureaucracy, there was no mistaking the intent or seriousness of the order he had been given.

It was already too late. Too late for the brumbies and too late for him. He didn't really care about the threat to his job. Much as he loved it, he would walk away if that would save the horses. But it wouldn't. In fact, quite the reverse. He wasn't going to walk away from his responsibility to the animals. This time he was going to follow orders that he hated. Orders that he believed were wrong. He'd do it to avoid a possibility of cruelty and suffering.

It would cost him everything – but he would do it.

Chapter Twenty-One

Quinn was woken by the sound of kookaburra laughing. She lay still for a few seconds, wondering what she and Dan would say to each other. Would she tell him how late she had sat by the campfire, knitting and hoping he would appear from the darkness? The almost completed garment lying on her rucksack was evidence of that. Would she tell him how disappointed she'd been when he didn't return?

She heard a car pull up and the sound of two doors slamming. Carrie and Justin. That meant it was unlikely she and Dan would have any private moments to talk about last night. She wasn't sure if that was a good thing or bad. Quinn rose from her camp cot and slipped on a clean top and shorts. She ran a brush through her tousled hair, before ducking through the tent flap. She looked across at Dan's tent. The flap was closed. His car wasn't parked in its usual spot. At some time during the night, he'd left. Again. Did he really find it that hard to be alone with her?

'Hi,' Carrie called as she walked past, a bale of hay balanced easily on her shoulder. 'You slept late.'

Quinn hadn't yet learned to judge the time of day by the position of the sun. She glanced at her watch and was surprised to see the time.

'I was up late,' she murmured as she set about lighting her gas burner. 'Coffee anyone?'

'No thanks, we've already had breakfast.' Justin was also carrying a bale of hay. 'We brought another load of feed. We're going to need it when we've got the brumbies in.'

Quinn made coffee and ate a muffin and an apple that

she found in Trish's latest care package. As she did, she watched the ease with which Justin and Carrie worked together. They had what seemed like a lot of horse feed unloaded by the time she had finished her breakfast. Then Justin caught one of the stock horses, saddled it and with a wave was gone, trotting away up the sandy bottom of the gorge.

It occurred to Quinn that she had never seen Carrie actually ride one of the horses. She frowned. That seemed wrong. She thought back to Ellen's visit with her kids. Carrie had seemed ill at ease just leading the horse around. Quinn watched Carrie and began to realise that the woman she had met in Coorah Creek lacked the confidence and enthusiasm to be a top jockey. Maybe that was changing a little, but Quinn thought Carrie had a secret she was not yet ready to share with any of them. A secret that might be the downfall of their mission.

Carrie joined Quinn and helped herself to an apple too.

'You're not riding with him. On the other horse?' Quinn asked.

'No. I thought I would wait. I assume Dan will be here soon. Then I can give him another lesson. That's important.'

'He said he really enjoyed yesterday,' Quinn said. 'You must be a good teacher.'

Carrie shook her head. 'He's a natural.'

Dan was many things, Quinn thought, and all of them tugged at her heart and her body.

'Is there anything useful I can do right now?' Quinn asked.

'Not really. Justin probably will have some bits and pieces he wants done when he gets back. But we are nearly ready, I think.'

'I have to go to the ranger station,' Quinn said getting

to her feet. 'I need a signal for my phone. I need to talk to my agent.'

Not just her agent, she thought as she got behind the wheel of her Humvee and started the engine. It was probably time she contacted her parents. It had been a while. She wasn't as close to them as she used to be, but they still worried about her.

And then there was Dan. She was glad they would be alone when she saw him again. Not that she had any real idea about what might happen. They had kissed. A good kiss. No – more than that. A great kiss. But still, just a kiss. They were adults not teenagers. So why should a simple kiss be so complex? And why did it cause her heart to flutter as she saw the ranger station appear on the road ahead?

When she pulled up at the station, Dan's jeep was parked beside the house. Quinn thought about going inside and asking to use his phone. Instead, she pulled her mobile from her pocket. There was signal. This was better, she thought. There might be parts of this conversation she didn't want Dan to hear. Everyone knew she was planning a photo essay about rescuing the brumbies. They'd all agreed to be a part of that. Even Dan. A positive story about a humane brumby rescue shouldn't upset his boss too much. In fact, quite the opposite. The part of this conversation she didn't want Dan to hear would be the part about her next assignment. The part about her leaving.

The conversation was brief. Her agent had some news for her about some of her book sales. A photograph she had taken had been shortlisted for an award, which made her absurdly proud. Then he asked when she was likely to have something from this project that he could look at. Then maybe he could start thinking about turning it into a photo essay. Or a book. Something that he could sell. After all, that was his job.

Then came the part she had been expecting. Her growing fame as a photographer meant she was in demand. There were publishers offering her projects. Magazines requesting her for high-end shoots. When, her agent wanted to know, would she be available? Which of the very attractive offers should he accept on her behalf?

Quinn was deliberately vague about how much longer she'd be staying at Coorah Creek. It wasn't that she was lying to her agent. She honestly didn't know herself. She was beginning to think that maybe she was in over her head – in more ways than one.

When she ended the call, she was scrolling down her contacts to her parents' number, when a sharp, harsh crack of sound made her freeze. A rifle shot! A few seconds later there was a second. And a third.

The shots were coming from behind Dan's house.

Quinn ran to the corner of the building. She emerged the other side just in time to see Dan swing the rifle back up to his shoulder and fire. Some distance away, a tree branch exploded into thousands of splinters. Dan lowered the rifle and checked the sights.

Horror swept over Quinn. This could only mean one thing.

'What the hell are you doing?'

He hadn't heard her approach. At the sound of her voice, he broke open the rifle and removed the load. Then he lowered the weapon. Strange that his hands were not sweating or shaking now that the decision had been made.

He heard her footsteps approach and could almost feel the emotion flowing off her like waves. He didn't want to face her.

'I'm just getting my eye in,' he said, not turning to look at her.

Quinn grabbed his arm and forced him to turn and look her in the face. Her emotions were written clearly in every line. Anger. Horror and shock. And they were all aimed at him.

'Why?' she asked, although he could tell she already knew the answer.

'I've had another e-mail from the department. Wanting to know why I have not resolved this yet. They want to know why I'm delaying the cull.'

'Can't you tell them we've got a plan to remove them to a safe place?'

'I did that a few days ago. They told me I had one chance to do that, and then they would take over. Now it appears time has run out. Just because some politician is facing re-election. They're sending an inspector out here to make sure the job gets done.'

'When?'

'I'm not sure. They're not impressed with the way I've handled this, so they probably won't warn me. He'll just turn up. He may already be on the way.'

'And what happens when he gets here?'

'If the brumbies are still here, he'll take matters into his own hands.'

'How?'

'He'll probably start shooting them himself. Or he'll bring in another shooter. I won't let that happen.'

'None of us will,' Quinn said firmly. 'We'll stop him.'

Dan wasn't sure whether he admired her determination – or wept for her naivety. 'You don't get it,' he said.

'Then tell me.' Her hazel eyes challenged him. She was so beautiful when she was all riled up like this. So alive. So passionate. How he wished he didn't have to do what he had to do.

'If the brumbies are still here, he'll simply fire me and close the park for a few days. He has that power and if it's the guy I think they are going to send, he won't hesitate to use it. He's ambitious and looking to make a name for himself. You will all have to leave. So will I. He'll order me out with the rest of you.'

'He can't do that!'

'Of course he can. His only concern will be clearing the park and culling the horses. He'll probably try to be humane, but shooting a moving target is hard. If the wrong person tries …'

He looked at Quinn, but could tell she couldn't understand. He had to be honest with her – brutally so.

'I am a military trained sniper. If I take the shot, it will be clean and quick. If someone else does …'

'No!' She was shaking her head. She didn't want to hear it, but she had to. He had to make her understand that he didn't want to do this. But it was the best option.

'The horses could be wounded rather than killed cleanly. If you had ever seen …' His voice broke as the memories washed over him again.

A little girl's dark eyes. Her face covered with blood. The smell of blood on the hot desert sand. Her screams as she died, slowly and in terrible pain. It wasn't his bullet, but it was his fault.

Dan took a deep breath. His heart was pounding as if he had run a marathon. His whole body was damp with sweat. He recognised the symptoms but was powerless to control them. 'If the best I can do is offer a quick end, that's what I will do.'

'No!'

Dan's hands started to shake as he felt his emotions running wild. Anger. Fear. The need to run or strike out at anything – anyone – near to him. It had happened before, and the army doctors had told him it would happen again. That he needed medication to recover. He hated the doctors and their drugs. He would control this himself. And he had. Until that e-mail arrived and sent him right back into his nightmares.

Gunfire. The smell of cordite. Stone chips slashing bare flesh as hot metal chewed away the wall protecting them.

'Withdraw. Get off the roof.'

A panicking voice shouting into a radio. 'We're taking heavy fire. We need cover. Get us out of here.'

Blood. So much blood.

And cutting through the gunfire, the sounds of a little girl's screams.

'Dan. Dan?'

A gentle sound. Quinn's voice pulling him back from the past. Back from the edge. He opened his eyes and looked at her. It was like taking a drink of cool water after the burning heat of the desert sun.

'What is it?' she asked him gently. She touched his arm. The smallest of human touches but to him, it was like a lifeline. 'What happened to you out there?'

He shook his head. He wanted to tell her. To share the burden that lay so heavily on him. But telling her wouldn't help him. And she would never understand. No one did, if they hadn't been there. Telling her would only drive a wedge between them. Whatever they had – friendship or something more – was too precious to let something as ugly as the past touch it. He bent to pick up the rifle that he hadn't realised had fallen from his hand. As he checked again that it wasn't loaded, he sensed his control returning.

'I will not let those horses suffer,' he said as he turned to walk back to the house.

'None of us will.' Quinn fell into step beside him.

She meant well. And God knew he appreciated her

support, but they were talking about different outcomes. He knew it, even if she didn't.

The uniform he wore now was different. But an order was an order. His military training had conditioned him to obey orders without question. But he hadn't obeyed that day in Fallujah. And the suffering that followed – the terribly inhuman suffering and loss of life – had been his fault.

This time, although he knew the order to be wrong, he would obey. The others would hate him for it. Quinn would hate him. Shooting those horses would destroy him. But this time the only suffering would be his.

Chapter Twenty-Two

'Hello, Finbarr.'

The chestnut gelding's ears flicked toward her.

Carrie leaned on the wooden rail and looked at the horse. He was a nice looking saddle horse, but nothing spectacular. Yesterday he'd proved himself a sensible and reliable creature. Nothing like the highly strung thoroughbreds she'd once ridden. He had given Dan an easy first lesson and been co-operative and gentle with Ellen's kids. He was a horse to trust.

'Fraser horses always have Irish names,' Carrie said to the gelding. 'One of these days Justin is going to run out of ideas.'

The gelding sighed, a long deep sleepy sound, and began to move towards her. He stopped just a pace away and stretched out his nose to sniff the very tip of her fingers. Sensing nothing untoward, he moved a little closer to do the same to her face and hair.

'You see, Finbarr, I have a bit of a problem,' Carrie said, gripping the rail tightly with both hands as she fought the urge to move away. To step back just far enough that the horse couldn't reach her. 'I used to ride, you know. I was a jockey once. But I fell off. And now I'm too scared to get back on a horse. Even one as quiet and gentle as you.'

Finbarr lowered his head and blinked. His huge dark brown eyes regarded her seriously.

'You have very long eyelashes, Finbarr. Has anyone ever told you that?'

The horse moved even closer, and began gently testing the ends of her fingers with his soft lips. The hair around his muzzle tickled her skin, and she smiled, despite herself.

It was very, very quiet. Quinn had left some time back, and Justin was still exercising the other stock horse.

'I suppose you need to be exercised too, Finbarr.'

The horse nickered and nudged her arm. He was looking for attention.

'Or are you just after a treat? Well, sorry to disappoint you boy, I haven't got any treats for you. I used to carry something in my pocket most of the time. But these last few months, I haven't needed horse treats.'

That didn't seem to deter him, and before she really knew what she was doing, Carrie was stroking the horse's broad intelligent face. Oh, but it felt good. It reminded her just how much she had always loved horses. Her mother used to swear that the first word her daughter spoke wasn't Mummy or Daddy – it was 'pony'. Carrie had always loved everything about horses. The way they looked. The smell of them. Their insatiable curiosity and intelligence. There were times, she always maintained, when her horses knew what she was thinking. And feeling. Did Finbarr know how she was feeling right now?

She was afraid – but not the same paralysing fear she'd felt before. There was no one here to see her fail. Of course, that also meant there was no one to help her if she needed it. But failure was the greater fear.

Trying very hard not to think about what she was doing, Carrie reached for the bridle hanging on the gate post. She slipped through the gate and in one smooth practised motion, she slid the bridle over Finbarr's head. The gelding didn't object and he stood patiently while Carrie lifted his saddle from the rail; and placed it on his back. Her hands were shaking so much; she fumbled twice while trying to get the girth tight. But still the horse stood motionless.

At last he was ready. But was she?

Carrie looked around. She was still alone. It has to be

now, she thought. If I don't do this now, I won't ever do it and I will regret it all my life.

Mustering every ounce of her courage, she passed the reins over Finbarr's head. She placed her foot in the stirrup and entwined her fingers firmly in his mane. Before her courage could fail her, she swung herself into the saddle.

Nothing happened. The horse just stood there. The furious pounding of Carrie's heart slowed just a fraction. The hands holding the reins were shaking a little. Her mind was in turmoil still, but her hands and her legs had not forgotten what she had learned as a child and loved ever since. Her body seemed to remember how to seat itself properly in the curved leather of the saddle. Her legs automatically closed around the horse's side.

She had done it! She was back in the saddle.

A part of her wanted to shout and cheer. But she fought that urge. She still had a long, long way to go before she could claim any sort of victory.

She gave Finbarr the gentlest nudge with her heels. He stepped forward. A surge of pure panic almost undid her. She wanted to fling herself off the horse ... but was equally terrified of falling.

Finbarr just continued to walk. He knew what to do, even without instructions from his rider. As he approached the fence he turned to circle the yard at a steady walk.

Carrie let out the breath she had unconsciously been holding. Instinctively her body flowed into the movement of the horse beneath her. She didn't have to think about it. In fact, it was better if she didn't. If she started to think – or to remember the last time she sat on a horse – the memories of her fall would cripple her.

Finbarr's ears flicked back and forth. He was getting bored and waiting for an instruction to trot. That should come next. When Carrie didn't move, Finbarr tossed his head and broke into a slow steady trot. Carrie gasped out loud. She lifted her hands and jerked back savagely on the reins. Finbarr slid to a stop, shaking his head at the unaccustomed harshness of her hands on the reins.

'Sorry, Finbarr,' Carrie said. 'I wasn't ready. I'm not ready. Not for that. Please have patience with me.' She stroked the horse's neck, and then gave him the smallest nudge with her heels. He started walking again.

It was nothing compared to what she had once done, but this quiet walk on a placid gelding was more than she had ever hoped she would do again.

Tears pricked her eyes and she turned Finbarr to walk in the other direction. He responded like the gentleman he was. Carrie's heart sang. Then Finbarr lifted his head and whinnied. Carrie only just managed to stop herself from grabbing the saddle for unnecessary extra security. She looked up and saw Justin riding towards her on his big gelding.

No! She didn't want him to see her like this. He remembered her as she once was, balanced on the back of a racing thoroughbred. A talented jockey – fast and fearless. She didn't want to see the disappointment on his face when he looked at what she had become.

She quickly slid from Finbarr's back, and buried her face in his mane so she didn't have to see the pity in Justin's eyes.

Justin had to almost bite his tongue to keep from cheering. She'd done it!

When he'd ridden out this morning, leaving Carrie and Finbarr behind, he had hoped beyond hope that she might take a small step towards finding herself again. She had done so well with the horse yesterday – with Dan and with Ellen's kids. But that had been from the ground. Actually getting back into the saddle was a huge step for Carrie. It had taken such courage. And she had done it. All by herself!

He felt proud of her – for her. This was the Carrie Bryant who had captured his heart that day at the races. And now she was doing it again.

He pushed his grey up to the fence and slid from the saddle. Tossing the reins over a post, he opened the gate and walked towards Carrie who still had her arms wrapped around Finbarr's neck. He couldn't see her face, but imagined she must be overjoyed. His steps faltered when he saw her shoulders heave and realised she was sobbing.

'Carrie?'

She didn't look up. She just shook her head.

He stepped to her side and gently turned her away from the horse. Her lovely face was streaked with tears, her eyes shining with them.

'Carrie, there's nothing to cry about.' He lifted his hand to gently wipe away the tears. 'You did it. That's wonderful.'

'No. No, it's not.' Her shoulders heaved. 'I could barely walk twice around the yard without panicking. It was pitiful. I was pitiful.'

'Don't say that.' Justin unconsciously pushed her hair away from her face. 'You were amazing. You took that first step back. And all alone. I am so proud of you!'

'But I was terrified,' she said in an unsteady voice.

'And that is the definition of courage – to do that thing which frightens you the most. Carrie, you should be proud of yourself.'

'Really?' As she looked up at him, the hope in her eyes almost broke his heart.

'Yes. Really.'

'But I ...'

'Just give yourself time. I'll help you. Together we can take all the time you need. You'll find yourself again, Carrie. I know you will.'

She held his eyes for a long, long moment, as if to convince herself of his sincerity. Then she raised herself onto her toes and reached up to kiss his cheek.

'Thank you,' she whispered.

The touch of her lips on his skin was as soft as a butterfly's wing. It made him feel ten feet tall.

'Let's get this pair unsaddled,' he said, his voice rough with emotion. 'Then I could murder a coffee. After which, I want to walk along the gully and look for places where we might lose the herd if they bolt.'

'Could you use some company?'

'I was counting on it.'

Carrie turned immediately to tend to Finbarr. There was not so much as a hint of uncertainty as she unsaddled the gelding. Finbarr lowered his head, tilting it so she could rub the tender spot behind his ear. Carrie laughed softly as she complied. Justin vowed at that moment that Finbarr would never be sold. The horse would have a good home at the Fraser Stud for as long as he lived.

The water was just starting to boil on the gas stove when they heard the sound of approaching engines. Dan's Land Rover and Quinn's Humvee pulled up and the two of them emerged. Justin took one look at their faces and knew something was up. He glanced down at Carrie, whose hands had paused in the act of making the coffee.

'What is it?' Justin asked.

Quinn dropped into a camp chair, leaving Dan to tell them about the e-mail notification. As he spoke, Justin's heart sank. He had promised Carrie all the time in the world. Now it looked like he was going to have to break that promise.

'How long?' he asked Dan.

The ranger shrugged. 'I'm not sure. A couple of days maybe.'

'Then we muster that herd tomorrow,' Justin said. 'We'll only have one chance, and we'd better get it right.'

Chapter Twenty-Three

'We're not ready,' Dan said. 'At least, I'm not. I won't be any use to you on horseback. I've only done it once before. There's no way I can actually muster anything.'

Justin was inclined to agree with him. Dan was a good man to have on your side. He worked hard. He was strong and resourceful. But he wasn't a horseman. One day, perhaps, but not yet. Not by a long shot. It had never been his plan that Dan should ride with him. He'd hoped Carrie might be ready. But it was too soon for her. Too soon for all of them.

'Maybe we can get some more help,' Quinn suggested. 'Get some people from Coorah Creek.'

She was right. They could call in outside help. There were some stockmen who could probably get here by tomorrow. Justin frowned. He didn't feel comfortable with that idea. He hadn't told anyone about the stallion. About Mariah's son. He wanted to make a bit of a splash *after* he had the horse safely back home. To get some publicity that would help re-launch the Fraser Stud. What if word got out that the horse was there and they failed in this attempt? He would look like a fool. Even worse, there was always the risk that someone else would go after the horse, and there would be nothing Justin could do to stop that happening. Justin looked at the faces around him. They were strangers who had become friends and were there to help him. And Carrie ... especially Carrie. This was their project. He didn't want outsiders here.

Justin shook his head. 'I don't know if that's a good idea. If there are too many people about and too much activity, the brumbies will just vanish. They'll find water somewhere else in the park and we'll never find them. Anyway, if we have to do this tomorrow, there's not really enough time to find people and horses and get them here. We'll have to do it on our own.'

There was a little scepticism in their eyes, but they believed him. They probably didn't want strangers muscling in on their project either. He tried hard to fight the frustration he was feeling. All they needed was time. Just a little more time. Time to teach Dan to ride. Time for Carrie to overcome her fears.

She had been very quiet during their conversation, sitting on a camp chair and sipping strong coffee from a tin mug. How he wished Dan and Quinn hadn't come back. If he and Carrie had been alone just a little longer ...

He was reading too much into a kiss on the cheek. He knew that. And maybe he was also reading too much into Carrie's short ride on Finbarr. Both were such tiny steps. He had no reason to feel as if the world was spinning onto a new and much better axis ...

'Justin? Mate! Are you with us?' Dan's voice brought him back to the present.

'He was just thinking about what he's going to do with that stallion when he gets him home,' Quinn said with a grin.

Quinn had one thing right. That's what he should have been thinking about. Recovering his father's heritage. Making the Fraser Stud what it had once been. That was the important thing. He had brumbies to catch and if that wasn't going to be hard enough, he then had to figure out what to do with them. He shouldn't be daydreaming about Carrie – no matter how strongly he was drawn to her.

'Right, let's figure this out.' Justin picked up a stick and began to draw a map in the red dust. 'Here's the billabong. The brumbies enter the gorge here – this is the line of the gorge. And we are here.'

He gazed at the few lines in the dust. In his head, he could see it all.

'We need someone there to block their retreat.' He drew a cross in the dust. 'And we need someone here at the yard, to get that gate closed once the horses are through it.'

Dan nodded as if the plan made sense to him. 'And we'll need someone here,' he suggested. 'The sides of the gorge are pretty shallow. They could easily veer away there.'

Justin agreed. 'We need someone on horseback driving them forward.' He was thinking out loud. 'If we had one person on horseback blocking their retreat – that person could run them forward. The second rider could be here ... blocking this gap. That's got to be you, Dan. Hopefully once they see you, they'll just turn down the gorge and keep running. If they try to escape – make as much movement and noise as you can to turn them back.'

'All right,' Dan said in a voice that betrayed his lack of confidence. 'I'll do my best. But my best may not be good enough.'

'I'll do it.' Carrie's voice was barely audible.

Justin's heart almost stopped beating as a wave of emotions rocked him. Shock and gratitude. Fear that Carrie might push herself too far. But most of all, an intense admiration for her courage.

A surprised silence fell on the group as all eyes turned to Carrie and Justin realised that they all knew. For some reason he'd imagined that he was the only one who had seen Carrie's fear. That was stupid of course. In just a few days working and planning together, the others must have seen what he'd seen. How hard it must be for Carrie to be out there like that. And now ...

'Carrie – are you sure?' Quinn asked.

'Yes.' Carrie's lovely face was still, hiding whatever emotions were raging inside her. That in itself told him so much.

Justin wanted to say no. He wanted to give her more time. If something happened because she wasn't ready, she might never ride again. She might never find her way back to the amazing woman she had once been. To the woman she should be. He couldn't bear the thought of that happening. But if he didn't support her now ... didn't believe in her ... he might damage her fragile confidence.

He was between a rock and a hard place. He needed her to save the brumbies – to capture the stallion and reclaim his heritage. But if it came to a choice – Carrie's future or his own past – which would he choose?

He looked across at Carrie. Her head was bowed and she was staring into her coffee cup. Her hair, falling forward, blocked her face and eyes from the startled looks of her friends. When at last she looked up, her eyes found his, and he had his answer. She was not the rider she had once been, but she was still the most amazing woman he had ever met. Her courage was astounding. He would not let himself doubt her. She deserved better.

'In that case,' the words came out a little roughly past the lump in Justin's throat, 'Dan, you will be stationed on foot here, at the billabong. Let them drink. The stallion will be the last to go down to the water. We need him to be with the mares, not up on the slope. Once he's there, right in the middle of the herd, I want you to use that rifle – but use it to get them running in the right direction. Then I'll come down the gap, blocking their retreat. I'll take up position behind them to keep them moving. Carrie – you'll be on the right side of the gorge at this weak point. I'll stay to the left – ready to move if they veer that way.'

'What about me?' Quinn asked.

'I know you want to take photos.'

'I do. But I want to help as well. Catching those horses is the most important thing.'

'Good,' Justin said. 'You'll be based here at the camp. Near the fence. Make sure they can't see you. You'll see them coming. In fact, you'll probably hear them before you see them. You might even be able to get some shots. Carrie and I will be behind them, but we'll pull back here, so they're not too panicked to stop when they reach the back fence. Your job is to run forward as soon as they are through and shut the gate.'

'I can do that.'

'As soon as they see the fence blocking them, they will turn and try to come back. The gate has to be shut by then. Carrie and I then come up pretty fast once they're through the gate. The gate is a weak point. We need to be there to strengthen it.'

Silence fell on their little group. All eyes were looking down at a few squiggles in the dirt. A few squiggles that represented a lot of hopes and dreams.

'We can do this,' Justin said. He looked across at Carrie. As he did, she raised her head and their eyes met. The fear was still there, bravely quashed, but there was a spark of hope too. 'We really can,' he said again.

What had she been thinking?

Carrie sat beside Justin as he drove homewards. Justin had talked her out of remaining at the gorge campsite. Her hands were clasped firmly in her lap. It was the only way to stop them shaking. The fear was back. The terrible, crippling fear. But this time it was a hundred times worse. It wasn't just the horses she was afraid of. It wasn't just the thought of falling beneath those pounding hooves again. It was more than just the remembered agony of her injuries. Or the humiliation of trying to return to her racing stables. She wasn't even afraid of the pity she might see in other people's eyes.

She was so afraid she would fail Justin.

Capturing that stallion was so important to him. So much of the future – the horses he would breed; the financial recovery of his property; reclaiming his father's legacy – all rested on the success of the brumby run. They'd worked so hard to put this plan together. It had just one flaw. One weak point. Her.

She was fooling herself to think she could do it. She couldn't. She had to back out now – before it was too late. She had to give Justin a chance to find someone else.

'Justin, you need to get some more help,' she said quietly as they drove through the gates of his home. 'I can't do this.'

Justin touched the brakes and the car came to a halt. He turned the engine off and turned to face her. He slowly reached out to place his hand over hers where they lay in her lap. Could he feel them shaking?

'Carrie, if you don't want to do this, I understand. I would never want you to do something you didn't want to. But don't say you can't do it. Because you can.'

'It's been so long,' Carrie said, blinking back the tears, 'and I am so afraid. Last time I rode – I mean really rode – the horse died. That beautiful animal is dead because of me.'

'No. Never say that. What happened that day was an accident. It was not your fault. I've seen you ride, remember? You were amazing. You are still amazing. You belong on the back of a horse, racing at full tilt. You need to get that back.'

'But what if I let you down? What if the brumbies get away? What if you lose that stallion?' It was a cry from the deepest part of her wounded heart.

He shook his head slowly. 'You won't let me down. Do you have any idea how thrilled I was to see you up on Finbarr today?'

The intensity of his gaze could have been overwhelming. But it wasn't. Because she saw something in his eyes that she had never thought to see.

'If I lose that stallion, Carrie, I'll survive. We can try again another time to catch him. If not, well, I'll just work a bit harder to rebuild the Fraser name. Yes, it's important to me ... but it's not as important as that step you took today. I would gladly lose every single one of those brumbies, if it meant you had found yourself again.'

Carrie could hardly breathe. The emotion in his voice reached deep inside her and curled around her heart.

When she leaned forward to kiss him, it wasn't on the cheek.

Chapter Twenty-Four

After Carrie and Justin left, the world seemed to go very quiet and still. There was nothing for Quinn and Dan to do. Nothing at all.

Quinn sat beside the fire pit in the camp, idly wondering if she should think about cooking some dinner for herself and Dan. But it was too early for that. Her thoughts flew to the bundle of knitting inside her tent. But for once she didn't go to fetch it. That wasn't the answer to the restlessness she was feeling.

Dan had gone down to the yard, to check that the stock horses had water. Quinn decided to follow him.

'At least this chap is now spared the job of carrying me around tomorrow,' Dan said as she approached. He was patting Finbarr's neck as the gelding dozed in the shade.

'You would have done fine,' Quinn said. 'I was surprised Carrie stepped forward like that, but really glad she feels up to riding again.'

Dan didn't reply, and Quinn could see his mind was a long way away. She guessed he was thinking about the next afternoon. The brumbies tended to head for the waterhole quite late in the day. That's when the action would start. She wondered if he had been like this – thoughtful and still – before his war-time missions.

'Are you heading back to the ranger station again tonight?' Quinn asked at last.

'No. I thought I might stay here. If I go back there might be more e-mails. I think I'd like to avoid them.'

'You're going AWOL?'

'There's a first time for everything. I left a notice at the ranger station for park visitors. If there's some sort of emergency, I have a radio in the Land Rover. The police in Coorah Creek or anyone at the station can get me on that.'

Quinn glanced up at the sky. The sun was low, but there was still quite a bit of daylight left. It was still hot, but not unbearably so. The tension she felt had other causes.

'I don't know if we should go swimming tonight,' she said, trying to keep the disappointment out of her voice. 'We might make the brumbies nervous if they see or smell us.'

'I wasn't thinking about going swimming,' Dan said. 'There's something I'd like to show you. A place I'd like to take you. We should make it by sunset.'

'All right.'

'Bring your camera.'

Dan drove. They didn't talk much, but the silence wasn't strained in any way. Dan liked that Quinn could just sit there watching the landscape roll past the open window, enjoying the beauty as he did. After a while, he turned off the road onto a track that was little more than two wheel ruts in the dust. The wheels of his vehicle fitted them perfectly because he was the one who'd made them. The overhanging trees scraped against the sides and roof of the Land Rover with a high pitched squeal that always made him hunch his shoulders as he thought of the damaged paintwork. He grinned when beside him Quinn also grimaced at the sound. He had to take it more slowly now, as the track became more difficult. They began to climb quite steeply, the engine roaring as he dropped down to the lowest gear. At last, even the four-wheel-drive could go no further.

'We have to walk from here,' Dan said as he turned off the engine. 'It's not far.'

Quinn slung her camera bag over her shoulder and followed him. It took just a few minutes. At the top of a barely visible path, a huge red sandstone boulder blocked their way. Dan swung himself easily onto the top and reached down to pull Quinn up beside him. Then he stepped to one side and was rewarded with an astonished gasp as Quinn took in the view.

They were standing on a huge flat chunk of sandstone at the top of an escarpment. Just a few meters in front of them, the escarpment dropped away to a flat plain that seemed to go on forever. Standing alone in the middle of the vast plain was a huge red sandstone outcrop. It was about two kilometres from the place where they stood. Its sides were steep and clean, as if cut by a giant's knife. The monolith was much smaller than Uluru, but with its sharp sides and jagged edges, it was more spectacular. The rock was a deep rust-red, but even as Dan watched, the rock began to change colour as the setting sun caught it. The red began to grow ever darker and change to violet. Each time he blinked, the stone seemed to change colour. This instant it was the colour of an amethyst. A few seconds later, the blue of a lorikeet's feathers.

Standing beside him, Quinn raised the camera to her eyes and began to take photographs. He moved away and crouched on his haunches. It was partly to give her room to work. And partly because he liked to watch her. She was so intent on what she was doing, he probably no longer existed for her. How he loved and envied that passion of hers. A passion to create something beautiful. Not to destroy.

This was a very special place to him and he was so glad to share it with Quinn, who clearly found in it the same magic he did. This was the place he came when the nightmares became too bad. The local aboriginal people believed there were healing spirits living in or around the sandstone monolith. Perhaps they were right. When he came here, he felt as if he were being healed. Never more than this evening, with Quinn by his side.

As the last traces of sunlight vanished from the western sky, Quinn lowered her camera. She turned towards him, her eyes shining.

'That was beautiful,' she said, her voice little more than a whisper. 'Thank you for sharing that with me.'

'There's more,' he said, reaching for the swag he had brought with him from the jeep. He unrolled a blanket and motioned for Quinn to sit beside him. Dan touched her shoulder, and gently drew her back, until they were lying side by side staring up at the darkening sky.

It was as if someone was scattering diamonds onto velvet above them. A handful here. Another group there until the sky was glowing with an ethereal beauty. And at its zenith the five bright jewels of the Southern Cross.

How Dan had missed that constellation during his time serving overseas. Iraq was an ancient country, and when he could close his eyes to the tragedy around him, he found it incredibly beautiful. The stars were as bright as those that shone above him and Quinn now. But the Southern Cross was not visible from the northern hemisphere. Those were the stars that called him home. Or they had been. Something else was calling him home now too. He moved his arm slightly, and touched the cool soft strength of Quinn's fingers.

He had never told anyone the full story of what happened that day. Not his superior officers. Not the doctors. Not even his family. He had vowed never to tell anyone because they would not understand. He had vowed never to tell Quinn, because he didn't want to drive her away by revealing that dark core of his soul. But as they lay there in the place he loved most in the world, he realised that Quinn was the only person he could tell the whole truth to.

'I was in Fallujah.'

He felt Quinn's breath catch beside him. Now the words were begun, he could no more stop them than he could have stopped what happened that day.

'I was assigned to an American unit. They needed a sniper. The target was the leader of an insurgent group responsible for at least a dozen US deaths. Even more of his own people. We had intel that he'd be attending a family gathering. A wedding. We took up station on a nearby rooftop. My job was to take him out as he left the family compound.

'It was late afternoon when he left. His car was waiting outside the gate. There was just one chance – a gap of about two meters he had to cross to get to the car. It was a long shot. A hard shot in failing light. I was on that roof because I was good enough to take it.'

The smell of spicy food cooking nearby.

The feel of sweat running down his back.

The tension is an almost tangible thing as they wait.

At last the door opens. His finger is already on the trigger. All it will take is the slightest pressure.

A little girl's face. Laughing as she looks up at the man holding her.

'When the target walked through that gate, he was carrying a child. His own, maybe. Someone else's. I never found out. She must have been about eight years old. I hesitated.'

'It's not a clean shot, sir. The child …'

'Take the shot. Damn you. Take it!'

'But … the child …'

'That's an order, soldier, take the shot!'

179

'I was ordered to take the shot anyway. A direct order. A soldier never disobeys a direct order. I had to do it. I'd been trained to do it.'

His finger tightens on the trigger. He can do this.

He is the best marksman in the unit. He can make the shot without hitting the girl.

He is the only one who can.

He blinks once and takes aim.

'I could have taken out the target without hurting the girl, but I … it was wrong. I don't know if she was his daughter, but she clearly loved him. She had her arms around his neck and was laughing. A daughter's last memory of her father should not be one of blood and pain and violence. I did something a soldier should never do. I disobeyed the order. I refused to take the shot.'

'Do it, soldier. Do it now!'

'No, sir. I will not.'

'You're a coward, Mitchell. You make me wanna puke.'

Quinn's fingers and his were now entwined. It gave him the courage he needed to say the words out loud.

'I was wrong. I should have done my duty.'

The sound of an engine.

'He's gonna get away. Take the shot. Someone take the damn shot!'

'Someone else took the shot. He wasn't a sniper. He wasn't as good as me. The bullet …' His throat contracted as if to cut off the words before they could be spoken. 'The bullet passed through the girl's body and into the target.'

Screams. A little girl's screams as she tumbles from her father's arms.

The smell of blood seeping into the hot desert sand.

'Oh God. No.' Quinn's voice was a whisper.

'That started a firefight. The worst I'd ever seen. We were pinned down on the roof. They were pinned down in the compound. It lasted a couple of hours. The target and the little girl were lying between us. On the road. It was a shooting alley. Neither side could get near them. He died quickly, but she ... she took a long time to die.'

The whine of bullets as they ricochet off the walls.

He could smell the sweat and fear on the men around him.

The stench of cordite.

And above it all, the sounds of a little girl dying just a few meters away.

'How did you get out?'

Dan's eyes were fixed on the glorious arc of the sky above them, but he was seeing a very different night sky. A sky lit by tracer rounds.

'Once it was fully dark, we started to pull back. But they followed us. It was a street to street running battle. Finally reinforcements reached us – but by then more than half the unit had been hit. We were struggling to get the wounded out. Two were dead, including the sergeant.'

There was so much more he could say. He wanted to tell Quinn how he had carried the wounded sergeant to safety. How he provided cover for the medics as they treated his brothers, despite his own wounds. But he wasn't going to do that. It would sound like he was trying to balance the scales. That his later actions could make up for a child's death. And they couldn't. Nothing could.

'You're a coward, Mitchell. You make me wanna puke.'

'I should have faced a court martial ... but it was complex. I was an Australian assigned to a US unit. The war had become pretty unpopular at home. It was a time when the US was under fire for some of its actions in the field.'

'I remember the photos from that prison – of Iraqis being tortured.'

'Abu Ghraib. That changed a lot of things. I think they didn't want this incident to hit the headlines. When I was discharged from hospital, I was—'

'You were wounded?'

He heard the concern in her voice.

'It wasn't anything,' he said. He knew she would disagree. That she would think two bullet wounds in his chest was a big thing. But compared to what others had suffered, it was nothing.

'I rejoined my Australian unit. I don't think I left the base again between then and when we were sent home. I knew by the time I got back, I wanted to get out. I think they wanted rid of me as well. I was granted a discharge on medical grounds.'

'PTSD.' It was a statement, not a question.

He nodded, knowing she wouldn't see the movement in the dark. But she didn't need to. She understood.

He could hear her breathing softly beside him. Feel the warmth of her concern. And friendship. Perhaps something more … things he didn't deserve. He raised himself into a sitting position and wrapped his arms around his knees, staring out over the park to the dark upon dark outline of the great sandstone monolith. The healing place.

'It's a common story. I had trouble fitting back into everyday life. I felt uncomfortable around people. Especially in crowds. Loud noises, even the smell of certain food cooking would send me right back to the rooftop. My family tried to help, but they didn't understand. The doctors did their thing, but mostly their help came in the form of little white pills. And I didn't want that. I thought that if I could find a place where I felt comfortable, given enough time I would sort myself out.

'The first real help came from you, Quinn. When I opened that book of yours and saw your photographs, I knew there was somewhere I could go. Somewhere I could learn to live with myself again. I believed that eventually the nightmares would fade. So I came here. It's been good. I sleep better now. I still sometimes see ...'

A little girl's face. Dark eyes looking back down the barrel of a rifle.

The smell of blood and the screams. The terrible, terrible screams.

'As I lay in that hospital bed in Iraq, I swore I would never harm another person. That I would never again look down a sniper scope at any living thing. Then this happened and I realised something.'

He paused. He didn't want to say the next words. But for the first time in a very long time, he was being totally honest. Not just to another person. But also to himself. He had to say what needed to be said. He could only hope that Quinn would understand.

'I don't want to do it. I will do my very best tomorrow to save those horses. But if we can't ... then I will do what has to be done. Because it's my responsibility. If the only thing I can do is make their deaths clean and as quick and as painless as possible ... then that is what I will do.'

He waited for her response. For her to get up and walk away from him and the terrible words he had just spoken.

Quinn sat up. He could feel her close beside him. Then he felt a gentle touch. Her fingers curved over his shoulder.

'It won't come to that,' she said softly.

'It might.'

'Then we'll deal with it. You are a good man, Dan Mitchell. The best. You'll do the right thing. And I'll be standing right beside you when you do.'

He turned towards her. Reflected starlight glinted in her eyes as she leaned slowly forward, and her lips touched his.

A soft, sweet touch that wrapped around his tormented soul and felt like cool spring water pouring into the deepest recesses of his heart.

After a few moments, Quinn pulled away, but only a hair's breadth. Just enough that she could look up at him. Her eyes were beautiful. Such eyes could steal a man's heart – or heal it.

Dan reached for her and pulled her close, his lips seeking hers with growing strength and desire. She was soft and warm, velvet wrapped around rich dark wood. Strong and beautiful; rich and supple and yielding.

It was like coming home at last.

Chapter Twenty-Five

Quinn could feel the touch of the sun on her skin, a gentle warm caress. It was not the only warmth surrounding her. She lay with her eyes closed, feeling the heat emanating from Dan, where he lay beside her, one arm curved around her ribs. One leg crossed over hers. Holding her tightly even as he slept.

She did not want to move. Or even open her eyes. She wanted nothing to break the spell that had begun on that high starlit rock. With the ancient open plains around them and the breath of the night wind on their bare skin, they had made love as if it was the first time for both of them. The nightmares of the past had been washed away by the touch of flesh on flesh. By warm breath mingling as they kissed. By the open, unfettered joy in their voices as they called each other's names.

Even now, the purity of it, the pleasure and the honesty of it left Quinn breathless.

Afterwards they had talked well into the night, lying together, their bodies entwined as they watched the million bright stars of the Milky Way circle above them. When the sun had risen just enough to light their way, they had climbed back down and driven back to the camp, to fall asleep together by the low flickering light of their campfire. The fire had died while they slept, but everything else about Quinn and Dan still seemed to glow.

Dan was asleep. She could tell by the deep regular breathing. At last she opened her eyes to study him. Was it her imagination, or were some of the lines etched into his strong face gone? He looked younger. Less worn down by care. Last night she had seen, caressed and kissed the physical scars that he carried from his time at war. Perhaps some of the mental scars had been eased as they lay talking into the night. Quinn still flinched at some of the things he had told her. The terrible things he had seen. But never at the things he had done. Somehow, in the midst of the horror that was war, Dan had never lost himself. He was a truly honourable man who had never stepped over the line, despite the strongest provocation. She admired that more than she could ever say.

Quinn closed her eyes and breathed deep the essence of Dan. The warmth of his skin. The faint smell of sweat. The smell that was uniquely his. Her body glowed with the remembrance of his hands on her skin. How good it felt to be lying here in his arms. Waking up like this was a gift she accepted with pleasure – but it came with pain too, because one day in the not too distant future, she was going to have to walk away from Dan Mitchell.

It wasn't that she didn't care. Quite the reverse. Last night, as they lay under stars, she knew that she was a little in love with Dan. More than a little. If you could fall for someone in just a few weeks, then that was what she had done. But she was still going to walk away. Because she had to.

Would it have been easier to leave if they hadn't spent this night together? Yes, it would. The last few hours had brought her more pleasure and more simple joy than anything else in her life as it now was. She would never forget it. And never stop wanting more. But at the same time she would never regret one moment of it. Except, perhaps, for that small part of her that knew she had brought more pain into Dan's life. Or she would when she left. And that was something she had never wanted to do. She would hate herself for that, but she couldn't change who she was. In her own way, her soul was as damaged as his. That small tissue wrapped parcel that she had carried with her these last three years was proof of that. And no man ... no matter how honourable ... could change what she was.

Dan flexed his muscles slightly in his sleep, pulling her close. Quinn relaxed her body and allowed him to. I'm spooning, she thought to herself, by a campfire in the middle of nowhere. With a man she had known for such a short time. Why then did it feel so very right?

Still mostly asleep, Dan nuzzled the base of her neck. It sent a chill of longing through her and she shivered. In response, Dan's arms closed even more firmly around her. As they did, Quinn heard the sound of a car engine. Carrie and Justin were returning.

What terrible timing. Clutching her rumpled clothing, she rose quickly to her feet and darted into her tent. Behind her, she heard Dan grunt with surprise as he was rudely awakened by her movement.

Inside her tent, Quinn struggled to bring her errant emotions under control. She reached out to stroke the soft yellow wool of the garment she was knitting, a replica of the tiny jacket that lay in the package in the back of her Hummer. She thought of a little girl with blue eyes like her father. She thought of an empty cot. An empty bed and a silent house. Shattered dreams that still hurt so much it was difficult to draw breath. She did not have the courage to face that again.

Strange that she should be the one to help a wounded man – but was herself beyond help.

Dan's mind reeled uncertainly for a few moments before dragging him back into reality. He was half asleep, still feeling the warmth of Quinn's body against his. Still tasting her lips on his. Still finding an unlooked for peace in the feel of her arms around him. He'd returned from his foreign war two years ago. Last night, he'd finally come home.

Dan didn't believe in miracles. He didn't expect the past to magically vanish, taking the regrets and the shame and nightmares with it. He had never planned to unburden himself to Quinn, but in doing so, he had lightened his load. In making love to her, he had found a joy he'd thought lost forever. From this point on, his load would be just that little bit less. Just that little bit easier to bear. All because of Quinn.

'Hey, Dan. It's almost lunchtime.'

Dan cautiously opened his eyes to see Justin's boot clad feet appear next to the campfire. 'What are you doing still asleep? I guess I'd better get the coffee on.'

Justin sounded ridiculously cheerful for a man facing what might be one of the greatest – or worst – days of his life.

Dan sat up, rubbing the sleep from his eyes. He glanced across at Quinn's tent just in time to see her emerge, looking so beautiful he could focus on nothing else.

'Morning all,' she said cheerfully.

Dan waited and a few moments later, her eyes turned towards him. She smiled. There was a softness to that smile. A gentleness that he had never seen before. If he had given her that, he was happy.

'Don't let that coffee take too long,' Dan said as he slid from his swag and headed for the water bucket to wash his face.

It felt so normal as he came back to sit by the fire and wait for the coffee to boil. Justin was trying to coax flame from their campfire. Carrie had walked towards the yard where the two stock horses were penned. She was feeding them, stroking their shining necks as she did. And

Quinn was making breakfast. She had taken some bread and bacon from the seemingly never-ending supplies that appeared somehow by magic (or by the workings of Trish Warren) in their icebox. He couldn't take his eyes off her. She had always been beautiful. But today, it was as if she shone – putting the sun to shame. He wondered if the others could see it. Would they guess what had happened last night? And then he realised he didn't care. He wanted to say or do something. Touch her hair. Take her hand. Something to reassure himself that last night had been real. He knew it was just his male ego wanting to stake his claim. To proclaim to the world that she was his.

Because deep down, he was afraid that she wasn't. When they lay in the moonlight last night, Quinn had listened to him talk about his demons, but not once had she talked about herself. In fact, she'd never said much about herself or her family or where she came from. She talked about her work, but not about herself. Dan realised he really knew very little about her – except that he … His mind froze for a second, as if fearing to let the words form, but the thought would not go away. He knew very little about Quinn except for the fact that he could love her. Did love her. He wanted to love her until they grew old together – if only she'd let him.

The fear that struck him then was more powerful than anything he'd felt in the army. No threat of attack or injury was half as devastating as the fear of facing the rest of his life without her.

At that moment, Quinn laughed at something Justin had said. Just the sound of her laughter was enough to lift his spirits. Whatever it takes, he thought to himself. Whatever it takes.

After breakfast, there was really nothing for the four of them to do. Their work would begin late in the afternoon.

Quinn pulled out her knitting and settled in the shade of a tree. Dan loved to see her like that. In his mind, he pictured her many years hence. Her hair would be grey. Or maybe she would colour it. There would be lines on her face, but that wouldn't make it one fraction less beautiful. And her eyes, those amazing tawny eyes would still dance in the firelight and set his heart racing. She would still be beautiful when she was sixty. He imagined her knitting in the living room of some home somewhere, while he read in an armchair opposite. The picture brought a smile to his lips.

And then he remembered. Quinn lived in her car. She refused to be bound to a single place. Would she ever bind herself to a single person? To him?

These disturbing thoughts ran through his mind again and again as they sat there, waiting for the day to pass. For the first time in this wild undertaking, a tension was starting to form in their little group. He guessed that was because there was really nothing more for them to do but wait. So when Carrie suggested he could have another riding lesson just to pass the time, he readily accepted. When he'd agreed to try to capture the brumbies, he hadn't expected to find himself riding a horse. Even less had he expected to find himself enjoying it. But he did. He liked being around the horse. He liked the feel of the silky coat over the strong muscles of the animal's neck. He liked the way it explored his hands and face with its nose and lips – and then seemed to readily agree to carry him. It wasn't a matter of bending the horse to his will, but rather, of becoming partners. He liked that too.

And he liked the way Quinn's eyes kept lifting from her knitting to watch him as, released from the school ground of the stockyard, he rode past their camp into the gully.

He was so caught up in what he was doing, he didn't hear the vehicle approaching. None of them did, until a figure suddenly appeared on the edge of their campsite.

'Is Ranger Mitchell here?' a curt voice asked.

Dan recognised the tone of the voice. The uniform this man was wearing wasn't military, but this National Parks department inspector was no less his superior officer than that sergeant in Iraq had been.

'I'm Dan Mitchell.' He swung down off the horse.

'Superintendent Thomas Lawson.' The man did not offer to shake Dan's hand.

Of course. He should have recognised the man's voice. Lawson was shorter than Dan, his dark hair greying at the temples. And while he wore the uniform of the National Parks Service, Lawson looked as if he would be far more comfortable in a nice clean office, with four walls and air-conditioning. He was too soft for the outback. He would be at home with rules and regulations, reports and budgets. Dan suspected he spent very little time in the parks he oversaw.

'I was expecting you, but didn't realise you would be coming today.' Dan bit back the word 'sir'.

'So I gather. I was expecting you to be at the ranger station,' Lawson said. 'If I hadn't stopped for directions at the pub, I wouldn't have found you at all. That garrulous woman gave you away.' The man took a deep breath and frowned. 'You were ordered to remove the horses from the park. I did not expect to find you actually riding one. Horse riding is not permitted here. You know that.'

'This isn't one of the brumbies,' Dan said. 'It's a stock horse. We are just getting ready to muster the brumbies. Once we've got them in that yard, we can remove them from the park, as per instructions.'

The tightening of the man's mouth indicated this wasn't

how he saw things. 'Can you hand that horse to someone and come with me, Mitchell? You have some explaining to do.'

Dan was very aware of the other three standing not far away, watching the conversation. He turned to hand the horse's reins back to Carrie, shaking his head slightly to deter them from stepping in. He didn't want them in the angry inspector's firing line.

He followed the man a short distance down the gully.

'Would you mind telling me just what's going on here? You were ordered to get rid of the horses – instead it seems you have brought more of them into the park.'

'We need the stock horses to capture the brumbies,' Dan explained, knowing as he did the man was not really listening. 'We are going to pen the brumbies this evening. Justin Fraser, who is helping with all this, is going to take the horses back to his property. Then the park will be free of them.'

'You were instructed to shoot those brumbies weeks ago. Why didn't you?'

'I decided it would be better to save them.' Dan looked the man squarely in the eye.

'It wasn't your decision to make.'

Dan shook his head. He had a terrible feeling of déjà vu. But this time, things were going to be different.

'I don't care,' he said. 'It was the right decision.'

'And it's going to make a great story.' Quinn stepped to his side, her camera in her hand. 'One way or another.' She raised the camera and took a couple of quick shots of the stupefied inspector.

'Who ... what?'

'I'm Quinn,' she said. 'I'm a photo journalist. I'm telling the story of these brumbies. It's your choice as to the type of story it is. It could praise your department and your minister for finding a humane solution to the problem. Or it could say something very different.'

Dan felt invincible with her beside him. With her support he could do what he knew to be right.

Lawson scowled, obviously very unhappy. But bureaucrat that he was, he was obviously all too aware of the power of good – or bad – publicity. He glared at the two of them, muttered a few words under his breath, and finally spoke out loud.

'All right. You've got twenty-four hours. I'll be back here tomorrow, and if those brumbies are still in the park, I'll find someone who is willing to take action. Do I make myself clear?' He turned and stormed back towards his car.

'We only need twenty-four hours,' Justin said as he and Carrie stepped closer. 'We can do this.'

'We'd better,' Dan said. 'Because there is no way I'm going to allow him or anyone else to shoot those horses!'

Chapter Twenty-Six

Justin shuffled his feet in the dirt. He was bored with waiting. It felt as if he had spent hours hidden among the boulders and scrubby trees above the gorge. He was so tense he was sure he was about to snap. The next hour would decide his future. He could see that future so clearly, it was as if it was already real. And he wanted it more than he could ever say.

He saw the brumby stallion, Finnegan's last, lost colt taking pride of place among the Fraser horses. He saw the stallion hard on the heels of a steer in a working horse competition, or winning ribbons at a breed show. He saw the foals gambolling in his paddocks. Foals with that same crooked white blaze down their face. He saw young horses with the Fraser brand blazing a trail across the competitions and racetracks. And in all these visions, Carrie was at his side.

Carrie.

Wherever he was and whatever he was doing, his thoughts always seemed to come back to Carrie. Not even something as important as recapturing the horse that was his father's legacy was enough to keep his thoughts away from her.

He wanted this venture to succeed – but if it had to fail, he would still consider himself well served – because it had brought him to Carrie.

He shook his head as he thought about her. The images flashing through his mind were so wildly different. There was Carrie mounted on a racing thoroughbred, crossing the winning line with one hand held high in victory. Carrie kissing the nose of a sweating horse, giving the animal more attention than the cheering crowds around her. The newspaper had carried a photograph of her terrible fall at Birdsville. To anyone who had ever ridden a horse, that photograph was shocking – a horse crashing to the ground as a small human form was tossed through the air like some broken and discarded doll. He had torn it up and thrown it away immediately, unable to contemplate such a terrible thing happening to a woman he admired so much – even if it was from afar. Far more shocking than that photo was the reality of her flinching away from his horses in fear. But the memory of her beautiful face, shining as she took those first tentative steps on Finbarr's back, could balance even the worst images.

She had found herself again. Found her way back from whatever dark and lonely place she'd been since that fall. He liked to think that maybe he'd helped her. If he had fallen a little in love with her the day he saw her triumph as a jockey, he had fallen even further now that he had watched her triumph as a person.

Justin desperately hoped that he wasn't asking too much of her today – to take such a vital role in the muster. Not that he was really asking it of her. She was asking it of herself. And that was what was so incredible about it. About her.

Justin removed his hat and wiped the sweat from his brow.

His horse, sensing his restlessness, moved uncertainly. It raised its head and its nostrils flared. Justin quickly ran his hand down the horse's nose, leaving his palm lying gently across the animal's nostrils. The last thing he wanted was the horse to whinny, or nicker and give away their hiding position.

His thoughts turned again to the wild stallion. In his head, he was already planning the steps he'd have to take to get the horse accepted into the stud book. His father had been part of one of the earliest equine blood typing programmes conducted by the University of Queensland. All the Fraser horses were blood typed. From those records, he should be able to prove the stallion's parentage. But even then, it wouldn't be easy. He couldn't recall another instance where an adult animal had been accepted under circumstances such as this. But he would try. If the people in charge of such things could only see the horse, they would know. Just as Carrie had known. Just as he knew.

His train of thought was interrupted by movement in the distance. Keeping his hand on his horse's nose, Justin watched as the brumbies appeared. They filed through the gap in the rocks on their way to water. They were a fine bunch. He would bet money that some of the mares were also runaways. Perhaps they had also escaped in the same bushfires that had caused Mariah to be lost. Several of the yearlings had the same distinctive while blaze as the stallion. Watching them pass, Justin thought that even if they were never accepted into the stud book, they could nonetheless develop into good sturdy work horses. He would train them and …

The stallion appeared. Just a few meters behind his mares, he was keeping a watchful eye as he followed them down to the billabong to drink. He really was magnificent. His mane was matted and dusty. His hooves unshod and rough-edged. But even unkempt and ungroomed, he was stunning and Justin was even more convinced that this really was Mariah's son and his future.

Justin remained frozen in his hiding place as the stallion walked through the gap and into the gorge and disappeared. He waited a few moments, then led his horse out from among the rocks. He fixed his hat more firmly on his head and took a steadying breath. He gathered the reins and swung into the saddle. As he settled himself firmly into the leather, he stroked the stock horse's neck.

'You had better be ready,' he said. 'We will only get one shot at this.' He was speaking to himself, as much as he was to the horse. And he was thinking of Carrie too. And Dan and Quinn. He hoped they were all ready. Because it was time.

He urged his horse a few steps forward, then halted just below the crest of the rise. From here, a few strides would see him breach the gap down to the gorge, effectively blocking the brumbies' retreat. But he didn't want to move just yet. He didn't want the horses to see him too soon. First he had to wait for Dan's signal.

Dan's fingertips touched the cold steel of the rifle where it lay on the ground beside him. From his place among the rocks he could see the wild horses approaching. They looked calm, and not unusually nervous, which he guessed was a good thing … but that calm was about to be shattered.

He had a good vantage point. This was the same place where he had last lifted the rifle to sight along the hard grey barrel at the brumbies. That time his goal was death … and he had failed. Partly due to Quinn's interference. He would be eternally grateful to her for that. This time he had no intention of hurting the animals, but it made no difference as he lifted the rifle. His heart began to hammer.

This was how it always began. The racing heart, followed by the sweat on his face and the palms of his hands. Then the voices in his head would begin and he would see a little girl's face.

He waited, eyes fixed on the horses as they waded into the billabong and began drinking.

His palms remained dry. The voices in his head were quiet. He closed his eyes, and saw nothing but darkness. And when he opened them again, he saw the landscape. He saw the horses. He did not see the little girl. He did not hear her screams.

The absence was as shocking as it was welcome. And he knew who he should thank for that.

Quinn.

Dan thought about the day he found that book that had brought him here. The day he had first learned her name. It had been such a dark time in his life when he had felt as disconnected from the people around him as if he had been on another planet. During his time here at Tyangi, he'd returned to that book often. Looking at the photographs and thinking about the unknown photographer. He'd never imagined Quinn was a woman; a beautiful woman, with a quick-fire mind and a heart to match. And he had certainly never imagined they would ever meet. It was nothing short of a miracle that Quinn had walked into his life, had become a part of it. She had become his friend and so much more. She had given him the gift of her body and her heart, and in doing so had healed some of his deepest wounds.

He wondered if the little girl with the brown eyes would ever come back, and realised that if she did, it would never be as bad as it had been in the past.

A squeal from the direction of the billabong dragged Dan's attention back to reality. He had a job to do and it was time he did it.

The brumbies were milling about, having drunk their fill of water. This was the moment Justin had told him to watch for. The stallion was in the middle of the mob, drinking and not on watch. Dan rose from his hiding place and stepped into full view. He could just shout and wave his arms. That would be enough to spook the horses. Instead, he raised his rifle. The shot would be a signal to the others that it had begun. He pointed the rifle at the sky and pulled the trigger.

The harsh crack of the shot bounced off the walls of the gorge. In a heartbeat the horses were moving. The stallion forced his way to the front of the herd, whipping his band to faster speeds with his teeth. As one, they turned back up the path they had come down, heading to the gap in the wall and escape into the wide open plain. Dan looked up at the gap in the rocks. There was no sign of Justin.

'Damn it!' Dan cursed as he watched the brumbies leaping upwards towards the gap and freedom. Had he moved too soon? A few more seconds and the stallion would reach the top of the rise and the mob would escape.

Justin appeared. His stock horse was quivering with excitement, but Justin held it in check with a firm hand and strong legs. He raised his arm above his head and the crack of his stock whip rang out as loud as any gunshot.

The stallion faltered in his mad rush as he saw the movement ahead. Then he tossed his head and darted forward, meaning to dash between Justin and the rock wall.

As Dan watched, Justin pushed his horse forward. It leaped into the gap, sliding onto its haunches on the loose surface. The brumbies slid to a halt, eyes white and wild, milling about. Justin urged his horse forward. It came leaping down the steep path, small rocks flying from its every stride. The stock whip lashed back and forth, making the gorge ring with its harsh voice.

The brumbies turned.

Dan strode down towards the billabong. He raised the rifle again and fired a second shot.

That was too much for the stallion. He spun and began

to race down the gorge. The herd followed, streaming out behind him. Then Justin was on their tail, driving them forward at a run. Driving them in the direction he wanted them to go ... along the gorge to where Carrie and Quinn waited.

Dan turned and began to run back toward the car he'd left hidden among the trees.

Chapter Twenty-Seven

Carrie froze when she heard the shot. She stared down the gorge. She was about two kilometres from the billabong with a clear view along the gorge. If the brumbies were coming her way, she didn't have much time. She turned to the horse at her side. Finbarr was alert, staring in the direction of the gunshot. Carrie felt her courage fail her. What had she been thinking? She couldn't do this. She was no longer that woman who could ride like she was born to it. Who could guide a horse with feet and hands and voice, bending it to her will and creating that magic partnership where two became as one. That woman had vanished under the slashing hooves of the horse that day she fell.

Beside her, Finbarr shuffled nervously and snorted. Her hands clenched the reins until she could feel her own nails biting into her palms.

Justin was relying on her. Justin who had been so kind and understanding. Justin who made her heart beat a little bit faster every time he was near her. Justin looked at her as if she was someone special; as if she was still that woman she had once been. She would never forget the look on his face when she'd offered to ride Finbarr today. The look of joy and pride. A look of admiration.

How could she fail him? How could she not?

A second shot echoed through the gorge. Her eyes widened. She hadn't expected a second shot. What was happening? Justin was going to need someone on this flank. He was going to need her. It was time to live up to the promise she had made. Trying to ignore the terrible fear threatening to swamp her, she thought of Justin and reached for the saddle. She slipped her foot into the metal stirrup and swung herself onto Finbarr's back. Feeling her tension, the excited horse sidled away, and her foot slipped out of the stirrup back to the ground. She stepped closer to the horse, but his growing excitement had Finbarr dancing away from her. Her hands were shaking too much to hold him. He would sense her fear and that would only make it harder for her to control him. Tears of frustration pricked her eyes.

She heard a noise, like a low rumble of thunder. Finbarr spun around to stare back up the gorge. The horses burst into sight.

The stallion was in the lead, his neck stretched out, nostrils flaring as he gasped for breath. He'd been running hard, and his sides were dark with sweat. The other brumbies were strung out behind him. The mares and foals were struggling to keep up the punishing speed their leader set.

Behind them, she could see a distant figure of a man on horseback. Justin. He was pushing them, but not too hard. He needed them to keep moving, without time to think. But at the same time, he didn't want them to stampede in a blind panic.

Finbarr began to prance beneath her restraining hand. He could see and hear and smell the wild horses. He wanted to run, too. It was all she could do to restrain him. She should be on his back now, and every second she waited, he grew harder and harder to control. A sob escaped her. She couldn't do this.

In the distance, Justin swung his stock whip once again. His big bay horse increased its speed and stumbled in the rough going.

It happened in slow motion. Carrie stopped breathing as the big bay stock horse fell to his knees and rolled over in dry creek-bed. Justin was flung from the saddle and rolled onto the sand right next to the thrashing feet of his horse.

'No!' The cry escaped from the deepest part of Carrie's soul. Without thinking, she turned and flung herself onto Finbarr's back. She gathered the reins and dug her heels into his sides, urging him into a gallop.

The stock horse lunged down the embankment, almost unseating her. Her heart clenched with fear, but instinct and years of training took over. She gripped more tightly with her knees and leaned forward, thinking of nothing but her need to get to Justin. She lost sight of where he lay as Finbarr began a strong, sure-footed race down the side of the gully.

A few seconds later, Finbarr flung his head high in the air and slid to a stop. Horses had appeared at the mouth of the gully. The brumbies were turning away from the main gorge, seeking escape. This was what Justin had feared. This was why Carrie was there.

Torn between the desire to do her job and the overwhelming need to get to where Justin lay, Carrie grabbed the stock whip that was hanging from the front of her saddle. Taking the reins in one hand, she shook the whip free and swung it.

The resulting crack echoed off the red rocks and brought the brumbies to a ragged halt. As the mares milled about uncertain of what to do next, the stallion pushed his way to the front. Carrie swung the whip again. And again. She was terribly afraid the stallion would decide to push past her, and she'd be powerless to stop him. She swung the whip one more time.

The mares broke, turning away from Carrie and back into the gorge. After a moment's hesitation, the stallion squealed and followed them. Moving faster than the rest he fought his way through the mob to take the lead. He stretched into a gallop, showing no sign of the exhaustion that was evident in the other horses. Behind him, the mares raced on, but those with young foals at foot were starting to falter. The yearlings too were showing signs of exhaustion.

Carrie guided Finbarr the last few strides down to the bottom of the gorge and turned his head away from the herd and back towards where she'd seen Justin fall. There he was, once more atop the big bay gelding, racing towards her as fast as the horse could go.

A sob of relief caught in her throat. Then she saw the blood on his face, and a terrible chill engulfed her.

'Carrie.' His voice echoed off the high rock walls. 'I'm okay. Let's go.'

Then he was beside her. Despite the blood on his face, he was grinning.

'You did great,' he shouted over the sound of horse's hooves.

Her heart swelled with joy and pride as the horses galloped side by side.

'I'll take the left flank,' Justin called. 'You take the right.'

'Okay.'

She pushed Finbarr to the right to take up her station. Justin moved towards the left. Ahead was the heaving sea of black and brown and grey bodies. The brumbies were moving a little more slowly now. Exhaustion was overriding fear. Some of the foals were falling behind, stumbling in the heavy sand of the gorge. Only the stallion seemed still full of energy. A gap was beginning to open between him and the rest of the herd.

'Try to push them up a bit,' Justin yelled. 'We don't want him to get too far ahead. We need to keep them all together.'

Carrie nodded. She pushed Finbarr to more speed and swung her whip. The harsh crack sent the mares lunging forward with renewed energy. The gap closed.

She glanced over at Justin, who waved his approval.

How good that felt. Carrie's heart was beating fast, her muscles straining as she rode with every ounce of skill she possessed. For the first time in months, she felt totally alive.

The gorge was growing even narrower, pushing the racing brumbies into a tighter mass. They were almost there. They had almost succeeded. The yard they had worked so hard to build was not far away.

It was up to Quinn now.

Quinn's fingers curved around the familiar shape of the camera. Her hands were still. Her arms poised. Every nerve in her body was alert for the first sight of the wild horses. She was carefully hidden among some boulders, just a short distance from the wide-open gates leading to the yard. The two metal gates had been partly obscured with small scrubby tree branches. The fence posts likewise had been disguised. The camouflage wouldn't stand up to close scrutiny, but hopefully the horses wouldn't see the trap until they were inside. It was Quinn's job to shut those gates, blocking the brumbies' escape back the way they had come. Carrie and Justin would be there too, on horseback, ready to block the herd if they turned. But the gates were the most important factor. Quinn had to get them shut.

She cocked her head, listening for the first sound of the brumbies' approach. She'd heard the two shots. Dan setting the horses on their way. But since then, there had been nothing but silence. The high walls blocked any other sounds from further down the gorge. Quinn would have sold her soul to know what was happening back there.

She lifted the camera and focussed on the place where the horses should emerge. This was the essence of being a photographer. Being prepared. This was the one important thing she had never failed at. It was who she was. Other women could be wives and mothers. Not her. That carefully wrapped package in the back of her Hummer was testimony to that. She was a photographer. Without that she would be nothing and no one. With her camera she could create beauty. It was the most important thing in her world. The only thing in her world.

She felt them coming, rather than heard them. A vibration running through the rocks. Her finger poised over the shutter release.

The stallion burst into view. In the zoom lens, she saw his eyes, wild and ringed with white. His nostrils flared as he gasped for breath. Again and again she depressed the shutter release ... pulling back to show his sweat streaked coat and straining muscles. Behind him, the herd came into view. Wide-eyed and exhausted, they were falling behind. The mares with foals at foot had dropped to the back of the mob which was starting to string out along the gorge. Quinn realised with a start that the stallion would likely reach the back fence of the yard before the rest of the brumbies were safely inside. The instant he scented the trap, he would turn and try to send the others back the way they had come. If she was just a few seconds late, they'd be gone. Or if the exhausted mares didn't respond, the stallion could simply bolt and escape alone. They might catch the rest of the herd, but lose the most important horse of all.

She lowered her camera, letting it fall the last few inches to the ground as she tensed her muscles, ready to run.

Below her the stallion shot past the gates without breaking stride or realising that he had run into a trap. Quinn forced herself to remain motionless until the first mares were in the gateway, then she leaped to her feet. She flung herself down the bank, and grabbed the first metal gate, swinging it shut behind the last of the trailing foals. But that one gate was useless without the other. Only when the two were locked together was the trap sprung. She darted to the other side of the gorge to pull the other gate forward. The branches used to hide it were now getting in her way. She tugged at them to free them, aware of every passing second.

Looking up, she saw the stallion halt in his headlong flight as he saw the way ahead was blocked. He reared high into the air, striking out with his powerful front legs, then he dropped to the ground and spun around, his eyes seeking an escape route back the way he had come. With a harsh scream, he flung himself back through the herd towards the gate, teeth slashing to clear his way. Quinn tugged at the gate and felt it give, then catch again. She wasn't going to make it!

Subconsciously she registered a sound of a car door slamming as she wrapped her fingers around one last branch and pulled with all her might. She was rewarded by the sound of snapping of timber as she dragged it free. Hoofbeats were approaching fast from behind her. Carrie and Justin were almost there. But almost might not be good enough. Then Dan appeared. He ran into the rapidly closing gap and stood there, arms spread wide to block the stallion.

It all happened so very fast.

Carrie and Justin bore down on horseback, whips cracking. But they were still just a fraction too far away to have any effect.

Dan let out a mighty yell and the big stallion suddenly stopped dead in his tracks. He swung his head, his eyes wild as he searched for escape. The only way out was past the man standing defiantly in the open gate. The stallion flattened his ears against his head and lunged forward, mouth open and teeth bared.

Quinn froze in fear. Get out of his way, she screamed silently in her head.

Dan moved. He jumped forward, towards the oncoming stallion. With movements almost too fast to see, he raised his rifle, pointed the barrel up at the sky and pulled the trigger.

The crash of the shot caused the stallion to shy away at the last possible second and hurl himself back through his mares looking for an escape in some other direction.

Quinn grabbed the gate and dragged it shut, dropping the metal latch into place with a loud clang. Beside her, Dan slid home the metal bar they had designed for extra strength.

It was done!

The stallion screamed in anger as he tore around the enclosure, desperately searching for a way out. For one heart-stopping moment, he ran straight at the back fence, gathering himself as if to jump to freedom. But at the last minute he swerved away. The rest of brumbies milled about, looking for a way out, but the race down the gorge had taken its toll. Mares stopped moving, their heads hanging in exhaustion as their foals collapsed beside them. The stallion trotted over to the steep cliff face that enclosed him, he pawed at the earth, but there was nowhere for him to go. He turned and followed the line of the back fence, searching for weaknesses, snorting his anger and fear.

Quinn turned to face Dan. He was standing there looking, not at the horses, but at her. His face was alive with emotion. Exhilaration. Joy. Relief. Then Carrie and Justin were with them. Quinn barely had time to notice the blood on Justin's face before he grabbed Carrie and lifted her high into the air. He spun her around and then dropped her back to earth so he could kiss her. There was much back-slapping and hugging all round, and when Dan grabbed Quinn and hugged her, she thought they would all explode with happiness.

Then she caught a glimpse of movement over his shoulder.

There was no congratulation on Thomas Lawson's face as he walked into their midst. He stood for a few moments watching the brumbies in the yard. The stallion was still searching for an escape. He flung himself from one side of the trap to the other, his head tossing, and his eyes wild. He slashed with teeth and hooves at the other horses around him. He crashed his sweat-streaked body against the wooden fence, then lifted his head and screamed in anger and frustration.

The park superintendent watched the furious horse for a minute then turned to Dan.

'So. You've caught him. Congratulations. But how the hell do you expect to get that wild animal transported out of the park?'

Chapter Twenty-Eight

The question hung in the air. Four people turned away from the park inspector, back towards the wild-eyed stallion. Quinn had to admit, it was a reasonable question.

'I'll get him there,' Justin said, quiet determination in his voice as he casually wiped a trickle of blood from his cheek.

'Yes, we will.' Carrie stepped to Justin's side.

Quinn had to admire their determination, but looking at the stallion, she had her doubts. He was pacing the fences, his coat a lather of sweat. His eyes still white ringed and fierce. Everything about the taut muscles of his body and the tossing of his head declared his wildness. Every few minutes he would let loose an almost human scream of anger and frustration. Even his mares were not safe near him. He vented his temper on them whenever they got too close.

'I'll truck them out,' Justin told the inspector.

'You'll never get that animal onto a truck,' Lawson said.

Another angry roar from the stallion seemed to underline the statement.

'Yes, I will,' Justin declared, his voice firm with determination. 'I just need a couple of days to get him settled.'

The inspector looked at Quinn and glanced down at her hands. He was looking for her camera. The camera she had carelessly dropped in the dirt as she ran to shut that gate. Quinn suddenly felt almost naked.

She stared back at the inspector anyway, trying to convey to him that just because she had no camera to hand, she could soon retrieve it, if there was any need to document what was going on.

'All right,' the inspector said. 'You've got two days. Then I'm taking over.'

Two days seemed a very short time to Quinn – but it was more than she had expected.

'I wish you luck,' Lawson said as he turned away. 'You're going to need it.'

The four of them stood silently watching him leave, taking with him the joy they should have been feeling at their success. Behind them, the thudding of hooves simply served to highlight the problem they now faced.

'I'd hoped to have a bit more time,' Justin said quietly.

'You can do it.' Carrie placed one hand on Justin's arm. 'I'll help you. Look what we've already done. We've got them now. No one is going to stop us.'

Carrie was speaking quite softly, leaving Quinn with a feeling that she was somehow intruding on a private moment. She turned and walked briskly back to her former hiding place. Her camera was there, looking a little forlorn in the dust. She picked it up and carefully checked for any damage. There was none. What on earth had possessed her to just drop her precious camera like that? That was just not like her. Her cameras were more than her livelihood. They were the only thing in the world that gave her any peace or satisfaction.

'Quinn?' Dan appeared at her side. 'Is everything all right? You just walked away.'

'I came back for this.' She held the camera up. Dan nodded but his face was sombre.

'Damn him!' Quinn said angrily. 'Why did he have to do that? Come back and spoil everything. We should be celebrating right now.'

'Yes, we should,' Dan said. 'And we're going to. Let's go and do whatever has to be done to make those horses safe. Then I need to take a look at Justin's head. Good thing Doctor Adam gave us a first aid kit.'

'I didn't know you were a medic,' Quinn said as they walked back to the others.

'In my unit we all had to have first aid training. To deal with field injuries.'

He said it in a calm, matter-of-fact way. Quinn glanced sideways at him. In the short time she'd known him, any reference to his military service had been accompanied by a tightening in his voice and a stiffening in his manner. Not this time.

'It's a good thing you've got such a hard head, my friend,' was Dan's diagnosis a few minutes later as he gently examined Justin's wound. 'You'll have a splitting headache for a while, but I think you'll live.'

'Thanks.' Justin winced as Dan applied butterfly stitches to close the wound on his head, while Carrie hovered in a protective fashion.

Dan finished and tossed a couple of bloodstained bits of gauze into the fire pit. 'I think we should head to the billabong to wash away some of the dust and sweat.'

This was a side of Dan that Quinn hadn't seen before. As they walked towards the cars for the trip to the swimming hole, Quinn realised what it was. Dan was happy. She'd never realised before that a veil of unhappiness had hung over him like a shadow. That shadow had been lifted. She guessed she had something to do with that, and was glad. She only hoped that when she left … No. This wasn't the time to think those thoughts. They had achieved their aim and captured the brumbies. They would all be working together a bit longer to get the horses back to Justin's place. After that ... well, after that could just wait. Dan was right. Tonight they deserved to celebrate.

As celebrations went it wasn't ever going to make the pages of some celebrity magazine. But to Carrie it was perfect. It had started at the billabong where the four of them had washed away the dust and sweat. They had romped about in the water, splashing each other like teenagers and laughing to rival the kookaburras. By the time darkness had truly fallen, they were back at their campsite, drying in the flickering light of a campfire.

Quinn surprised them all by pulling flour and salt and herbs from her supplies in the back of her Hummer. With the help of some butter remaining in their icebox, she quickly mixed up a thick dough. She wrapped the dough in foil and cleared a space for the damper on the glowing coals. From the icebox they also took the last of Trish Warren's offerings – a tub of some sort of meat stew – and set that to cooking on the fire. It wasn't long till the rich smells of the food filled the cool night air.

Carrie took no part in the cooking. Quinn had it all under control. Dan and Justin were doing the blokey barbecue and beer thing, talking together slightly away from the womenfolk. They had retrieved the last few cans of beer and were obviously set on incorporating that into the celebrations. In typical male fashion, they were thinking only about the moment. And she wasn't going to deny them that. Justin had achieved something really important today. He had forged his own future. He deserved to celebrate.

Carrie had a lot to think about and was glad to sit quietly, slightly removed from the others. Because she had done something really important today too. She had escaped the past and opened new chances for her future. She just wasn't sure what she wanted that future to be.

She could ride again! For the first time tears welled up behind her eyes. After all these long months when she felt so lost. So unlike herself. She had found that thing which was at the very core of her soul. When she saw Justin's horse fall today, all her fears had come flooding back. Memories of that dreadful day at the races had threatened to overwhelm and paralyse her. But all she knew was that she had to get to Justin. So strong had that need been, she could barely remember leaping onto Finbarr and sending him racing down the gully. Her feelings for Justin had thrown off the shackles of fear and humiliation and despair that had left her crippled since her fall at the Birdsville Races. She had done it to help Justin – but in doing that, she had saved herself. Tomorrow she could walk up to Finbarr and swing herself onto his back without the slightest hesitation or doubt.

She wasn't ready to be a jockey again. She needed exercise and hard work to bring her muscles back to race fitness. But she could do it easily. The trainers and owners she knew might hesitate to hire her at first, remembering the past. But once they saw her ride again, they would welcome her back. She could become that woman Justin had seen steer that big grey horse to victory. The woman he had admired from the sidelines. The woman a lot of people had admired and cheered. And she should not forget the financial reward that waited for her if she returned to top form.

If that was what she wanted.

Carrie heard movement from the direction of the stockyard. She got quietly to her feet and slipped away from the campfire. Two large forms loomed up out of the darkness. The stock horses had been fed and hobbled just outside the yard where the brumbies were held. Justin hoped they would be a calming influence on the wild horses. It had worked on the mares, but not on the stallion.

Carrie patted Finbarr and moved past him to stand at the gates.

There wasn't much moonlight, but there was enough for her to see the stallion pacing restlessly around the big yard. The other horses had moved towards the middle. Some were munching on the last of the hay bales that Carrie had tossed over the fence earlier in the evening. Others were sleeping on their feet. The foals and the older mares were lying down, exhausted after the run through the gorge. Mariah's son wasn't resting. He stopped and raised his head, sending a harsh scream out into the night. He turned and began pacing back around the fence. He saw, or sensed, Carrie standing by the gate and launched himself at her, ears flat back, mouth open to show his teeth gleaming in the moonlight.

Carrie stood her ground. There was a gate between them. He couldn't reach her. And she was no longer afraid. The stallion slid to a stop and twisted his head, ears flattened and eyes rolling.

'I'm not scared of you,' she said in a soft voice.

The stallion squealed.

'I'm really not,' Carrie said again. 'So you stop all that palaver.'

The stallion's ears flicked forwards as he listened to her voice.

'You've been out there in the wilds for far too long. You're not really a brumby. You're not wild at all. You're a thoroughbred and it's time you started acting like one.'

The horse took a tentative half step forward.

'That's what we are looking for,' Carrie crooned gently. 'That's what we expect from a Fraser horse.'

The stallion took another step. He stretched out his

neck, his nostrils flaring as he sniffed hesitantly at Carrie's hand on the rail between them.

The whiskers on his muzzle tickled the soft skin of her wrist.

'I know what it's like to be lost,' Carrie told him softly as he looked at her with big liquid brown eyes. 'I was lost too. But I'm finding my way back. You could too. It's time you came home. There's a place for you with Justin. That's where you belong.'

'There's a place for you too, if you want it.'

Carrie hadn't heard him approach.

'I mean it, Carrie.'

As Justin moved to stand beside her, the stallion's nerve broke. Flattening his ears again, he made a threatening lunge at the two humans, then turned away to resume his ceaseless pacing along the far rails of the yard.

Once Carrie might have run away too. But not anymore. She turned to face Justin, tilting her head by way of asking a question.

'I'm serious. We make such a good team,' Justin said. 'What do you think about maybe making it a bit more permanent?'

Carrie's heart gave a little flutter. 'What do you mean, more permanent?' she asked.

'Well, after we get them home, these horses are going to need a lot of work. I'm going to want to get the youngsters trained and ready to sell. I'll never get stud book registration for them, but they should make good saleable work horses once they are broken in. We could work on that together.'

Carrie frowned. Was he talking about her working for him?

'Wouldn't you like to finish what we started here?'

Yes she would – but she didn't think she and Justin

were on the same wavelength. He was thinking about the horses. She wasn't. Maybe she needed to turn his thoughts in the right direction.

'I was thinking ...' she said slowly, watching for his reaction. 'I could start racing again. It wouldn't take me long to get race fit. I could go back to being a jockey.'

'If that's what you want, then that is what you should do. Just let me be there with you.' He almost whispered the words in her ear.

'Are you sure you don't just want someone to work for you – for free?' Carrie grinned cheekily up at him, and was rewarded by an answering smile that lit his whole face.

'Well, yes. That too. Just think of the extra money people will pay for horses that I've bred and you've trained.' He ducked as Carrie playfully punched his arm. 'But this was more what I had in mind.'

He pulled her close and kissed her. It was a strong, passionate kiss. A kiss filled with longing and wonder and excitement. Carrie was swept up in a moment, wrapping her arms around his shoulders and standing on her toes to get even closer to him. How she loved the feel of his strong but gentle hands on her body. He tasted ever so slightly of the beer he had drunk. But more than that, he tasted and smelled and felt like the other half of her soul.

A bloodcurdling scream ripped through the air close by. They fell apart and spun to see the stallion just a short distance away, rearing on his hind legs, as if he was challenging them. His screams set the sleeping horses scrambling to their feet or racing to the far corner of the yard.

'I think maybe he's jealous,' Justin said.

'Oh, hush you,' Carrie told the horse. 'Your life is about to get a whole lot better – so stop fighting it.'

Chapter Twenty-Nine

If only he could hold back the day and tell the sun not to rise. For the first time in a very long time, the darkness held no fear for Dan. Once more his sleep had been dreamless. The little girl with the huge dark eyes had not haunted him. For two nights now she had left him to sleep in peace. Dan lay by the dying embers of the campfire, staring at the orange glow … waiting. Waiting for the ghosts to come. But they didn't.

He knew the reason. He moved his head ever so carefully and brushed his lips across the top of Quinn's head.

He wasn't quite sure how this amazing woman had come into his life. But he was so grateful that she had. Last night, this world famous photographer, the woman who could have been a supermodel had she chosen, had happily cooked damper on a campfire. The four of them had eaten a meal of stew sent from the Coorah Creek pub and warm damper. No restaurant meal had ever tasted so good. They'd washed the food down with a can each of warm beer. Not exactly a Château Laffite which, he had read somewhere, was the world's most expensive wine. But warm beer would be more than he would ever want, as long as he had Rachel Quinn sitting beside him while he drank it.

Carrie and Justin had left after the meal, heading back to Justin's stud, brimming over with plans for the future. They hadn't stopped talking about how they would train the brumbies and sell them on. How the stallion would become a part of the Fraser Stud and how they would launch him upon an unsuspecting world. They talked a lot about horses, but it was easy to see those plans were also about the two of them. Dan and Quinn had said very little about the future. But Carrie and Justin had been so caught up in their own dreams, they hadn't noticed.

Only Dan was awake. Quinn lay with her head on his shoulder, her long slow breathing telling him that she was fast asleep. If he could hold one moment of his life forever untouched by time, it would be this one. Lying beneath the dawn sky, the gentle sounds of the bush around him. Quinn asleep beside him, her warm body curled against his, her hand lying on his chest. For the first time in so very long Dan was at peace with the world, and with himself.

That day in Fallujah Dan had lost everything he believed in. He had lost faith in humanity. In the triumph of right over wrong. In himself. These past few days had given much of that back to him. Dan was a realist. He didn't believe in miracle cures. But he knew his life had turned around and there was a future for him now.

Quinn started to wake. She murmured something softly. He thought he caught the sound of a name. Kim. Dan brushed the hair back from her face, and gently kissed her. She smiled, and then her eyes flashed open. For a few seconds he saw something there he hadn't seen before. Something wild. Like an animal caught in the headlights. Her breath caught in her throat for a moment. Then she caught herself, she smiled and kissed him back.

Dan kissed her, wanting to lose himself in the taste and smell of her. He kissed her hard, with every bit of the yearning he felt for her. He kissed her to make her forget whatever it was he had just seen in her eyes. He pulled her closer and rolled his body over hers. He could feel her move beneath him and he wanted to pull the clothes from her body right there and make her his. To love her so hard and so much that she would forget everything else.

To love her so much she would stay with him.

'Well, good morning.' The voice from the other side of the campfire caught him by surprise. Justin and Carrie were back. Feeling both embarrassed and disappointed, he pulled himself together and sat up. Quinn took a moment longer before she too faced their friends.

'I don't suppose there's room service bringing coffee?' she asked Dan.

'I guess not. I can boil a billy if that helps,' Dan said, shaking the last vestiges of sleep from his head and getting to his feet.

Quinn vanished to do whatever it was women did in the mornings when they were camping and didn't have a bathroom to spend hours in. Justin and Carrie were checking on the horses. Dan set about making coffee and warming some of last night's left over damper.

'I knew I recognised a couple of the brands on those escaped mares,' Justin said as he returned.

'I guess that means you'll have to give them back to their owners.'

'True,' Justin agreed. 'But from our point of view, those mares will be easier to handle than true brumbies. They'll settle quickly. And if they settle it will help the stallion settle. Getting them on a truck to get them home might not prove so difficult.'

Dan handed him an enamel mug full of steaming coffee. 'That's good news,' he said, but he didn't mean it. Getting the horses safely back to Justin's place was the end of their mission. There would be no reason for Quinn to stay after that.

Dan saw the light that shone from Justin's face as he looked at Carrie. It was reflected in hers. He was happy for them. Particularly for Carrie. He'd recognised the fear in her that first night they met. PTSD was not just for war victims. He knew the dark place she'd been lost in, because he'd been there too. Justin had lighted her way out, just as Quinn had done for him.

But Quinn didn't live in Coorah Creek. Quinn lived in the back of her Humvee. And that Humvee could take her anywhere. It could take her away from him. He didn't know if he would be able to stop it.

'We've got a busy day ahead of us,' Quinn said as she re-joined them and dropped to a crouch to place a frying pan on the fire. 'I need a decent breakfast. Any other takers?'

She received a chorus of affirmative replies.

'What's the plan?' Dan asked as he sipped his coffee.

'There are too many horses to fit in a single journey,' Justin said. 'And some of them are truly wild. They will have to be forced onto a truck. For that, we need to build a proper race and loading ramp.'

'That sounds like a lot of heavy lifting,' Dan said. 'More than we can do in a day. And we only have two.'

'I know.' Justin grinned. 'So I did the only thing that you can do when faced with an impossible task.' He paused for effect. 'I called Trish Warren.'

'Trish?' Quinn's voice rose a couple of notes. 'How is Trish going to help transport a wild horse herd?'

Justin grinned. 'Wait and see. We'll know in an hour or so. In the meantime, Carrie and I are going to take the stock horses home. That will be one job done.'

'If we've got a bit of time, and nothing constructive to do, I probably should go somewhere where I have phone signal and Internet,' Quinn said. 'My agent will think I have dropped off the face of the planet. And if I don't e-mail my mother soon she'll probably report me missing to the police.'

'We could go back to the ranger station,' Dan suggested. 'I should check in too. I've still got a job and a park to look after.'

'Will the horses be all right here alone?' Quinn asked.

'I don't see why not. They have food and water – and it's not as if anyone is likely to disturb them'

When they got back to the ranger station, Dan walked over to his office, while Quinn went to the house and set up her computer and camera on the kitchen table. She plugged everything in to start re-charging, and began downloading the photos onto her laptop. As soon as she could she started flicking through the images.

'Yes!'

The exclamation was repeated several times as she perused her work. There were some excellent shots that really captured the story of what they were doing. Quinn paused at a wonderful shot of the stallion, looking wild and untamed. That was a cover shot if ever she saw one. The shot of the brumbies running down the gully, Carrie and Justin on horseback behind them looked like a scene from a wild west movie. Quinn was soon thinking about how she would crop the images, maybe tweak the lighting just so. She was beginning to decide how many images to send to her agent and in what order they should be presented. It was his job to sell the photo essay to a magazine. Perhaps *Australian Geographic* or *Outback* magazine if *National Geographic* weren't interested. Her agent had also been talking about selling her photos for an outback scenes calendar. There were definitely a couple of suitable shots of the brumbies.

Quinn flicked through to the next image and stopped.

Dan's face filled the screen. It was the shot she had taken very early on in their adventure, as they set up their campsite. Dan's face was in part profile. The clean strong lines clearly lit by the angle of the sun. It showed what a handsome man he was … and more than that. Every line of his face showed his character – the strength, his struggle against the horror of war. It was the face of a troubled man.

It was a wonderful portrait – but it was not a shot that Quinn would send anywhere. This image was for her alone. When she was gone.

That sobering thought stilled her fingers. The time was nearly upon her when she would have to leave. Of course, she could stay for a while. Spend some time alone with Dan in this beautiful park. It was tempting. She had no other assignment booked – at least none that she knew about. Quinn reached for her phone before she could find an excuse not to.

'Quinn,' her agent said as soon as he answered the phone. 'So good to hear from you. How did it go?'

'Really great,' she said. 'I'm just reviewing the images now. They should be easy to sell. The big colour glossies should love them.'

'Excellent. Can you send me a couple so I can have a look?'

'Sure. I'll e-mail something shortly.'

'Great. Are you done?'

'Almost. I need one more shot to finish the story. That should happen in the next day or two.'

'Great. When are you coming back east? I guess you'll want a few days off.'

'Have you got anything booked for me?' Quinn avoided the question.

'There's nothing here that is really worth hurrying back for,' he said. 'So if you want to take some time, go right ahead.'

It was not the answer she'd been hoping for. A big job waiting for her would make it so much easier to leave. She knew that the longer she stayed, the harder it would be to drive down that dusty track and away from this beautiful wild landscape. Away from Dan. But she couldn't stay forever. She wasn't the woman to stay in one place. She didn't need – or want – a home or a family.

'I don't think so,' she said. 'Have you got anything that starts next week? Or the week after that?'

'There are a couple of things. I'll e-mail you some details. Well, get some shots to me today and let's see where all this goes. Let me know when you're on the way back. Talk soon.'

As she ended the call and dropped the phone back on the table Quinn looked up to see Dan standing in the doorway. She wondered how much of the conversation he had heard. Judging from the look on his face, he'd heard enough.

'So, you'll be leaving soon,' he said slowly.

'I guess so,' she replied. After all, leaving was what she did.

Chapter Thirty

Justin dimly heard the sound of a vehicle arriving, but it wasn't enough to take his concentration off Carrie and the stallion. She was mesmerising. His head didn't believe what his eyes were seeing, but his heart did. He stood rock still a few meters from the stockyard. He was barely daring to breathe in case he interrupted the magic – there was no other word for it – that was occurring.

Carrie was inside the yard with the brumbies. Carrie, who just a few days ago was too afraid to even get close to one of his stock horses, was standing face to face with the wild stallion. She wasn't being foolish. She was close to the gate, ready to slip through to safety if needed. But Justin didn't think she would. Obviously some sort of connection had been formed when the stallion touched her hand last night. The first human touch the horse had ever felt. Now something was happening that he had heard about, but never seen in all his years working with horses.

Justin heard Dan and Quinn approaching. He twisted his body and waved urgently at them to silence them. They understood the message and slipped slowly and silently to his side.

Inside the yard the stallion took a hesitant step forward. He was listening to Carrie talking, his ears flicking back and forward. He pawed the ground with one front leg, clods of earth flying away with the force of each stroke. His head was never still, tossing and twisting as if he wanted to break away – but couldn't. Carrie didn't move. Justin clenched his hands as the horse took another hesitant half step towards Carrie. The stallion was close enough that a simple lunge would take him to her. If he chose to strike out with those front hooves ... Or slash with his strong white teeth ... Justin knew very well the threat posed by a vicious horse. A part of him wanted to call her back to safety. The stallion might have been born a blue blood, but he was still a wild thing. He was dangerous. The thought of Carrie being hurt again was almost too much to stand.

He bit his lip to force himself to remain still.

Beside him, Quinn ever so slowly and carefully raised her camera.

In the stockyard Carrie waited.

For once the wind stilled and a strange silence settled over the gorge.

The stallion tossed his head, and took another step forward. He reached out his long elegant head, nostrils flaring as he breathed in Carrie's scent.

Justin tried not to think about the danger in a horse's bite ... a bite that could break skin and crush bone. The animal towered over Carrie. She looked so small and so utterly vulnerable as she stood rock still while the stallion touched her face gently with his nose.

He barely heard the soft whir of Quinn's camera as the stallion snorted, the force of his breath raising Carrie's brown hair. Still Carrie remained motionless. The horse shuffled just a fraction nearer, so he could run his muzzle over her face.

That's when Carrie moved for the first time. She slowly raised one hand and placed it on the stallion's gleaming muscular neck. She ran her hand down the firm ridge of muscle, stroking the gleaming hide that had never before known the touch of human hand.

'What is she ... some kind of horse whisperer?' Quinn asked as she took another photo.

'She's just Carrie,' Justin said, not caring if Dan and Quinn heard the awe and love in his voice.

Inside the yard Carrie was rubbing her hand down the stallion's face. The big horse was quivering with tension as he lowered his head to accept her hand.

'Is that dangerous?' Beside him Dan voiced the fears that Justin was holding so tight inside.

'Yes.'

Carrie was talking to the horse. They could hear the soft murmur of her voice, but not the words. The stallion's ears twitched as he listened to her. She pulled a few twigs from his matted mane and straightened the thick forelock hanging between his eyes.

'Is it because he's not really a brumby?' Quinn asked. 'Is it some kind of race memory? Generations of domestication coming to the fore to remind him that humans are his friends?'

'Maybe,' Justin said. 'Or maybe it's just Carrie's special gift.'

The three stood silent for a few more moments, until Carrie dropped her hand from the horse's coat. The stallion tossed his head and snorted, but it wasn't the angry sound they had heard before. One of the mares stepped closer to him, and he turned his head, nipping her on the rump as she moved past. She flicked a hind leg at him, but the kick passed harmlessly between him and Carrie. The spell was broken. The stallion shied, and leaped away. Carrie began moving slowly backwards, her eyes never leaving him as she slid through the gate. Justin was already there. As he dropped the latch behind her, Justin let out the deep breath he had not even known he was holding. Carrie too seemed to visibly relax.

'Wow, he's really something,' Carrie said, her voice tinged with awe.

Justin shook his head, quite unable to put into words the immense feeling that was swelling up through him. His fear for Carrie's safety had given way to anger that she should take such a risk. At the same time, he was so happy for her and proud of her. And over all other emotions lay a fierce love.

He took Carrie by the shoulders, and stared down into her shining eyes. He wanted to yell at her. To tell her never to do that again. To remind her that wild horses were dangerous and she could have been hurt again. But she knew all that. Those were not the words she needed to hear from him.

Instead he kissed her, long and hard. His heart sang as she kissed him back with equal passion.

'That was amazing,' he said at last in a voice that was not quite his own. 'You had him eating out of your hand.'

'Not quite,' Carrie's voice was bubbling over with joy. 'But I don't think it will be long.'

The lump in Justin's throat was the size of the red cliffs around them. He pulled Carrie to his chest and wrapped his arms around her, holding her tightly, as if he would never let her go. Because he wouldn't.

The silence that followed was finally broken by the sound of a car engine. Of more than one engine. Dan looked towards the sound and caught a glimpse of a dust cloud.

'Perfect timing,' said Justin as he released Carrie. 'That would be the cavalry.'

Cavalry? In his mind, Dan saw a convoy of military vehicles, with uniformed and disciplined men waiting to leap into action. The convoy that appeared down the rough track was nothing like that.

The lead vehicle was a truck with some sort of small earthmover loaded onto its flat bed. Another small truck followed behind, loaded down with timber. Jack North was there with his ute, the tray back full of tools. One of the two cars that followed held four men dressed in working gear. When the last car of the convoy pulled up, Trish Warren hopped out.

Jack parked his car and ambled over to shake Justin's hand. 'I hear you need to build a loading ramp. Could you use a hand?'

'I sure could,' Justin replied. 'Thanks for coming.'

'Have you ever known me to take no for an answer,' Trish said as she approached. 'Now, show me these brumbies I've heard so much about.'

Dan hung back as the others walked over to look at the horses. There was much back-slapping and congratulations for Justin. One of the men recognised his own brand on a mare in the herd, a cause for another round of congratulations. Dan knew that kind of sharing. It was the same brotherhood he had been gifted with in his unit. The willingness to help one another. To share the good times and the bad.

'I always wanted a Fraser horse,' the owner of the mare chortled. 'And now I have Fraser bloodlines for free in that colt of hers.'

'Not quite for free,' Justin pointed out. 'First we have to get these horses out of the park. So let's get to it.'

The group of townsfolk lacked the discipline and training of his old army unit, but when they set their minds to something, it got done. Justin outlined his need for a safe and solid earthen ramp, with strong high rails at the sides, growing ever narrower. The brumbies would be pushed up this race into the back of a truck.

'It's how we handle cattle, rather than horses,' Justin said. 'But we don't have time to do it any other way. The horses have to be moved tomorrow.'

The men responded quickly. Rails and shovels appeared. Pliers and fencing wire were produced. The sound of the small digger biting into the earth startled the brumbies, but after a few minutes' panic, they came to accept it wasn't about to hurt them.

Dan winced when the digger's blade bit into the earth for the first time.

'Don't worry,' Jack said as he walked past, a timber rail balanced on his shoulder, 'we'll put it back the way it was after the brumbies are gone. No one will ever know.'

A short distance from the construction site, Trish Warren gathered Quinn and Carrie under her wing, and set about providing food and water for the workers. They soon had a billy boiling over the fire pit, and another of Trish's endless stews bubbling in a camp oven. The smell of cooking damper wafted down the gorge.

By the time they stopped to eat, the loading ramp was taking shape. As the men ate, they discussed how many trucks they would need the next day to load the whole mob of brumbies. They agreed that all the horses would be taken initially to Justin's property. After that, owners could claim the escapees. Justin freely offered any of the workers their choice of the yearlings as a reward for their help.

Dan sat with them, enjoying the camaraderie. He had always kept himself a little apart from the town. He had felt a stranger who didn't really belong. He could see now that was of his own making. The townsfolk accepted him. They always had. He had friends among them now.

While Carrie divided her time between work at the stockyard and Trish's camp kitchen, Quinn remained a little aloof. Dan knew that was partly because she was once more wearing her photographer's role. Capturing the event, rather than being a part of it. But he had a suspicion there was another reason too. A reason that sent a wave of sadness deep into his heart.

'Can I have two coffees, please,' he asked Trish.

Trish poured the steaming dark liquid into two enamel mugs and cast a meaningful glace to where Quinn was seated part of the way up the side of the gully.

'How do you want them?'

'Both black, please.'

Dan carried the mugs over to Quinn and the two of them sat on a boulder, drinking in silence.

Even when the mugs were empty, neither of them showed any desire to move. Quinn held the camera in her lap, her hands finally still.

After a long moment, Dan spoke. 'It looks like they'll be gone tomorrow. Then all we have to do is pull this lot down and it's over.'

'You've done a remarkable thing,' Quinn said softly.

'No. I haven't ... we all have.' Dan paused for a few seconds. 'I guess you'll be going to Justin's place to get some shots when the brumbies finally reach their new home.'

Quinn nodded.

'That will be the end of your story, won't it? You'll leave then.'

Dan's heart seemed to stop beating as he waited for Quinn's answer. He knew what it was going to be, but that did not ease the knife thrust of pain he felt.

She turned towards him and Dan saw sadness there in her eyes. 'Yes, it is time I moved on.'

He'd known it was coming, of course. But somewhere deep inside had been the hope that she might stay. Twice now Quinn had given him gifts that had lifted him out of his despair. A third time was too much to ask. He would have to give to her the only thing he could – he would have to let her go.

The silence hung between then. Then Quinn got to her

feet. 'I'm not needed here. I think I'm going to go and take some general shots of the park while I still have the time.'

Dan collected their mugs. 'If you need to use the phone or the Internet, the back door of my house is open.'

He walked away, back down to the camp to hand the mugs back to Trish. She raised a questioning eyebrow as she watched Quinn walk away towards her Hummer.

Dan couldn't face her questions. He quickly strode back to join Justin unloading more timber rails from a truck.

Justin paused in his work and together they watched the Hummer drive away. 'Look, Dan, I know it's none of my business but are you just going to let her walk away?'

He was right, of course. Dan knew that. But ... 'I can hardly force her to stay.'

'Mate, I know if it was Carrie, I wouldn't let her go quite so easily.'

Easily? It wasn't going to be easy. It was going to be unbearably hard to let her go. But he hadn't given up hope. Not yet. He had one chance – one night – to change her mind.

Chapter Thirty-One

She had lied to Dan. For the first time. She hadn't really been taking additional photos in the park. The photos of the brumbies and their capture were done. She had no real need to take photographs at Justin's property. There was no reason for her to stay. Except for her desire to watch as Carrie and Justin took the brumbies home. Except for her desire to spend one more night with Dan.

It was cruel of her. She knew that. She should walk away now and not give Dan the false hope that there could be more than one more night for them. But she wanted that night so much. It was more than she could do to leave. Somewhere in the night, she would find the courage to tell Dan what he needed to know. So that he would let her go. So that he would be glad to let her go.

And then she would turn towards … not home. She had no home. There was only her work and the Hummer … and that small tissue wrapped parcel stored so carefully inside it.

So she had spent the day in Dan's small home. She had borrowed his Internet, his electricity and his shower. She had to admit it felt good to have a nice hot shower. It was a strangely intimate thing, to borrow another person's shower when they were not around. Dan used a plain, unscented soap. But she had known that. When she lay with her head on his shoulder, she breathed deeply of a scent that was all Dan. She'd borrowed some of his shampoo too. She had found clean towels neatly stacked in a bathroom cupboard. For a man, he was extremely tidy. She guessed that was a hangover from his life in the military.

After showering she sat on Dan's sofa with her mug of coffee while she checked her e-mails. There were several from her agent, suggesting possible assignments when she returned to Brisbane. There was also one from her mother, wanting to know how she was, and when she would be coming back. She ignored them as she flicked through her book – the one Dan had bought all those months ago back in Sydney. The one that had led him to Tyangi Crossing National Park … and eventually to her.

She had promised him she would sign the book. She found a pen and sat there, with her hand poised over the page, wondering what to write. She had done book signings a dozen times before. Always she had scribbled an easy phrase on the page. I hope you enjoy the book. And she had always been sincere in that hope. But what should she write for Dan? She sincerely hoped he would be happy when she left. That the ghosts that haunted him would fade in time. That he found peace and happiness. But all of those thoughts simply highlighted one thing – she would not be with him.

She got up and took her empty cup into the kitchen. The business of boiling the kettle gave her hands something to do. While she waited she stood in the doorway and stared across the room at the book. Finally, in a sudden quick motion, she crossed the room again and picked up her pen. She simply wrote two words – Rachel Quinn – and firmly closed the book.

She didn't bother going back for the coffee she really didn't want. Instead, she sat back against the softness of the sofa. She felt so very comfortable in Dan's home. For all it was part of the ranger station, it did feel like a home. She'd had a home once. Four walls with pictures, not unlike the ones that hung on Dan's walls. And bookshelves that, like those around her now, groaned under the weight of the books they carried.

She could close her eyes and pretend she hadn't lost all that. But eventually she would have to open her eyes again and acknowledge that this was not her home. She had no home. She'd be back on the open road again soon. And that was the way she liked it. She never stayed more than a few days in any place without feeling restless. Just because this sofa and these four walls felt good – well, that was an aberration. She would never have the house with the white picket fence, two kids and a dog. But if she did, Dan would fit very nicely into the picture, with his gentle strength and his brilliant eyes. Their kids would probably have his red hair ... maybe freckles ...

Quinn's eyes flashed open. She must have been dozing. For one moment there she had seen the future she had once wanted – but now could never have. Quickly she got to her feet and headed to the kitchen. Coffee. That was the answer.

Inside the kitchen her eyes fell onto the coffee maker sitting on one corner of the worktop. Proper coffee! There was a thought. Not that she hadn't enjoyed the billy tea and the instant coffee they made on the campfire. But real percolated coffee would be a treat. She was sure Dan wouldn't mind.

It was the work of just a minute to find the coffee and set the machine going. As she did, she realised the kitchen was rather well equipped. It would be a pleasure to cook there. Quinn liked to cook. She had enjoyed making the damper on the campfire for the others. Enjoyed the pleasure on their faces as they ate it. Enjoyed the glow in Dan's eyes as he bit into the tasty dough and enjoyed the warm feeling of satisfaction that had given her. There had been a time when she cooked a lot. For friends and family. She realised now she had missed that.

She breathed deep the smell of the percolating coffee.

Knowing she was simply being nosy, she opened a cupboard. It was well stocked with food. Everything from dried mushrooms to jars of sundried tomatoes. She raised an eyebrow in surprise. Dan obviously liked to cook. The next cupboard revealed dried pasta, and couscous and rice. Not only did Dan like to cook, he kept an organised kitchen. Suddenly Quinn was on a mission. She would cook dinner tonight. Here, in Dan's kitchen. Then she would take it to the campsite to serve her friends in this, their last night together. She ignored the stab of pain that thought gave her, choosing to focus on what she would cook. By the time the coffee was made, she was pulling ingredients from the cupboards, and digging through the packets of meat in Dan's freezer, her mind running through her favourite recipes.

Quinn was not a tidy cook. She cooked like she did most other things, with joy and enthusiasm. By the time she had a meat sauce bubbling away on the stove, the kitchen was in a certain degree of disarray. This bothered her not one whit. The house was beginning to fill with delicious smells. Her T-shirt was slightly grubby, but Quinn was happy. She wished briefly that she had brought her knitting. It would be nice to knit as she waited for the dinner to cook. But her needles and wool were back in her tent at the campsite. She was determined not to turn on her laptop. Instead, she pulled one of the books from Dan's shelves and curled up to read it.

She was still there when she heard the sound of a vehicle pull up outside. She stood up, wondering if it was a park visitor. Instead she saw Dan walking towards the door.

She felt a sudden urge to comb her hair. Or tidy the kitchen. And she was suddenly very aware of the cooking stains on her T-shirt.

Dan opened the door. As he walked through a smile lit his face. 'Hi.'

Quinn felt an answering smile on her own lips. 'If you say "Honey, I'm home", I will throw something at you.'

'And if you ask "How was your day?', I might just throw it back.'

They both chuckled and the room around them seemed to brighten and grow warm.

'What smells so good?' Dan asked.

'I thought I would cook something and take it back to the campsite. We could all share dinner.' She left out the word 'last'.

'That's a really nice thought, but Carrie and Justin have gone back to his place. There's just the two of us.'

'Oh.' For a moment Quinn wasn't sure if she was disappointed or pleased. She looked at Dan's handsome face and broad shoulders and felt a little twinge deep inside her. She was glad they were alone.

'I tell you what,' Dan said. 'Let's go crazy and have dinner here. We could eat at a table for a change.'

Quinn laughed. 'That sounds good. It's nothing special. I made some pasta sauce. And I found your stash of frozen bread. So I thought I might make garlic bread. You do have garlic, don't you?'

They walked through to the kitchen, where Dan produced the required garlic from his well-stocked cupboards. While Quinn made the bread, Dan went about setting the table. When Quinn walked through to the dining room she was startled to see candles glowing brightly in the dimly lit room.

'The solar batteries sometimes run flat,' Dan explained. 'I always keep a couple of candles about just in case.'

Quinn raised an eyebrow at the wine glasses. 'We have wine?'

'I don't keep much alcohol in the house. The doctors thought it was a bad idea for someone like me – especially as I live alone. For once I agreed with them. However, I do keep a couple of bottles here. In case of guests.' He opened a corner cupboard and reaching into the back produced a bottle of red wine. He frowned as he looked at it. 'It's been there a while.'

'Well aged then,' Quinn said. 'Come on. Let's eat.'

The meal was everything Quinn no longer had. She and Dan sat at the table, talking easily – about books and places, about the brumbies and Coorah Creek. In some ways they were like some old married couple. Comfortable together. But when Dan's eyes met hers, Quinn felt that stirring deep inside brought on by the promise of the night to come.

Before that, though, Quinn had to tell Dan why she was leaving. She owed him that. She hated the thought of spoiling their last few hours together. But she had to do it. If only she could gather the nerve …

'So,' Dan said at last. 'Tell me whatever it is you have to tell me.'

'How do you know I have something to tell you?'

Dan reached across the table to take her hand. 'I just do.'

Quinn swallowed and gathered all her courage. 'I want you to know that all this has really been special for me. The brumbies. Working like this to save them, with Justin and Carrie …' She paused and held his eyes for a very long time. 'You.'

'I know.'

She nodded, hearing the words he hadn't spoken. It had been special for him too. And now …

'I have to go tomorrow,' she said. 'I can't be what you want me to be. Do what you want me to do.'

'And what do you think I want you to do or to be?'

'This.' Quinn motioned with her hand to encompass the

room, the table with the remains of the meal. The whole house. 'I tried this once. It all went terribly wrong.'

There, the words were out.

Dan said nothing. He simply sat, holding her hand. Waiting for her to continue.

'I was married.'

His eyes registered his surprise, but his gaze never wavered. Nor did he release her hand.

'We were very young and so very much in love. I was still working in the fashion industry. He was a teacher. We met through friends and fell in love. We were going to have it all. A beautiful home. A family. Everything ...' Her voice trailed off as the memories surfaced. A little girl with blue eyes like her father.

'What happened?'

'We bought our dream house. It was a stretch to afford it, but we did it anyway. Then I found out I was pregnant. I kept working as long as possible. We needed the money ... The baby came early. Too early. She was so beautiful but so weak. We called her Kim. She had blue eyes. And she died.'

Dan squeezed her hand so tightly it hurt. Quinn welcomed the pain. At least that would end.

'She was only a few days old. And it was my fault.'

'How was it your fault?'

'If I hadn't been working so hard ... she wouldn't have been premature. She would have been strong enough to survive.'

'You don't know that.'

'Yes. Yes I do.' Quinn wrenched her hand away from Dan. 'My husband knew it too. He blamed me and eventually he left. My parents blamed me too. I couldn't stand the accusation in their eyes, so I left. Even now, when I go back, I can feel them blaming me. I know they love me, but they loved their granddaughter too. I'm better on my own. This is the life I have chosen. That's why I have to leave. I cannot risk another relationship. A marriage. Another child. It would destroy me if that happened again.'

Fighting back the tears Quinn thrust back her chair, grabbed their dirty plates and almost ran through into the kitchen.

Dan watched her go, his heart aching for her. He understood Quinn's pain. It was the sort of pain that could haunt a person their entire life. Unless someone helped them, as she had helped him.

He stood up and followed her. She was standing by the sink, her shoulders shaking as she sobbed. Dan thought it might be a very long time since she had allowed herself to cry like that.

He crossed the kitchen and wrapped his arms around her. She leaned back against him, still sobbing.

'That's why you knit those little baby things, isn't it?' he said softly.

She nodded. 'I knitted her a little pink jacket. When I was pregnant. It took such a long time to knit, but I just loved doing it. She was going to look so beautiful in it. But she died before—' Her voice trailed away.

He slowly turned her towards him, and with one finger tilted her chin so she was looking at him.

'Sometimes terrible things happen, Quinn. They happen to people who don't deserve them, but there's nothing we can do to stop them. It's not your fault. It's not anyone's fault. It just happened.'

As he spoke, he realised he was talking about and to himself too.

'Your life is more than just this one thing. Mourn your

little girl, but let go of the guilt. Life is too precious a gift to waste it in guilt and anger. You taught me that.'

'She was my daughter.' A world of grief poured into four words.

He pulled her to him, wrapping his arms around her and holding her tightly. He leaned forward and pressed his lips to her forehead, in the hope that if he loved her enough he could take away some of her pain, as she had done for him. And maybe, if he loved her enough, she wouldn't leave.

Chapter Thirty-Two

'Where are they?' Carrie turned slowly around. The campsite was deserted. The horses moved restlessly around the yard, but otherwise the gorge was silent and still. There was no trace of smoke or heat in the campfire and no cars to be seen.

'It looks like they didn't spend the night here,' Justin said.

'I hope that's a good thing,' Carrie said. 'I hate the thought of Quinn leaving.'

Justin put his arm around her shoulders and pulled her close. 'I know. But we can't keep her if she doesn't want to stay.'

'I don't think she wants to leave,' Carrie said. 'I just don't think she knows *how* to stay.'

'If Dan hasn't been able to show her that, no one can.'

Carrie nodded. There was nothing she could do, but she didn't want to lose a friend. Quinn had done so much for all of them. Because of Quinn, Justin had reclaimed his father's heritage. Dan had escaped the nightmare of shooting the wild horses. And Carrie herself had found not just her love of horses and riding again, but she had also found Justin. She would always be grateful to Quinn for that. The four of them had shared so much in such a short time that it felt as if they had been friends forever.

'Come on,' Justin said taking her hand. 'We've got a big day ahead. We need to get those brumbies feeling well-fed and lazy before we try to load them.'

'All right.'

They set about opening two bales of hay to distribute to the brumbies. The branded mares who had escaped from their owners had quickly come to terms with their capture. They were crowding close to the fence, waiting for their breakfast. The foals were more than happy to take their mothers' lead and accept there was no danger in the humans. They were even a little bit curious about these two-legged creatures who provided food and water. The stallion was standing a little to one side. He was no longer careering wildly around the yard, but he was keeping himself aloof, tossing his head as he watched Carrie approach.

'So, you're going to be a tough guy, are you?' Carrie said to him. She moved quickly to an empty place on the fence and dipped her hand into her pocket. The carrot she produced was bright orange and very crisp. She broke it in half with a snap and placed the two halves on her open palm. She held it out, crooning softly. The stallion started moving towards her. He was still wary, but much of his fear and hesitation had vanished. She felt his lips touch her hand, his whiskers tickling as they touched the sensitive skin at her wrist. His lips curled around once piece of the carrot. In a trice it was gone. There were a few loud crunching sounds and then the second piece of carrot followed the first.

'See, I told you he'd be eating out of your hand,' Justin said as he moved quietly to her side. The stallion squealed and danced away.

'He doesn't like me,' Justin said with feigned sadness.

'He's just jealous.' Carrie winked broadly and chuckled.

'He should be.' Justin grabbed her and pulled her close for a quick, powerful kiss.

Carrie felt her heart skip in her chest as she responded to the kiss with all the emotion surging through her. When Justin would have pulled away, she wrapped her fingers through his hair and pulled him back to her.

When they finally broke apart, they were no longer alone.

Quinn was at the campsite. She raised an arm in salute, and then turned her attention to her tent. She bent over and with a sudden heave pulled up a peg, the guy rope still hanging from it. Dan was walking towards them; the look on his face told Carrie everything she needed to know. She glanced at Justin and saw from the tight line of his mouth that he too had read the signs.

'I guess we should get this done,' Dan said in a clipped voice that suggested he was struggling to keep a tight hold on his emotions.

'I guess so. I'll bring the truck over now.' Justin laid a hand on Dan's shoulder briefly as he moved away.

'She really is leaving?' Carrie asked Dan in a hushed voice. 'You couldn't convince her to stay?'

'She has her own reasons.'

'Maybe she'll change her mind and come back,' Carrie said, forcing a hopeful note into her voice.

'Maybe.' He didn't sound at all like he believed it.

Further conversation was stalled by the arrival of Justin and the truck. He backed it towards the yard and the newly constructed loading ramp. As he did, two more trucks appeared on the dirt track. Yesterday's helpers had returned.

Some of the horses milled wildly about as the truck grew closer, but a certain calm was maintained by the branded mares who'd no doubt seen many trucks before. The stallion stood back, eyeing the vehicles with suspicion.

Justin leaped out and began checking the back of the truck. It was firmly wedged against the loading ramp. He opened the sliding gate to expose the interior of the truck.

'So, how do you get them on board?' Quinn joined them. She stood close to Dan's side. Carrie saw them exchange a glance that almost broke her heart.

'We push them into the race. Once there, the horses at the rear will push those in front of them forward. There's nowhere for them to go but into the truck. Hopefully a couple of the older more sensible mares will lead the way and just step on board. They must have done it before.'

'They won't all fit in one load, will they?' Dan asked, although his mind was clearly elsewhere.

'That's where we come in,' one of the others said. Carrie knew him as the owner of one of the branded mares. 'There are four of us coming today with trucks. That should be plenty to shift them all.'

'We'll take them all to my place,' Justin said. 'Give them a few days to settle down then you can cut out your own stock and take them home.'

'That works for me.'

'I'd like the stallion to go in the first load,' Justin added. 'If he's left behind he'll only get more worked up and stressed. That'll make him even harder to deal with.'

As they gathered by the gate, ready to start manoeuvring the horses, Carrie noticed something strange about Quinn. It was a few seconds before she realised what it was. Quinn was not carrying a camera. She was not photographing this final act of the story. Somehow that was more upsetting than anything else. Carrie tried to think of something she could say or do to change what was going to happen. But there wasn't anything. Quinn had obviously made up her mind.

'Let's go,' Justin called her back to the job at hand. 'I think four of us inside the yard will be enough. Dan, can you stand by to slide the truck gate shut when I give you the signal?'

'Sure.'

'Carrie, the stallion knows you, so I need you in the yard.'

Carrie nodded, thrilled that she didn't feel the slightest fear or hesitation.

Justin gave instructions to two of the other men, then turned to open the gate into the yard.

The mares began milling about.

'Try not to stir them too much,' Justin said in a low voice. 'But we have to keep pushing forwards.'

Their arms spread wide, the four of them advanced. The stallion pushed his way through the bunch of horses until he was at the front, staring up the ramp into the dark entrance to the truck.

'Push them,' Justin instructed. He gave a sharp yell. Carrie followed suit, flapping her hands. A small group of the mares shied away.

'Leave them,' Justin instructed. 'Push the rest.'

Waving their arms and making loud noises, they moved forward another few yards. The stallion glanced about one final time, wild-eyed and uncertain. He lunged up the ramp, two huge leaps that carried him into the back of the truck.

'Quickly,' Dan shouted.

Three of the mares gave way before the human pressure and bounded up the ramp, effectively blocking the stallion's retreat. Some others followed, their foals close behind. At a shout from Justin, Dan darted forward and slammed the gate of the truck.

'Yes.' Justin punched the air. He grabbed Carrie and spun her in a wide circle. She was almost lost for breath when he put her down again. 'We've done it!'

This declaration was accompanied by some hugging and back-slapping. Inside the truck, the horses moved restlessly, but there was nowhere for them to go. The stallion roared in frustration, and several loud bangs suggested he was venting his anger in other ways too.

'This was the hard one,' Justin said. 'We better get moving before he kicks my truck to pieces.'

'With him gone, the mares and foals should be easy,' the other men agreed. 'We should be right behind you with the rest of them.'

Dan watched the truck leave, wishing he could tell Justin to stop. The horses were not the only thing he was taking away.

Quinn turned and walked silently back to the campsite where she continued to pack her things into the back of the Hummer.

Dan simply watched her. He could not bring himself to help her leave. Instead, he maintained his place at the yard, helping where he could as the rest of the horses were loaded.

As the last truck drove away, with assurances that the men would return the next day to help dismantle the yard and ramp, the gorge became terribly quiet.

Dan watched as Quinn carried the last of her things to her Hummer. He tried to imprint everything about her on his mind. The way her hair shone as the sun hit it. The strong lines of her body. The way she moved with such energy and confidence. The care with which she stowed everything in the back of her vehicle – that well-designed and organised part of the vehicle where she stowed her whole life and all her memories. Did she have anything there that would remind her of him?

Quinn locked the back door of her vehicle; it was as if she was locking away her heart as well. For a heartbeat she stood with her back to him, staring at the door lock.

'You don't have to go,' he said.

She didn't turn. It was as if she couldn't bear to look at him. 'Yes. I do.'

'You say you can't be what I want. But you can. You are. I want you, Quinn. Not some formula dictated by convention. I don't need a house and a white picket fence. I don't even need children, if that's how it turns out.'

She was shaking her head. Dan took her by the shoulders and turned her to face him. There were tears in her eyes.

'I just need you, Quinn. Nothing else. Just you.'

'She was my daughter, Dan. Surely you of all people understand. She was my daughter. I cannot forgive myself for that.'

He knew then there was nothing he could do.

'Yes, you can,' he said softly. 'And you will. One day.'

He kissed her one last time. A long slow soft kiss that would have to last him a lifetime. Then he let her go.

Her shoulders were shaking slightly as she turned away. She opened the door of the car and got behind the wheel. The engine roared and slowly the Humvee began to move away. Dan kept his eyes fixed on the driver's side window. But she didn't wave. She didn't look back.

'Some day you will forgive yourself, Quinn,' he said to the retreating car. 'And when you do, I'll be waiting here for you.'

The gold Hummer vanished, leaving only a trail of dust in its wake. Dan stood silently watching until the last of the dust had settled back to the earth, leaving no trace of her passing.

Chapter Thirty-Three

'What are you going to call him?' Carrie asked as a loud crash emanated from the back of the truck. The stallion was not enjoying his journey. 'Were there any famous Irish boxers? That would work.'

'You've already named him,' Justin said.

'I have? When?'

'That first day when you came to me with Quinn and Dan you said you had found Mariah's son. That's his name. Mariah's Son.'

There was another crash from the back of the truck.

'See, he approves,' Carrie said.

They were halfway to their destination, travelling slowly because of the horses, when Carrie happened to glance in the truck's side mirror.

'Justin,' she said, interrupting his buoyant outlining of his plans to re-launch the Fraser Stud. 'Isn't that Quinn's car behind us?'

Justin checked his mirror. 'Yes. I guess she decided she wanted some more photos after all.'

When they pulled up at Justin's yard, Quinn emerged from the Hummer, camera in hand. And alone.

Carrie jumped down from the cab of the truck, leaving Justin to back it into position to unload the horses.

'Dan didn't come?' Carrie asked Quinn.

'No.'

The flat tone of her voice made Carrie want to cry.

There wasn't time left for any more conversation. Justin had the truck in position. Carrie opened the back and stepped back. There was nothing for a few moments, just the noise of shuffling hooves inside the truck. Then a brown nose appeared in the doorway, sniffing the air. One of the mares stepped hesitantly out. Her foal followed with a giant leap that made Carrie and Justin laugh.

Quinn of course was taking photos, but it seemed to Carrie her usual joy and enthusiasm was missing.

A few more seconds and the horses were all streaming out into Justin's securely fenced paddock. The stallion immediately raised his voice in a strident whinny. An equally loud challenge echoed from the stables.

'I guess Beckett knows there's a new man in town,' Justin said with a smile.

'Beckett?' Quinn asked, although Carrie could tell her mind was elsewhere.

'He's Justin's current stud,' she explained. 'But he's getting on in years.'

'What are you going to do with him? You won't …' Quinn asked, suddenly pensive.

'Of course not,' Justin said. 'I'd never do that. I know someone who has admired him for a while. One phone call and I'm sure I'll find a buyer for him.'

'That's good.'

The three of them stood for a few moments watching the horses as they began to explore their new home. The mares were mostly interested in the water trough and in tasting the sweet green grass. The foals skittered about, short fluffy tails wagging in excitement. As for the stallion, he began to check out the fence line. He broke into a long flowing trot, head held high, his knotted mane and tail streaming out behind him. He looked magnificent and very much a blue blood. Carrie squeezed Justin's hand. This should have been a joyous moment, but it wasn't. At last Quinn broke the silence.

'The other trucks will be here soon with the rest of the

mob, but I think I'd better get going. I have a long drive in front of me.'

'You're heading back tonight?' Carrie asked, really beginning to understand just how much she was going to miss Quinn.

'It'll be easier that way.'

Carrie threw her arms around Quinn and hugged her hard. 'Are you sure?' she whispered.

She felt Quinn nod. 'I'll stay in touch,' Quinn said. 'And … look after him.' Her voice broke.

She wasn't talking about the stallion.

'I will,' Carrie said. 'You take care of yourself.'

Justin hugged Quinn too, and then she climbed into her golden Humvee and drove away. The last thing they saw was a hand waving through the window as the vehicle was enveloped in a cloud of dust.

'I can't believe she's gone,' Carrie said softly. 'There's so much I have to thank her for.'

'We both do,' Justin said, squeezing her hand. 'Maybe she'll come back for a visit sometime.'

They both knew she probably wouldn't.

A sound behind them brought their attention back to the horses. The stallion was standing close to the fence, his head raised as he surveyed his surroundings. His ears twitched as he heard the sound of another truck approaching. He whinnied loudly.

'Here comes the rest of his harem,' Justin said.

Within a couple of hours, it was over. The brumbies were all safe in Justin's well-fenced paddocks. The foals were sleeping off the exhausting journey. The mares were enjoying grazing the sweet grass. Even Mariah's Son had begun to settle. One by one the other trucks had left, with agreement to meet up at Tyangi next day to undo any damage done to the park.

But Carrie didn't want to wait that long. 'Let's get back there,' she said, and Justin agreed, knowing it wasn't the brumbies or the work she was thinking about.

The drive to the national park had never seemed longer. When they got to the gorge, Dan's Land Rover wasn't there.

The campsite was barely recognisable. There was just an empty place where Quinn's tent had been. Her camp stove and other little luxuries were gone. The fire pit was black and cold. Only Dan's tent remained, standing alone on the bare earth.

'I wonder where he's gone?' Justin said.

'Maybe he went back to the ranger station,' Carrie responded. 'We could stop there on the way out. Make sure he's all right.'

'He's not all right,' Justin said, moving close to her and placing a comforting arm around her shoulders. 'I wouldn't be if you left.'

'There must be something we can do to help him.'

'There's nothing you can do.' Justin squeezed her gently. 'I love that you want to try. But you're not the one he needs right now.'

Carrie nodded, knowing he was right.

'Let's give him a day or two. Then we can make sure he isn't too lonely. Maybe you can get him riding again or something.'

She didn't think that was likely. She was afraid Dan would slide back into the solitary life he had led before Quinn came. She was determined that was not going to happen. After all, she had made a promise to Quinn, and she intended to keep it.

Chapter Thirty-Four

It didn't take long for nature to take back her own.

Dan stood in the gorge, looking for some sign of what had happened there. The stockyard was gone. He'd taken that down in a fury of hard work in the first few days after Quinn left. He'd hoped that sweat and exhaustion would help him sleep at night.

It hadn't.

He'd lain in his bed, listening to the sounds of the night, and thinking of that last night with Quinn. Wondering if there was anything more he could have said or done to hold her – and knowing that there was not.

Jack and Doctor Adam and some of the men from town had come to the park to help demolish the yard and cart the timber and iron back to the mine from where it had come. Dan had a feeling they had come to keep him company too. Justin and Carrie had seemed determined that he should not spend too much time alone. Even after the work was done, Carrie had dropped by to see him a couple of times. She had invited him to dinner with her and Justin. She'd even talked about continuing his riding lessons. He could feel her sympathy, and while he appreciated the efforts, he wanted none of it.

Since the yard had vanished, he had spent his days alone. Doing the job that he loved. Thomas Lawson had vanished back into whatever government office he'd come from, muttering darkly under his breath, but too afraid of adverse publicity to take action against Dan. There was a perverse irony in that. Once again, public opinion had saved him from retribution after disobeying an order.

He'd looked after some visiting tourists and cut another

firebreak. The latter activity had made him more restless, not less. With each swing of the axe, he remembered the last time he'd cut a firebreak.

What sort of park ranger are you?

Quinn had been all fire and indignation in that second meeting. Who would have thought they would have ended up as lovers ... not just lovers ... in love.

There was nothing left of her now. Just his memories and her name scrawled in his book. He had found that the day after she left. How like Quinn to always keep her word.

Dan turned away from the place where the campsite had been and drove down to the billabong. Now that the brumbies were gone, the grass was growing quite lush and green by the waterhole. The kangaroos were enjoying having the place to themselves again. They were appearing now in even greater numbers than before. They turned their faces towards him as he approached, then bounded away, tails held high.

He sat on the high rock, from where he had once taken aim at the brumby stallion. He remembered the feelings as he raised the rifle to his eye. The sweating and the shakes had left him now. The memories still came in the dark of the night, when he was lying awake and alone. He still saw the little girl with the dark eyes, but the debilitating guilt had been replaced with a simple sadness. The accusing voices were not so loud now. They had no more power over him.

That was Quinn's great gift to him – and he would always thank her for that.

Dan raised his eyes to squint at the sun almost directly above him in the cloudless blue arc of sky. Now that the roos had left, the billabong was his if he felt like a swim. But there were memories waiting for him down by the water as well. Feeling restless, he left the billabong and began driving further into the park. The wheel ruts were still there, perhaps a little more overgrown due to lack of use. He hadn't been back to this special place since the night he came here with Quinn. He climbed to the edge of the escarpment, and sat down on the big flat rock.

He looked out over the vast plain to the sandstone monolith, which now seemed stripped of all its healing powers. He thought about the night he had brought Quinn here. How she listened when he told her about Fallujah. About the little girl who died. She hadn't judged or condemned him. He loved her for that. Images began crowding his mind of Quinn as they made love here under the starlight. His body ached for her now. His heart ached. His very soul ached.

Dan got to his feet and left the high place. There was no peace for him there now, without Quinn.

He got back into his car and began driving. He headed out of the park and onto the road that lead to the Fraser Stud. When he arrived he didn't have to look far to find Justin and Carrie. He walked over to the big exercise yard, and leaned on the fence to watch.

Justin was inside the wooden railed exercise yard, leaning back against the rails, his hat tipped back from his face. He was watching with critical eyes as Carrie guided her horse in wide, smooth circles in the centre of the yard. The brumby stallion was instantly recognisable – but he was a different animal now. His coat gleamed from regular brushing. His mane and tail floated on the air, free now of knots and dust. His hooves were neatly shod, and his muscular body exuded good health and loving care. But the change in him was more than just physical. The big horse was bending himself happily to Carrie's gentle control. As he moved, his ears flicked back and forth, listening for her voice. He was just as magnificent as he had been – but he was no longer a brumby. It was a remarkable transformation.

'It's hard to believe that he was wild such a short time ago,' Dan said as he leaned on the fence rails beside Justin.

'She's some sort of witch,' Justin said, waving Carrie over. 'She has us both under her spell.'

'Isn't he wonderful.' Carrie's eyes shone as she slid down off the horse and patted his neck. She was rewarded with a playful shove that sent her cannoning into Justin, who caught her easily.

'I sometimes think it isn't me she loves, so much as the horse,' Justin said with mock despair, as he draped his arm around Carrie's shoulders.

Carrie jabbed him in the ribs with her elbow, and he laughed.

Dan was pleased to see them so happy, but it only served to heighten his own loneliness.

'I don't suppose you've heard from Quinn?' The words were out before he could stop them.

Justin and Carrie exchanged a glance.

'We e-mail,' Carrie said hesitantly.

Dan clenched his fist. He wasn't sure how that news made him feel. He was glad she hadn't lost touch with her friends, but it hurt that the others still had something of her – while he had nothing.

'It's all right,' he assured Carrie. 'I was just wondering how she was doing.'

'Fine, I think. She's been staying with her parents between jobs, trying to reconnect with them a bit.'

He was so pleased to hear that. 'And the story about the brumbies?'

'It's due to appear in *Australian Geographic* in a few weeks,' Justin told him. 'We are using that as a launch pad to bring Mariah's Son out of hiding and back into the world.'

Justin's voice was full of hope and enthusiasm. He was achieving his dream. Dan was happy for him.

Carrie glanced up at the sun. 'It's early, but we can finish this now,' she said. 'We're so pleased to see you, Dan. Please stay for dinner.'

'No. Thanks. I just came by to see how things were with the horses.' That was a lie and they all knew it.

Justin and Carrie spent some time showing him how well the brumbies had settled. Some of the mares were gone. Justin had found their owners. The younger brumbies were starting to behave like civilised animals, and Carrie had high hopes that most would make good stock horses given time. They would never be stud book animals, but many did carry unofficial Fraser blood. They'd bring good money when they were ready to sell.

It seemed the story had a happy ending for almost everyone.

'Do you want me to pass a message to Quinn when we e-mail?' Carrie asked in a whisper as they said their goodbyes.

'No,' he said.

Driving back to the park, Dan paused at a crossroads. To his right was the park, where he could continue his solitary and safe existence. If he turned left, the road would lead him to Coorah Creek. He'd been uncomfortable around people ever since his return from Iraq. Apart from those days he had spent with Justin and Carrie and Quinn. Maybe it was time he re-joined the rest of the world. He slipped the vehicle into gear and turned left. He would go to the pub for a beer and some of Trish's fine cooking. If there were people there he could talk to them. If not – well, he'd spent enough nights alone. Another one wasn't going to kill him. At least he was making an effort. Quinn would be pleased if she knew.

Chapter Thirty-Five

'Rachel, there's some mail here for you.'

Quinn's mother had always refused to call her daughter by anything other than the name she had given her at her christening. Quinn had long since become used to it.

She had often stayed with her parents between jobs. After all, she had no place of her own. The house she'd shared with her ex-husband had been sold long ago. It seemed foolish to spend money on another house, or even a flat, when she was never there. Her parents' home in an affluent Brisbane suburb was large enough to accommodate her visits but this was the longest she'd ever stayed between jobs and she and her mother were starting to get on each other's nerves. They'd always had this tendency to rub each other the wrong way. Especially since Kim's short time with them.

Quinn's agent had come up with some ideas for her next project. He'd also suggested a couple of magazine jobs. They only took a few days and they paid well. Quinn had accepted a couple of them, just to get away for a while. She'd done her job well as she always did, but nothing had inspired her. Her agent had looked at the photographs, which were good, but lacked her usual brilliance, and suggested some time off.

She'd rented a holiday flat at the beach for a few days, just to give herself and her parents a break from each other. But that had proved to be a pretty bad idea. During the day, she had sat on the beach, looking out at the vast expanse of shining blue water, thinking about Coorah Creek and the rugged beauty of the outback. At night, she had simply lain awake in the big, empty bed, thinking about Dan.

'Rachel? Did you hear me?' Her mother's voice betrayed her impatience.

'Coming,' she called, and unwound herself from her position on the couch. She put her laptop on the coffee table and headed for the kitchen.

'What is it?' she asked as she walked into her mother's immaculate domain. Like her daughter, Margaret Quinn liked to cook. But unlike her daughter, she cooked in a restrained and methodical fashion, so that even in mid-preparation the kitchen never seemed less than spotless. She was busy now preparing food to take to a neighbour's party. Quinn guessed that like most of her mother's meals, this would be wholesome and well presented, but unlikely to have people asking for the recipe.

'Here you go.'

Quinn barely glanced at the brown manila envelope her mother had placed in the centre of the table. She had been expecting this for a few days now, and wasn't at all sure she wanted to open it.

'Thanks.'

'Is that your latest article?'

'Yes.'

Quinn could feel her mother's frustration

'Aren't you going to open it?'

'Later, I guess.' Quinn walked to the fridge and opened it, not looking for anything in particular, but rather trying to avoid the conversation she knew was coming.

'May I see it?'

She wanted to say no. She really didn't want to open the envelope. She knew exactly what she would see. She'd written the story and prepared the photographs soon after her return from Coorah Creek. There had been a lot of heartache in every one. Heartache that had not faded in the weeks since.

But refusing to open the envelope was not going to stop the pain.

'Sure.' She pulled the water jug from the fridge and went in search of a glass.

Her mother opened the envelope, her carefully manicured nails bright against the plain brown wrapper. She removed the glossy magazine and flicked quickly through the pages.

'Oh. You're the feature article!'

Quinn didn't say anything. She tried to avert her eyes, but the pictures leaped off the page at her. The brumbies. Carrie and the stallion. Justin, every inch the stockman as he galloped behind the fleeing mob. And Dan …

'Oh, my. These are very good, Rachel. But wasn't it a bit difficult, camping out there in the wilds?' Her mother was never happy if she was more than a kilometre from the nearest hair salon.

'Not at all, Mum,' she said. 'It's very beautiful out there.'

'I don't even want to think about what you had for a bathroom.'

Quinn drained her glass and rinsed it in the sink. There was no way she would ever discuss camping ablutions with her mother. Margaret would probably have palpitations.

'The people look very nice,' Margaret continued. 'You talked about this girl, Carrie. And Justin. But you never said much about this ranger … Dan.'

Quinn saw the speculative look on her mother's face. Margaret was no fool.

'He's a good man,' Quinn said, trying to keep her voice sounding normal. 'An ex-serviceman. He served in Iraq and it's left him with some unpleasant memories.'

'We all have those,' Margaret said softly. 'We just have to deal with them as best we can.'

Quinn felt her heart twist. She knew what her mother meant, but they never talked about those days. There was nothing in the house to remind them of Kim. At least, nothing that Margaret knew about. There was a small box of things among Quinn's belongings under the bed in the room she used when she stayed. And of course, there was that tissue wrapped package in the back of her Hummer. But Margaret had removed every trace of her grand-daughter from her life. That hurt. It hurt so very much.

'So,' Margaret took a deep breath. 'I was thinking, the weather is so nice; perhaps we could have a garden party.'

'You mother means a barbecue.' Quinn's father entered the kitchen, pausing to kiss both his daughter and his wife on the cheek. 'And I think it's an excellent idea.'

'We'll invite all the neighbours. And Richard, you must invite that nice young lawyer from your firm. You know, the new one.'

'Mother!' Quinn said. 'Don't do this again. Don't start matchmaking.'

'I'm not matchmaking,' Margaret said. 'I just think it wouldn't hurt for you to meet someone new. You're still young and—'

'Don't!' Quinn was starting to get angry. 'Don't you dare say I'm still young enough to marry again and have another family. Don't ever say that to me.' She was quivering with anger and hurt and surprised by the intensity of her own reaction. She should be immune to her mother's hints by now.

'Rachel,' her father cut in, his voice gentle as he took on the familiar role of peacekeeper. 'Your mother didn't mean that.'

'No, Richard, I did mean that.' Uncharacteristically, Margaret shrugged off the comforting hand her husband had laid across her shoulders. 'We have tiptoed around this long enough. Rachel, it's time you stopped running away and got on with your life.'

Quinn was stunned into silence.

'What happened was a terrible tragedy. But you can't give up on happiness because of that.' Tears ran unheeded down Margaret's cheeks.

Keeping a stranglehold on her emotions, Quinn stormed out of the kitchen into the living room. She was so angry she was afraid she'd do or say something she would later regret.

'Rachel. Please. You have to get past this.'

Quinn spun to face her mother, who had followed her from the kitchen. 'Get over it? Like you did. You forgot Kim so quickly. It's as if she never existed. Do you even remember what she looked like?'

'Remember her?' Margaret was crying openly now, something Quinn hadn't seen her do since the day of the funeral. 'Of course I remember her. How could I ever forget? I think about her every day.'

'So do I, Mother. So do I.'

Margaret crossed the room and opened the drawer on a polished mahogany sideboard. Carefully she removed something and thrust it at Quinn. Quinn looked down at the silver frame and the photograph in it. The photo showed a mother and her child. A smiling fair-haired woman and a little girl with big beautiful blue eyes. Quinn felt tears coming. She gently stroked the glass covering her daughter's photo.

'It usually sits on the bookshelf,' Richard said quietly. 'There's another photograph of the two of you in our bedroom. Your mother puts them away when you come to visit.'

Quinn dragged her eyes away from her daughter's face and looked at her mother. 'Why?'

'At first it was because I didn't want to upset you. Then it was because I didn't know how to behave differently. You have been so locked away inside yourself all this time, Rachel, I didn't know how to help you.'

In the silence that followed Quinn looked at her mother. Really looked at her for the first time in a long while. She saw the lines either side of Margaret's brown eyes and the faint trace of grey hair that the next trip to the salon would hide. In contrast to Quinn's work-roughened hands, Margaret's were carefully manicured. But they were beginning to look a little fragile. Her mother was not a young woman any more. Quinn looked more carefully at her face, and saw the shadows put there by the same grief Quinn herself had suffered.

Quinn began to wonder if what she had thought was blame was simply grief. Grief that, like Quinn's, had never faded.

'Mum—'

'It's time, Rachel. You have got to move on.'

Margaret stepped forward and slowly wrapped her arms around her daughter, pulling her close. Neither spoke for a few moments, but Quinn was left with the feeling that the barrier between them was beginning to fall away.

Her father came and placed his arms around them both. Quinn could feel the dampness of his cheek. She had been so wrapped up in her own grief; she had forgotten that her parents had also suffered when Kim died.

Quinn still held the photograph tightly in her hand. She gently stroked the glass covering her daughter's photo. She walked over to the bookshelf and set the frame down.

'Leave it,' she told her mother with a faint smile. 'It looks good there.'

'Yes. It does.' Her mother dashed a hand across her eyes.

'Wait here, I'll be right back.' Quinn darted outside to where her Hummer was parked in the driveway. She opened the back and carefully removed the tissue wrapped package from its place.

Back inside the house, she handed the package to her mother. Margaret carefully opened it. Inside was a delicate pink baby's jacket. Knitted with care and a great deal of love. It had never been worn. Quinn reached out her fingers to stroke the soft wool.

'This was the last thing I knitted for Kim,' she said. 'Can I leave it here with you?'

Margaret nodded. Ever so carefully, she rewrapped the parcel and placed it in the drawer where the photo frame had rested.

'I'll keep it there …' she didn't finish the sentence, but Quinn knew what she was going to say. Until there was another little girl who needed it. Quinn wasn't ready to go that far yet. Neither of them was. But they had made a start.

'So,' Quinn said, taking a deep breath and forcing a smile onto her face, 'when were you planning on this barbecue?'

'You'll come?' Margaret asked, her eyes shining.

'No, but I'll stay a few days longer. After that,' she glanced through the open doorway to the kitchen table, where the magazine lay open, 'there's somewhere I have to go.'

As always, Quinn was glad to be back on the road. But this time, it was a little different. She wasn't running away from anything. She and her parents had become much closer during the past few days. They had talked about Kim. The small box of photographs and other mementos had come out from under Quinn's bed. They had talked and shared and better understood their grief. Quinn had even talked about Dan. Now she was on her own again, but she wasn't alone.

Once more she had everything she needed with her in her Hummer. Her cameras and laptop. Her knitting. She frowned. Actually, not so much knitting. She had finished her last project and given that to Ellen as she passed through Coorah Creek on her way home. She hadn't started another yet. She needed to get some wool before she found herself in a place where there was no wool to be had. She knew the location of almost every yarn store for several hundred kilometres. She would get what she needed as she passed through the next town.

Quinn walked into the big room no different from a dozen others she had encountered in her travels. The walls were lined with brilliant coloured balls of yarn. Sample knitted garments hung in the window. And in the middle of the room was a large table covered with pattern books, needles, balls of wool and the other tools of the knitter's craft. A group of women, all holding knitting needles, sat around the table chatting. One of them was heavily pregnant, and was working on a garment not unlike the ones Quinn always knitted. They all looked up as Quinn entered.

'Hello,' a friendly dark-eyed woman said. 'Welcome. Can I help you with anything, or do you just want to browse.'

'I'll just browse, thank you,' Quinn said.

'That's fine. If you need anything, I'm right here.' The woman settled back to her knitting and her friends.

As she always did, Quinn headed for the section of the shop featuring baby wools. The colours here tended to be more pastel. The yarns were finer and softer. She didn't pause at the patterns. She didn't need one. She knew what she was knitting. She picked up a ball of multi-coloured yarn in cream with pale pink and green highlights. She touched it to the skin of her face. It was beautifully soft and would knit up well. She picked up a similar yarn, but this time in shades of blue and caramel. Something that might suit a little boy. She seldom knitted pink wool. As she fingered the soft wool, the conversation behind her began to filter through to her mind.

'… never really liked a redhead, but I might make an exception for him.'

'Trust you, Jean. The story is about the horses, not the man.'

'I know. But there's no crime in looking. And that's a man well worth looking at.'

'It's that photo,' said a third voice. 'It's almost like a love song to him. I wonder who the photographer was. Whoever it was, they obviously have a thing for him. It shows in every inch of that photo.'

'In that case, I hope it was a woman,' replied the woman called Jean. 'Because if it was a man, I might have to change my mind about how gorgeous this park ranger is.'

Quinn turned around slowly. The magazine lay in the centre of the table, open to her photo of Dan. How well she remembered taking that shot. It was a wonderful portrait of Dan, the strong clean lines of his face silhouetted against the sky. Her heart did a long slow tumble. The woman was right. The photographer who took that shot was desperately in love with Dan. It had just taken her a long time to figure it out.

'Excuse me,' she said to the owner of the shop. 'I think I do need some help after all.'

'Of course. What are you looking for?'

'I am thinking of making a change. I usually knit for

babies, but now I need a pattern and yarn to knit a man's jumper. Something that would look good on an outdoors type of man. One with red hair.'

The woman looked down at the magazine again. 'A bit like him you mean? You lucky girl.'

'Yes, I am lucky,' Quinn said. 'I'll need a lot of yarn because where I'm headed there aren't any yarn stores.'

A few minutes later, Quinn was packing a large bag of yarn and needles and pattern books into the Humvee. She didn't need to consult a map. She knew exactly where she was going.

Chapter Thirty-Six

Dan was due to meet Justin and Carrie at the pub for dinner. The outing was rapidly becoming a regular event. After the success of the brumby run, his friends had refused to let him withdraw back into himself. Although he'd fought it at first, refusing their invitations, he was glad now that he had decided it was time to re-join the world.

He enjoyed Justin and Carrie's company, although it was sometimes hard to watch the love they shared growing stronger every day. Each time they met he would ask Carrie about Quinn. She told him just enough for him to know the woman he loved was all right. He hadn't given up hope that one day she would come back to Coorah Creek. Back to him. But first, he had to give her time to resolve the issues that isolated her as much as PTSD had done to him.

He knew he was finding his way back from his dark place. He hoped Quinn was doing the same.

He was only halfway up the stairs when the pub doors swung open and a crowd of people surged out towards him, talking loudly. He made to step aside, but Trish Warren grabbed his arm.

'Dan, that's great. You're just in time.' She turned him around. 'In fact, you can drive. Unlike the rest of this lot, you haven't been drinking.'

'Ah … Okay.' Dan allowed himself to be led back to his car. 'But all these people will not fit in my car.'

Just then, Justin's car pulled in beside him.

'Excellent timing,' Trish said as if she personally had organised it. 'Half of you go with Justin. The rest with us.'

Trish got in beside Dan, as her husband and a couple of people he didn't know crowded into the back seat.

'Just where am I driving too?'

'To the hospital,' Trish told him. 'Jack and Ellen's baby has come. He just rang. They have a little girl.'

Dan started the engine. 'That's great.'

'We're going down to see her, and to congratulate them.'

'And who is looking after the pub?' Dan asked as he backed out of his parking place.

'That doesn't matter. Everyone will be at the hospital. We'll come back later for a party.'

Dan shrugged and turned in the direction of the hospital. In his rear-view mirror, he saw Justin fall into place behind him.

As he pulled up at the hospital another vehicle pulled into the car park. He recognised the driver as the mine manager who had helped with their brumby muster. The back of the vehicle was filled with men who, presumably, knew Jack from his work at the mine.

'Good news, eh?' said Chris Powell as they all made their way up the steps into the small hospital.

'All right you lot, stop right there.' A smiling Adam Gilmore was standing in the hallway.

'Hey, Doc, how are they?'

'Mother and baby are fine,' Adam said. 'I'm not so sure about Jack. He looks as if someone has hit him with a brick.'

There was a murmur of laughter.

'Can we see them?' Trish asked.

'Of course, but I think maybe not all at once. Ellen is tired and the room is not that big.'

Trish was, of course, the first one through the door. Dan held back. He wasn't really a part of this community. He didn't want to intrude. He leaned against the wall, hoping for a chance to congratulate Jack. Then he'd leave.

'Is that Dan Mitchell out there?' a gentle voice called from inside the room. 'Dan, come in here. There's someone you should meet.'

Ellen was lying in a big bed that did not look at all like it belonged in a hospital. She looked tired, but very happy. Sitting beside her, Jack looked not only happy, but stunned. The two kids, Bethany and Harry, were there too. It was such a perfect family picture; it brought a lump to Dan's throat.

'Come and meet our little girl.' Ellen waved him forward.

The child in her arms was impossibly tiny, and looked as ugly as all newborns do to anyone who is not a parent.

'She's lovely,' Dan said, meaning it.

'Have you got a name for her yet?' Trish Warren cooed from the other side of the bed. She had taken up residence in the room's only chair and showed no signs of making way for anyone else in the near future.

'Not yet,' Ellen said, glancing up at Jack. 'We're still arguing about it.' The love that shone from her face put a lie to the words.

Dan glanced around, looking for a way to tactfully back away from this family moment, and his eyes fell on something lying on top of the chest of drawers on the other side of the room. Something pale yellow and soft.

'Quinn gave it to me before she left,' Ellen said quietly, following his gaze. 'It's beautiful. I thought it would be perfect for the christening.'

Dan nodded, remembering the care Quinn had put into knitting the garment. If he closed his eyes he could still see her, sitting by the gas light, her hands moving quickly and surely. Muttering his congratulations, he left the room and walked to the other end of the hallway, where he leaned against the wall. He missed Quinn so much he could hardly breathe. He missed the way a flash of her eyes could make his heart skip a beat. The way her cheeky grin could lift his spirits. And he missed the warm comfort of her body in the night, when his memories made sleep impossible.

When he opened his eyes, he was looking through an open door into an empty, darkened room. For a moment he thought he saw someone there. The little girl with the big dark eyes who haunted him. He had seen her face in the darkness or in the flames of a campfire. But he'd never seen her like this. Standing there, looking almost real. Almost as if she was still alive. And this time, for the first time, the little girl was smiling at him.

He blinked and she was gone, but he knew what he had to do. He'd probably known all along. It had just taken some time for his thick brain to accept it.

Pushing himself off the wall, he strode back through the hospital. The first person he saw was Dr Adam.

'If anyone is looking for me, I'll be away for the next few days,' he said. 'There's something I have to do.'

Chapter Thirty-Seven

Where were they? Dan stared down the track leading from the ranger station back towards the main road. It was empty.

'Come on, Justin,' he muttered under his breath as he glanced at his watch for the twentieth time.

As if called into being by the words, a slightly battered and dusty utility appeared on the road, followed by another smaller car.

'At last!'

The two cars pulled up outside the ranger station. Justin emerged from the first, a huge grin on his face. The door of the second burst open and Carrie darted out, to wrap Dan in a bear hug.

'You're going to get her?' Carrie asked.

'Yes,' he said, his heart lifting at the mere thought.

'Just as soon as you let him go,' Justin added.

Carrie unwrapped her arms from Dan's neck. 'We brought you my car. It's not exactly what you're used to, but it's reliable. It'll get you where you have to go.'

After leaving the hospital two days ago, Dan had driven straight to the Coorah Creek police station to tell Max Delaney, the sergeant, that he would be gone for a time. He didn't know how long. The park, he said, would remain open. Another ranger would arrive to take his place until he could return. Organising that other ranger had taken far more time than Dan expected. When he'd phoned the department, he'd ended up talking to Thomas Lawson. When he heard the man's voice on the other end of the phone, his heart had sunk, but if finding Quinn meant losing his job, so be it. Lawson had, surprisingly, accepted

Dan's explanation of a personal emergency. A temporary replacement ranger was not that easy to find, however. Dan had chafed under the delay, but leaving the park unattended just was not an option. Visitors needed to have someone to help them – a lifeline in case of emergencies. Dan wasn't going to just abandon his responsibilities. But at last the parks service informed him that a ranger was on the way to cover for him.

Then another barrier had dropped into place. The car. He drove a park service Land Rover. He couldn't just take off in a vehicle that wasn't technically his. He had to leave that for his replacement. A phone call to Justin and Carrie had solved that one. He explained his problem and, with Carrie cheering wildly in the background, Justin had offered to lend him a car.

Looking at the car now, Dan did not care how old or battered it was. If it took him to Quinn, that would be enough.

He opened the car door and tossed in a rucksack with some clothes and a few other necessities. He then carefully placed the book on the front seat. The book in which Quinn had written her name.

'I don't know how long this will take me,' he said to Justin and Carrie as he opened the driver's side door.

'Keep it as long as you need it,' Justin said. 'We've still got the old ute.'

'Just bring her back with you.' Carrie planted a kiss on Dan's cheek.

He nodded at both of them and got behind the wheel of the car. Without wasting another minute, he was heading for the park exit. Carrie and Justin kept him company for a short time, and then sent him on his way with a blast of their horn as they turned onto the gravel road that led back to their home.

Dan continued driving until he reached the intersection with the main highway, then he pulled over and turned the engine off. The road now led south to Coorah Creek, and then turned east towards the east coast and Brisbane. Quinn's book lay on the seat beside him. Once before, that book had guided him to the place he needed to be. Now it was doing it again. He wasn't sure exactly where he was going. But he was going to find Quinn.

Finding her might not be all that easy. She was a celebrity of sorts, one who protected her privacy. The book listed her agent, giving him an office address in Brisbane. Dan would start there. He had thought about phoning the agent, or e-mailing, but decided against it. He wouldn't give the man a chance to refuse to tell him where Quinn was. He would simply go to the agent's office and stay there if he had too – until he was told what he needed to know.

It wasn't much of a plan, but it was the only one he had. He wouldn't stop looking until he found her. He would ask nothing of her until she was ready. She needed to come to terms with her past, just as he had done. Quinn had helped him do that and if he could, he would help her too, even if that help was nothing more than letting her know he was there for her if she needed him.

He was not prepared to countenance the chance of failure. He needed Quinn in his life in the same way that he needed to breathe. He needed to wake in the mornings and watch her sleep beside him. He needed to hear her laugh. He needed her to be the home he still did not have. And he needed to fill the same role in her life.

He glanced at his watch. The drive from Coorah Creek to Brisbane would take him nearly twenty hours. He wouldn't make it today, but that was all right. He'd find a motel somewhere for the night. He settled himself more comfortably in the unfamiliar seat, took a firm grip on his concentration and restarted the engine. As he pulled back onto the highway, he began trying to find the words he would say to Quinn. The words that would make her realise that they belonged together. The words that would make her change her mind.

He drove south to Coorah Creek. He didn't stop in the town. He reached the intersection with the east-bound highway and turned. In a few minutes the town vanished into the haze behind him. He briefly wondered if Trish Warren knew what he was doing. Probably. And if she knew the whole town would know. Strangely enough, that didn't bother him. Maybe their good wishes would help his cause.

It was early afternoon, and the sun was beating down mercilessly on the car. He'd only been driving for a little more than an hour, when he saw something emerge from the heat haze on the road ahead. At first he thought it was a mirage, brought on by the heat. But it wasn't. His heart skipped a beat as he recognised the low boxy shape coming towards him. He'd seen too many Humvees emerge from the desert heat not to know one when he saw it. But this was not the vehicle of his nightmares. It held all his dreams.

Dan flashed his headlights twice, and then braked. He pulled the car over to the side of the road. He was getting out when the Hummer swept past him. A second later, he saw the glow of the red brake lights as it pulled up about fifty meters further down the road. Dan stood next to the car, his heart pounding, and waited. The Hummer began reversing back up the road. It angled onto the red dust verge opposite him and stopped.

It was dark inside the vehicle against the brightness of the sun. Behind the tinted windows, Dan could only see the outline of the driver. But he didn't need to see her. His heart told him she was there.

The door opened and she got out. She was sweating in the heat. Her hair was a mess and her clothes rumpled from long hours of travelling. She was so beautiful, she took his breath away. All the carefully planned words vanished from his head.

She closed the car door behind her, and moved towards him. Dan took two steps into the middle of the road and she was in his arms.

Kissing her was like drinking ice-cold water under the heat of the desert sun. It was like coming home and it was a very long time before he could bring himself to stop.

'I know there's not a lot of traffic out here,' Dan said roughly when he was finally able to speak again. 'But at some point, perhaps we should move off the road.'

Quinn nodded. Keeping his arms around her, so that her body was close to him, Dan led the way back to the Hummer.

Quinn leaned back against her vehicle and looked across at Dan's car.

'I almost didn't stop,' she said. 'I didn't know it was you.'

'I borrowed it from Carrie. I had to leave the Land Rover behind.' Dan held her hand tightly. 'You were coming back.' The wonder of it was almost overwhelming.

She nodded. 'Yes. And you were coming to find me, weren't you?'

'Yes. I had to tell you that I love you and when you are ready to share your life again, I want to be with you.'

Quinn didn't hesitate. Her face was serious as she spoke. 'I love you. I want to be with you. I am ready to move on with my life, but was too afraid to say that before.'

'There's no reason to be afraid,' Dan said. 'Ever.'

'I know. I've realised something. All those dreams I had as a girl. Home and husband and family. I still want all those things.'

'And you can have them. We can have them, together.'

'I let my work get in the way once before. I won't this time.'

'Don't say that.' Dan took her by the shoulders and held her so he could see her face clearly. He spoke slowly, with utter surety. 'Your work is important to you. You can't give it up. I will never ask you to. In fact, I would never allow you to. It's a part of who you are – part of what makes me love you.'

'But it'll take me away from you.'

'That's fine. Just as long as you come back to me. I'll always be there for you, Quinn. Wherever and whenever you need me.'

He kissed her again.

Neither of them heard the roar of an approaching engine. With a long loud blast of an air horn, a huge truck roared past, breaking their embrace.

'You were coming after me,' Quinn said again, her voice dancing with joy. 'Why? What made you decide to do that now?'

'Missing you. Loving you and wanting to be with you,' Dan said, and then his mouth spread into a wide smile. 'And Jack and Ellen had their baby – a little girl.'

'I'm really happy for them.' This time there was no shadow in her eyes. No flash of pain.

'Looking at the little girl made me realise something,' Dan said. He lifted one of her hands and gently kissed the soft skin on her palm. 'Love is a gift. A rare thing that is too precious to throw away. It's wrong to turn your back on it. Even if it lasts for just a day, love is worth it.'

The tears he saw in her eyes were all the answer he

needed. He kissed her again, because it was beyond his power to stop.

'I suppose I should tell my agent not to take any bookings for me for a while,' Quinn said a long time later. 'I have a feeling I'm going to be busy.'

'Take a job if you want to,' Dan said. 'Never say no to something you want to do because of me. It will always be your choice, Quinn. And besides,' he chuckled, 'you make a lot more money than I do, so your work is our retirement fund.'

'Retirement fund? Retirement is a whole lifetime away.'

'Which will be almost, but not quite enough time to spend together.' He kissed her again, loving the taste of her lips and the softness of her body against his. And loving the joy he felt surrounding the two of them like an aura.

'So,' Dan said when they could both talk again, 'are you ready? I've got a feeling the whole town is probably waiting to welcome you back.'

Quinn smiled and nodded.

Dan walked back across the road, and got behind the wheel of the car. He started the engine and did a U-turn. Quinn got into her Hummer. As she pulled back onto the highway, Dan slid his vehicle into place behind her. Driving the car that was no longer her only home, Quinn led them both back towards Coorah Creek.

About the Author

Janet lives in Surrey with her English husband but grew up in the Australian outback surrounded by books. She solved mysteries with Sherlock Holmes, explored jungles with Edgar Rice Burroughs and shot to the stars with Isaac Asimov and Ray Bradbury. After studying journalism at Queensland University she became a television journalist, first in Australia, then in Asia and Europe. During her career Janet saw and did a lot of unusual things. She met one Pope, at least three Prime Ministers, a few movie stars and a dolphin. Janet now works in television production and travels extensively with her job.

Janet's first short story, *The Last Dragon*, was published in 2002. Since then she has published numerous short stories, one of which won the Elizabeth Goudge Award from the Romantic Novelists' Association. She has previously published three novels with Little Black Dress. Her Choc Lit novels include *Flight to Coorah Creek*, *The Wild One* and *Bring Me Sunshine*.

https://twitter.com/janet_gover
https://www.facebook.com/janetgoverbooks
http://janetgover.com/

More Choc Lit

From Janet Gover

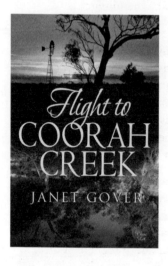

Flight to Coorah Creek

Book 1 in the Coorah Creek series

What happens when you can fly, but you just can't hide?

Only Jessica Pearson knows the truth when the press portray her as the woman who betrayed her lover to escape prosecution. But will her new job flying an outback air ambulance help her sleep at night or atone for a lost life?

Doctor Adam Gilmore touches the lives of his patients, but his own scars mean he can never let a woman touch his heart.

Runaway Ellen Parkes wants to build a safe future for her two children. Without a man – not even one as gentle as Jack North.

In Coorah Creek, a town on the edge of nowhere, you're judged by what you do, not what people say about you. But when the harshest judge is the one you see in the mirror, there's nowhere left to hide.

Visit www.choc-lit.com for more details including the first two chapters and reviews, or simply scan barcode using your mobile phone QR reader.

Bring Me Sunshine

Sometimes, you've just got to take the plunge …

When marine biologist, Jenny Payne, agrees to spend Christmas working on the Cape Adare cruise ship to escape a disastrous love affair, she envisions a few weeks of sunny climes, cocktails and bronzed men …

What she gets is an Antarctic expedition, extreme weather, and a couple of close shaves with death. And then there's her fellow passengers; Vera, the eccentric, elderly crime writer and Lian, a young runaway in pursuit of forbidden love …

There's also Kit Walker; the mysterious and handsome man who is renting the most luxurious cabin on the ship, but who nobody ever sees.

As the expedition progresses, Jenny finds herself becoming increasingly obsessed with the enigmatic Kit and the secrets he hides. Will she crack the code before the return journey or is she bound for another disappointment?

Visit www.choc-lit.com for more details, or simply scan barcode using your mobile phone QR reader.

Introducing Choc Lit

We're an independent publisher creating
a delicious selection of fiction.
Where heroes are like chocolate – irresistible!
Quality stories with a romance at the heart.

See our selection here:
www.choc-lit.com

We'd love to hear how you enjoyed *The Wild One*.
Please leave a review where you purchased the novel
or visit: **www.choc-lit.com** and give your feedback.

Choc Lit novels are selected by genuine readers like yourself.
We only publish stories our Choc Lit Tasting Panel want to
see in print. Our reviews and awards speak for themselves.

Could you be a Star Selector and join our Tasting Panel?
Would you like to play a role in choosing which novels we
decide to publish? Do you enjoy reading romance novels?
Then you could be perfect for our Choc Lit Tasting Panel.

Visit here for more details…
www.choc-lit.com/join-the-choc-lit-tasting-panel

Keep in touch:
Sign up for our monthly newsletter Choc Lit Spread for
all the latest news and offers: www.spread.choc-lit.com.
Follow us on Twitter: @ChocLituk and Facebook: Choc Lit.

Or simply scan barcode using your mobile phone QR reader:

Choc Lit
Spread

Twitter

Facebook